EPIDEMIC

Wanda Landry

Copyright © 2014 by Wanda Landry
First Edition – 2014

ISBN
978-1-4602-3887-5 (Paperback)
978-1-4602-3888-2 (eBook)

All rights reserved.

No part of this publication may be reproduced in any form, or by any means, electronic or mechanical, including photocopying, recording, or any information browsing, storage, or retrieval system, without permission in writing from the publisher.

Epidemic was written by Wanda Landry. Published by her husband and children (making a dream a reality). Epidemic has been published "as is" (as book was left) at time of Wanda's passing.

Produced by:

FriesenPress
Suite 300 – 990 Fort Street
Victoria, BC, Canada V8V 3K2

www.friesenpress.com

Distributed to the trade by The Ingram Book Company

Table of Contents

Chapter 1	1
Chapter 2	3
Chapter 3	11
Chapter 4	15
Chapter 5	21
Chapter 6	25
Chapter 7	37
Chapter 8	49
Chapter 9	57
Chapter 10	63
Chapter 11	69
Chapter 12	75
Chapter 13	83
Chapter 14	93
Chapter 15	99
Chapter 16	105
Chapter 17	109
Chapter 18	123
Chapter 19	125
Chapter 20	133

Chapter 21	147
Chapter 22	157
Chapter 23	161
Chapter 24	167
Chapter 25	173
Chapter 26	177
Chapter 27	185
Chapter 28	191
Chapter 29	199
Chapter 30	205
Chapter 31	209
Chapter 32	215
Chapter 33	223
Chapter 34	231
Chapter 35	235
Chapter 36	241
Chapter 37	245
Dear Reader:	249

Chapter 1

Day One - Monday

Consumed with dread, and fear of their human frailty, highly acclaimed scientists watched the image of a stone faced man transmit to them across a large screen mounted on a white wall. He soberly asked, "What happened?"

Dr. Lee answered, "A sample we were working with spilt. When Dr. Yen was cleaning the spill, he discovered a slight puncture in his glove. He thinks it was a defect from the factory, which was overlooked by the staff assigned to inspecting our equipment prior to us using it."

Granite features remained emotionless. The superior they were speaking with was only one member in the chain of command. Dr. Lee and his associates at the lab answered to him, he answered to his superiors, and the links continued connecting all the way to carefully planned presentations to the public.

Slicing through strained silence, he asked, "What is the incubation period for the disease you are researching?"

The scientists looked at each other with glazed eyes. The last few months had been devoted to an unfamiliar viral strain discovered in early human remains found perfectly preserved under thick ice in the Antarctic. Researching the primitive virus was of great scientific significance. Ecstatic excitement had held them captive when they had watched it thaw to vibrant life after enduring hostile conditions for millenniums.

"Tests indicate an incubation period of twelve days." Dr. Yen answered, and then corrected, "In an ideal environment the virus would thrive and the incubation period could be much less, especially if the host has a weak immune system."

"You will all remain quarantined in the lab for two weeks. Nobody will enter the building, nor will anybody leave the compound. After the incubation period has passed, if there are no symptoms among you, the quarantine will be lifted. Groceries and other necessary supplies, including medical equipment, will be dropped at the compound for you. Hopefully this is only a precautionary measure and in two weeks the lab will return to normal operations." His grave expression intensified as he decreed, "This accident is classified as top secret. All information relating to it will be withheld from the world."

Outside, forgotten and unnoticed, members of the cleaning staff were climbing into a white company van. The oldest crew member, Lee Yates, prickled with anxiety. He was glad his blunder had gone unnoticed. He would surely lose his job if anyone knew what had happened.

He calmed his unease by assuring himself the lab was secured with fully modern technology making accidents almost impossible. Still, it had been foolish to pick up the paper towel negligently discarded outside the 'no sharp' zone. The blood soiled towelling should have been treated with rigid procedures, and the contaminated vicinity should have been diligently sterilized.

It was the first time he had ever encountered a situation resulting from a scientist making an error, even one so slight as negligently dropping a small piece of garbage The scientists were paid big dollars for being impeccable and handling the most minute details with perfection. Lee consoled his action of plucking the paper towel off the floor and throwing it in the garbage as an ordinary and appropriate response for an average person. He was a janitor, and that made him average, so he decided his decision had been appropriate. Anticipating the savoury meal his wife was sure to have prepared, Lee let his mind drift to pleasant thoughts.

Day Two - Tuesday

The next day, Lee Yates found himself with an unexpected holiday due to an emergency closure at the lab. He boarded a plane bound for Canada and was anticipating an overdue visit with his brother.

Chapter 2

Day Ten - Wednesday

'how r u?'

Staring at the screen, Arista briefly doubted there was any purpose in wasting her time with what she was doing. She had nothing else to do and nowhere to go, so she responded, "good. how r u?"

'i m dave. wanna cyber?'

Chilled at the rude perversion, she considered numerous deterrents. The stranger online could be someone she knew, or a relative, or some maniac serial criminal. Endless strings of unappealing possibilities leapt to mammoth proportions in her imagination.

She responded, 'na. bye.' About to click offline, she glanced at the abrupt appearance of a box on her screen.

'u asked what we do for enjoyment'

Choosing to ignore the response her previous question had brought, she keyed, 'g2g bye'. Got to go, was one of the few things she knew the internet abbreviation for. The person logged in as Sulf had sent a second message, and it popped up immediately after she pressed her send button.

'i have a nook tucked away from everything except nature, fresh air, and clear mountain streams. i go there to unwind.'

His choice of wording sounded educated despite the poor grammar befitting to the popular code used on the internet. The thought of being beside a bubbly creek instead of rushing civilization fanned Arista into dreamily longing for the tranquility of such a place.

'u still there?'

'ya. it sounds perfect.'

'it is. I go fishing under the stars and laze in my own natural spa. it's something u would have to c to appreciate.' Leaning heavily against the back of his chair, Hauk closed his eyes to a vision of his wilderness where wolves howled at night and sunlight winked on clear streams during the day. He was in greater need of rest and relaxation than words could describe.

'y u not cybering?'

'cause. bye.' She clicked Dave's screen closed and clicked out of the chat room.

'where r u?' Sulf's message popped onto her screen.

'spain.'

'what time is it over there?'

She didn't know what time it was in Spain. Dodging his question she keyed, 'time to get a cup of coffee.'

Correctly interpreting the admission to her lie, he keyed, 'i c'

'where r u?'

'the west coast of Canada. air smells like sweet pine, birds sing to the sunrise and sunset, and water is crystal clear.'

'ohhhhhhhhhhh............ groan...........................'

'groan?'

'ya. where i live i smell traffic exhaust while listening to blaring horns and screaming sirens.'

'lol.'

Arista did not know the meaning of lol. The natural thing for her was to feel immediately intimidated. She thought it might be some rude slang aimed to offend. After staring at the screen for uncomfortable seconds, she decided her reaction of feeling insulted and defensive was ludicrous, and she asked, 'what does lol mean?'

'laugh out loud.'

Slightly taken back by the error of her initial reaction, she keyed, 'thank you.'

'sometimes i go whale watching.'

Remembering she was supposedly from Spain she made a feeble attempt to even the score by jibing, 'we have fantastic dances.' Lacking knowledge about the way of life in Spain she hoped she was right.

'i bet u do. i enjoy dancing. and singing. r u musical?'

'no. do u have voice?'

'yes.'

'will u sing now?'

Hauk pressed buttons, opened the file of music he had recorded onto his laptop, chose a title, and played it through the microphone.

In a couple of minutes a guitar strummed. His voice came across to her in rich male tones as he sang a classic rock song telling of dreams and love. Her stomach dove with pleasure as she imagined a face to match the voice. Of course, the ideal body also came to mind. His words drew a picture, and she drifted into a fantasy of a private dance for two, surrounded by the heavy sultry air of a warm evening, under shimmering stars, in a faraway place of perfection.

When he was finished, she keyed, 'your song was wonderful.' Stopping at the sound of constant beeps coming over her speaker she assumed he was being bombarded by impressed females seeking his attention. After waiting for him to send her a return message, Arista guessed he was busy talking to other women and decided it was a good time for her to leave.

'i have to go now. bye.'

'bye.'

She clicked out of the message box.

It popped back up. 'it was nice talking to u. may i add u to my list?'

'sure.'

'what is your name?'

'April.'

In seconds a different box gave her the choice to accept or decline the addition of her to his list. She accepted.

'xoxoxoxoxoxoxo.' His lengthy farewell blinked onto her screen.

She disconnected her computer from the internet, turned her computer off, and went to bed with the lingering whisper of a faraway dream. She didn't know who Sulf was, what he looked like, or anything about him, except the sound of his voice, and even that had been distorted by her speakers. She was free to build him into any fantasy she wanted him to be.

Drifting on the tides of imagination, she evaded the cold night stretching ahead. She rarely managed to sleep for more than a few scant hours, and even those were frequently interrupted with stretches of being awake. She hated going to bed. It was the loneliest time in the world when darkness descended, traffic dwindled away, and, she lay awake while the entire world seemed to sleep.

Sulf was working his seventeenth consecutive hour and everything he had told Arista on the internet was true, right down to his upcoming holiday.

Static crackled from the intercom followed by, "Code Blue, H Unit, Code Blue, H Unit, Dr. VanLiev report to H Unit, Dr. VanLiev Report to H Unit."

Swinging the white lab coat off the back of his chair and onto his shoulders he pushed his arms into the sleeves as he raced down the hall toward 'H Unit'. He already knew the call was for Mr. Kad Yates. The elderly man was a longstanding patient of his who suffered from chronic but mild asthma. He had been admitted earlier in the evening with an unusually aggressive attack stubbornly resisting treatment.

Entering Kad Yates room at a brisk walk, almost a run, Dr. VanLiev announced a string of orders to the staff already performing emergency procedures. Medications were administered and the blueness in Kad Yates' skin slowly regained normal hues. Strangled breaths hissing through tight windpipes led to violent coughing.

The elderly and gentle man looked at Dr. VanLiev with haunted hazel eyes. "I don't want to go back to sleep." He shook his head dismally. "It is not a nice feeling waking up unable to breathe."

"No. It wouldn't be." Dr. VanLiev's lips pinched against the inability to relieve his patient's difficulty. "I wish I could say your condition is under control."

"I know it is not." Reaching for his glass of water, he glanced at the numerous machines continuously monitoring his vital signs. "This irritating itch always comes before the coughing starts."

"Itch?" It was the first time the symptom was mentioned. "Do you have food allergies?"

"I don't know of any." Hazel eyes winced as the dry itch intensified. "I think they must have tested me for everything by now." He swallowed huge gulps of water.

"When did the itch start in your throat?"

Kad Yates closed his eyes and thought back as he continued swallowing and trying to wash down the aggravation. "It's been about four days."

"Your asthma has been getting progressively worse for the last few days?"

"Yes. I have never been afraid of it before. Now, it scares me."

"I suspect there is more than your asthma involved. I want you to take an antibiotic." He charted instructions. "You have signs of a mild case of bronchitis setting in." Dr. VanLiev extracted a chest x-ray and carefully examined it. "So far there is no permanent damage. Certain viral and bacterial infections are capable of intensifying, or even causing, chronic asthma. The medication I'm prescribing is for preventive treatment. It probably will not reduce the symptoms you are feeling."

"Do I have a bacterial infection?" Kad Yates was slightly confused about what it meant to suffer from bacteria, but he knew it sounded serious.

"If I give you a swab, and the lab gets the culture tested, it may not show an infection even if one is present."

"What do you think I have?"

"How have you been feeling between coughing bouts?"

"I've been tired since this started. Until tonight, I have been fine between the attacks of coughing and have been going about my days as usual. But, when the coughing starts," his eyes clouded with fear, "it gets so bad it puts me down on my knees and usually makes me vomit."

"How many coughing spells do you get in one day?"

"Sometimes there are two or three. Some days there aren't any." He stopped talking and swallowed large gulps of water. Then, he launched into another episode of coughing.

Dr. VanLiev handed him his puffer.

Struggling, Kad Yates straightened, breathed in, and quickly shot a blast of medication down his throat. For the briefest second the whistle left his breathing, and then the harsh attack escalated severely.

Medical staff waiting for orders from the doctor gave him quizzical looks when he stood silently watching his patient gasp for air. The gasping continued for a few minutes before Kad lurched into violent coughs emptying his lungs of air followed by him sucking in huge gasps only to be attacked by more shuddering coughing until it left him shaking and vomiting.

The nurse brought Kad a warm moist face cloth. He took it and mopped the sweat from his face. Avoiding eye contact with the people around him, Kad Yates stared down at his mattress. He swallowed, breathed, and regained some of the strength drained by the attack. When he was recovered enough to talk, he looked at Dr. VanLiev, "Is my asthma going to be like this for the rest of my life?"

"I don't think so." The lack of a proven diagnosis made the outcome uncertain. Dr. VanLiev suspected Whooping Cough, but remained cautiously noncommittal. "You appear to be handling the coughing bouts equally well with or without medication. Is that accurate?"

"The puffer helps."

"Have you tried other cough remedies?"

"When it began, I tried cough candies and syrups."

"Did they help?"

"No."

"I still want you to take antibiotics to prevent complications. I'm prescribing a different puffer, one with steroids to reduce the swelling in your respiratory system."

"Are you sending me home?" Hazel eyes silently pleaded against spending the remainder of the night by himself in his house. Kad wished his brother was still there, but, Lee had taken the first flight home after his wife had telephoned to tell him his grandson was seriously ill with a mysterious virus.

"No." Dr. VanLiev took hold of Kad's wrinkled hand in a show of friendship and comfort. "We are going to keep you here until you feel better."

"What do I do if I go home and this happens?"

"Then you need to come back to the hospital. You should go to the emergency unit anytime you have a health problem and the clinics are closed." Dr. VanLiev explained that he expected the attacks of coughing would diminish in frequency and severity. He reinforced his advice to seek further medical aid if the cough worsened. Then, he left his patient in the nursing staff's efficient care.

Making his round of examining patients proved time consuming despite the small size of the quaint hospital. It never ceased to amaze him how each patient and every condition held unique qualities. His patients ranged from newborn babies and their recovering mothers, to elderly people awaiting admission into care homes where their needs could be provided for, to the terminally ill being relieved of as much discomfort as possible.

He was trained to diagnose and treat disease, and conditioned to preach healthy lifestyles. With every answer there were always uncountable questions. Despite the continuous string of uncertainties Dr. VanLiev knew one unwavering fact, he wanted to help people.

When he reached the staff lounge, he saw Dr. Nam seated at the computer. A wave of exhaustion washed over him the instant he realized his replacement had arrived. After giving Dr. Nam a briefing on the last two shifts, he went home to bed and fell into an exhausted sleep.

Day Eleven - Thursday

Arista awoke to the cheery greeting of morning sunshine. Sometime during the night she had dreamt that a very attractive man with black hair and blue eyes walked up to her and asked, "You don't talk to anybody do you?" She scornfully thought of Guy's condescending, arrogant, selfish, and shallow responses to everything. And she knew a great number of people that were the same as Guy. She spat her answer, "No! What do you think? I'm Stupid?" The stranger walked away and disappeared. She wished she had talked to him. He looked like the kind of person she could trust with her deepest secrets. She wished she knew someone like the man in her dream.

The vague wistfulness of silent longing crept with her relentlessly as she stepped into her routine. Arista showered with perfumed gel, painted a fresh coat of subtle colour to perfectly manicured fingernails, brushed her shoulder length mass of thick hair into a sheen of raven black waves, carefully applied shimmering hints of colour around dark eyes, and shone succulently full lips with flavoured translucent gloss. Then, before plunging into her busy day, she took time for a freshly brewed cup of steamy coffee, laced with thick cream.

She patiently manoeuvred her car through streets congested with morning rush hour, and, as always, bedlam assailed at nine o'clock sharp. At a turn of the door locks, customers forming disorderly lines instantly swarmed with hurried demands and endless complaints.

She smiled and nodded when customers grumbled, "This bank should open earlier." When they complained, "We would have liked to have been on our way an hour ago, but we had to wait for the bank to open." When they confessed, "I snuck away from work to get this done, please hurry before my boss notices I'm missing."

Equal monotony absorbed Arista's evenings. This evening, like all evenings, she pulled onto her driveway expecting only to crash onto her sofa in a tangle of frayed nerves and eat something unwholesome. Sitting in her car, she thought about her life.

Sometimes Guy would come over. Other times he wouldn't. Arista was happiest when he stayed away. Guy was a jerk, a control freak, insulting, overbearing, overly stupid, overly underachieving, and overly annoying. Her friends described him as a stale crumb when they advised her to look for someone new. They suggested she might be able to find a full loaf.

Regardless of what her life consisted of, and lacked, she forced herself to do a daily exercise regime of light weightlifting, an abdominal circuit, and a brisk forty minutes on her treadmill. She crowded in chores of laundry and housekeeping. Though she was worn out by the end of each day, she still suffered continuous nights of lying in bed and staring at the ceiling for excruciatingly long hours as sleep eluded her.

Those hours often held an illogical glimmer of something, almost tangible, like she was missing someone she had never known. There was a rooted longing to hold a hand she had never felt and share a smile with someone she had never seen. She figured it must be some kind of emotional mirage, and she wondered what was wrong with her to make her hanker over something she had never had.

Her thoughts drifted to Guy. He is a born traitor. He likes watching for weak moments in people, and running about with the attitude 'guess what I know and can't wait to tell'. He loves belittling her, and anyone else, including his best friends. He believes he is making his grand superiority obvious and undisputable by pointing out the flaws of other people. Guy's recounts of situations are usually embellished with dramatic additions created by his imagination.

Guy loves being around when people are hurting. He digs into fresh wounds with predictably snide insults like, 'What else do you expect to happen? You bring these things on yourself.' Or, he refuses to offer support, and snubs with, 'Suck it up.' She passionately loathed that phrase. Guy never displays empathy, compassion, or wisdom. He reliably degrades, embarrasses, humiliates and spreads twisted and malicious rumours about the people he knows. Guy generously bestows hatred on his family, his friends, and all other people unfortunate enough to meet him.

Guy's favourite past time is waiting for down moments in other people's lives. He then pursues cajoling material items, or favours, or extracting vengeance for some past injustice he is harbouring resentment about. Guy's feelings of being wronged may stem from factual deeds, or they may be delusional. Whatever darkness is swirling in his heart, he is always quick to rant with angry and vile loathing. He never displays remorse or love.

Having recently embarked on radically restructuring her life, Arista had moved, and landed a job at the bank, and met Guy.

Twisting the key in her ignition she turned the engine off, got out of her car, locked the doors, and moved into her evening.

Chapter 3

"Hello, my sweet fortress of solitude." Sulf whispered adoration at inanimate objects. His appreciation was heightened after having been away for longer than usual. The glorious wealth of nature thriving around him provided a paradise. Sunshine radiating from a clear blue sky caressed his ruddy skin with soothing warmth. In the shade of sturdy pine trees wildflowers trembled into mats of riotous colour as a breeze waltzed over them. Each tiny member was the liking of a small gem forming clusters of jewels adorning the majestic crown of craggy mountains jutting into lofty heights and claiming their snow capped glory.

Melding with his surroundings, Hauk approvingly contemplated the nickname his elementary school friends had given him many years ago. He reminisced over the teasing he had been subjected to after making a playful swoop at the white mouse their grade one teacher had as a class pet. Uniqueness was added by the incorrect spelling of grade one students.

Sebastian, the name bestowed on him by his parents, was more conventional and decidedly more appropriate for his profession. The title Dr. Sebastian VanLiev had an appealing ring. He spared only a fraction of a second to puzzle over why his friends still preferred to call him Hauk. With a chuckle, he thought of the many friends liberally using his nickname. If they were to see the hovel Hauk cherished, those gentler folk would surely deem him insane. Quite the opposite of embracing nature's grand design, many of his associates preferred to worship arrogant pedestals in a concrete and glass world promoting plastic lives.

Hauk absently appreciated the differences in people as his thoughts drifted over the tedium too much similarity would create. If solitude and nature were to gain popularity it would generate an annoying infringement for him by contaminating his getaway with a crowding problem. With a grin, Hauk realized it was the first time in many months he had had the luxury of idle time where he could wander aimlessly with equally inconsequential thoughts.

Breathing the sweet pine scent impregnating crisp air, Hauk made a conscious attempt to push thoughts of his everyday life into as remote a section of his mind as possible. Still, the complications of upcoming change stubbornly crept into his thinking. He was comfortable with his present lifestyle, and working alongside admirable colleagues, and having a routine organized to perfection. He had spent years pushing himself through twenty four hour days while establishing his practice. He keenly recognized the value of having leisure time.

He almost wished the career opportunity had never presented itself. It had come from one of the finest hospitals in the country, with highly coveted doctors whose skills were enviable. The knowledge he would gain from those people would be invaluable. It was greatly appealing to imagine having access to the superior technology at the elite research hospital. Another strong attraction was the luxurious salary they were offering.

Something deep in his heart drooped with sadness instead of lifting with elation. The higher income level appealed to him more than he liked. He scorned himself for allowing the material aspects to entice him. Greed was something he disdained.

The rat race always seems to offer more to strive for and more to want. Just when a person thinks they have everything they could possibly need, there is someone to say there's more to be gained. The never ending competition spurs society into perpetual motion going nowhere. For some unfathomable reason almost everybody is highly susceptible to the invisible prods pushing on with ceaseless persistence.

He disliked admitting that he was as vulnerable to the influence as anyone else. Studying his awesome surroundings, he knew no amount of money was able to buy anything comparable to the true magnificence of even one mature spruce tree much less the splendid pine forest stretching around him. His soul relaxed in the glory of nature liberally adorning his world under the vibrant brilliance of the clear blue sky.

The tranquil gurgle of a nearby brook mingled with the melodies of song birds and soothed the pains of his deliberations. He fetched his fishing tackle. After hours spent fishing peacefully, he melted a thick slab of butter in a deep pan. He coated two fish fillets with salt, pepper, and flour. Hot butter spluttered as he laid fillets in the preheated frying pan. Taking a deep breath of the succulent aroma filling his kitchen, he glanced out his window at white puffs of clouds floating lazily in the sky. An awareness of life's frailty nudged him into absorbing as many sights, sounds, and sensations as possible. Even something so small as an itch was worth experiencing.

Busy days robbed him of taking time to pay heed to precious details. Hectic work schedules forced him to gulp his meals down without having time to sit for one mouthful. Today he was leisurely savouring the flavours of buttery fish, smooth mashed potatoes, and sweet creamed corn.

Full and content, he went outside and built a fire in the stone pit he had made three years ago. It had been his first renovation to the property he had acquired after making a lengthy search for the owner who had left it deserted. Hauk had then presented him with a generous offer to purchase, which was instantly accepted with enthusiasm.

Needing time to make the dwelling liveable, Hauk had pitched a tent and built the fire pit for himself. Even then he had valued every moment he spent in this secluded wilderness. It gave him time to think and reacquaint with himself. Whatever he stood to gain for his career, the need to relocate and sacrifice close proximity to this retreat was a severe loss for him.

Chapter 4

Day Twelve - Friday

Arista was drastically less content then Hauk. She fumed with frustration while vowing to treat the next customer with rudeness equalling what she had been receiving. Setting her chin in square determination, Arista refused to smile, and spat, "Next, please!"

True to Arista's standard luck, an elderly woman, leaning heavily on a squeaky walker, teetered toward her wicket. "I am sorry I am so slow." Her lips lifted in a sheepish and gentle smile. "If only I could walk properly."

Arista's determination to be abrupt with her customers dissolved in guilt. "There's no need to rush." Soft reassurance warmed her voice.

Frail and wrinkled hands fumbled shakily in her purse. She pulled out an envelope bulging with papers. "Could you please take those out for me?" She put the envelope on the counter and slid it to Arista. "I am so sorry to be making such a nuisance of myself."

"You are not a nuisance." Arista removed the papers and began unfolding them. Trying to be friendly, she resorted to a mundane comment about the weather. "It's sure been windy outside lately."

"Every day is wonderful though. I'm happy just to be alive."

Trying to concentrate on doing her job, Arista's mind reeled at the unexpected comment. It was true, she was also happy to be alive.

The elderly woman continued, "At my age one never knows if they will see another day. If I had known how I was going to be feeling at eighty nine, I might have done things differently. Oh well. We really don't have control over some matters."

Rendered speechless, Arista quickly stamped the assortment of bills, calculated the total on her adding machine, and filled out the signed cheque she had pulled from the envelope. After shoving receipts back into the envelope, Arista handed it to the woman.

"Oh, Deary, I would also like three hundred dollars, please?"

"I will help you with that right now." She read the woman's account number from her cheque and copied it onto a withdrawal slip. After filling out the form, she handed it over for a signature.

"Oh." Reaching a trembling hand back into her purse, the woman pulled out her chequebook. "Could you please use one of these? My daughter looks after my finances, and if I don't use one of my numbered cheques she doesn't know I've taken money out." She waved her hand impatiently. "I don't understand why she is always so picky."

When the transaction was complete, the woman began to move away slowly, and Arista summoned, "Next!"

Arching both brows, she watched a customer approach. It was all of ten o'clock in the morning and the unshaven, overweight, middle aged man was staggering in an obvious state of intoxication. A burning cigarette dangled between his lips.

"You can't do that here."

"Whattttttt?" He slurred.

"Smoking is not allowed in this building."

He stared at her, blew a cloud of smoke into the air, took the cigarette in black stained and thickly calloused yellow fingers, threw it on the floor, and crushed it under the heel of his boot. Looking back up at her, he asked, "Is this better?"

"Much." She refrained from laughing at the sudden burst of humour she saw in his intrusive behaviour.

His squinted eyes studied her from under heavy brows. "Give me fifty dollars."

Pulling out a withdrawal slip she asked, "What is your account number?"

"Here." He pulled his chequebook out of his shirt pocket and put it down on the counter. She prepared the cheque, gave it to him, he signed, and she counted the money out to him.

Watching customers filter through the doors for endless hours, glancing down at the aged yellow floor tiles and hating the rancid smell clinging to money, Arista was suddenly overwhelmed with stifling dissatisfaction. She found temporary escape by using the tired but unarguable excuse of needing the 'ladies' room.

Irrational frustration curdled in her veins as she glared at the loathsome door. It could hardly be called a 'ladies' room since five female employees and two male employees made use of the same facility, and the men left telltale lines running down the outside bowl of the toilet. Shimming away from the filth she went to the sink. Rinsing her hands under soothing warm water, her finger brushed against caked scum layering the ceramic sink.

Her stomach growled aggressively. Glaring at her wristwatch, she mumbled angrily to nobody, "Six hours done and two to go." She ground her heel into the tile. "No lunch breaks." Her chin squared, "No coffee breaks." Adding frustrated pressure to her foot snapped the heel off her shoe.

She marched back to her wicket with her broken shoes dangling from her hand. It was her second week of being smoke free, and she was unable to remember feeling even slightly happy since taking up the war against her addiction.

Every time she got into her car at the end of a workday, her immediate reaction was to open the ashtray and then forlornly remember the absence of her vice. An illogical attachment to the habit made her sad about leaving it behind. The nicotine cravings were keeping her as cranky as a bear. A couple of difficult days had been expected, but this was two relentless weeks with no relief in sight. Taking a deep breath, she refreshed her determination to win the battle she was fighting.

Forcing professional behaviour from herself, Arista removed the 'closed' sign at her wicket, plastered on an artificial smile, and using a friendly voice announced, "Next."

Her craving for a cigarette quickly became unbearable. She soothed it with nicotine laced gum. It slowly brought relief. The hungry grumbles in her stomach transformed to nausea.

"Hi, Honey." A lanky man with dark blond hair fastened into a ponytail at the nape of his neck swaggered over with a cocky grin, coughed into his hand, used the same hand to pull a stack of money from his pocket, and handed it to her.

Grossed out with his action, she took it from him and wished she didn't have to touch his germ laden money. The notes were wrapped in a bank bundle complete with what was likely to be a script. If her suspicions were correct, it was a sure sign of his having very recently robbed a bank.

"I would like to have my money exchanged to U.S. bills." Turning his face from the wicket, he coughed violently.

The rate was calculated, she gave him U.S. cash, and she wished him a nice day.

He made a feeble attempt to respond, but his breath hitched on the cough assaulting him. He took the money and continued coughing fiercely as he walked past the waiting line of customers and out the door.

Then, she told the manager about the suspicious transaction.

The manager informed her, "We would have no way of tracing the script."

Stunned at the response, Arista asked, "He could rob a different bank and come here to change the money?"

The manager shrugged indifference.

Arista went back to her wicket with growing vexation. One of her regular customers, a dark haired man in his thirties, stepped up. His transactions were always simple, tidy, and rarely incorrect. Seeing him, and expecting smooth simplicity, her smile came easily.

"Good afternoon." Mike's cheeks bunched in a friendly grin as he slid his deposit book across to her.

Folded neatly on top of it was a cheque order slip. Glancing at it, Arista stopped when she saw the request for his cheque numbers to begin at one. Looking up at him, back down at the order form, and up again her brow arched.

"Is there something wrong?"

"Are you sure you want your cheque numbers to go back to one?"

"Yes." His smile broadened with confidence.

Although the easiest solution was to do as he asked, she explained, "Companies don't usually like to use low numbers. Even when first opening, they will often start with a much higher number."

"Why?"

"It makes the company appear credible."

"What does a cheque number have to do with credibility?"

"It makes it look as though they have written out more cheques than they have. The appearance of having done ample business transactions gives the impression of reliability."

"A higher cheque number is good for appearances?"

Attempting to add logic, Arista spouted, "It could get confusing if a bunch of cheques come back with the same numbers."

"It would take years for me to use the entire order and get back to this number." He took the order form, scribbled out the request, changed it to start at the number where his old order left off, and his eyes scorned the system. "Now I know why every business in the country has astronomically high cheque numbers. It keeps up appearances."

Instead of screaming, 'Just like this stupid smile on face', she maintained control of her composure and processed his transactions.

Then he gave her a personal cheque, and asked, "Will you please give me twenties for this?"

"Sure." She counted out ten twenty dollar bills from the money she had just exchanged to U. S., and it irked her to be handing out money she was sure had been stolen.

Finally the work day crawled to an end. She sidled into her very welcoming, very comfortable, very plush, car. At a twist of her key the engine purred to life. She habitually opened the ashtray, stared at the shiny cleanliness, sighed, and closed the ashtray. She cautiously reversed away from her parking spot.

Pulling into the driveway at her home brought a wave of appreciation for her small space of privacy. A stop at her mail box produced a fistful of bills. Quickly opening and assessing them, she realized, as was becoming the norm, her costs were beyond her salary. Her paycheques were rapidly deteriorating under the pressure of ever increasing inflation, and for the life of her, she had no immediate solution for the problem. How much downsizing was humanly possible? Unfortunately, like everyone else, she needed food, heat, water, clothing, and the almost unaffordable use of her vehicle. At the rate she was going, her substantial savings account was going to disappear far too quickly.

Annoyance brought her thoughts around to Guy. Although he lazed in her apartment as though it were his own, ate her food without constraint, borrowed her car regularly, and helped himself to anything he might find convenient, he was the stingiest person she had ever met.

Suddenly dreading the possibility of having Guy descend on her evening with his arrogant and boorish antics, Arista got back into her car. She drove aimlessly. When a fast food restaurant came into view she pulled into the drive through and purchased a cheeseburger, french fries, and a diet cola. Then, she parked and ate in her car while deciding where she should go next.

Chapter 5

Having driven the short jaunt from town to the summit, she embraced a rich reward of sultry air hanging in the eerie silence unique to mountain tops. Filled with an intense need for solitude, she sought it by walking into the thick pine forest. Other than the gas station/café/convenience store along the only highway weaving over the mountain, there was no sign of civilization for miles.

Absorbed in self pity, feeling dry twigs snapping under her feet, Arista took a deep breath of pine impregnated air. Beginning to relax, she whispered, "This," a smile finally toyed with her lips, "is the closest thing to Heaven on Earth." She couldn't remember the last time she had noticed a single detail of the natural pleasures abounding throughout creation.

Circling around a large patch of snow, she bent down and smelt wildflowers, giggled at a pair of squirrels racing up a tree, and walked, and walked, and walked. Frosted crests stretched gracefully into the brilliant blueness of sky, wildflowers danced with the wind in a colourful ballet, and resilient pine trees spiced the air with fragrant abundance.

"The best things in life really are free." She cooed.

Intoxicated with the bliss of pure tranquility, Arista lost herself to the dreamy sense of stolen freedom. Hugging her arms around her waist, she twirled, glanced once more at the sky, and stopped as she glimpsed pink hues splashing the brilliant blue.

For the first time in a long time, she was noticing the splendour of a sunset. She wished she could stay here forever. She turned to the direction she had come from. On her way, she illegally plucked a handful of wildflowers to bring home. They would remind her to do this for herself oftener.

Twigs crackling under her feet haunted her with the feeling she had walked much further than she thought. The snowy patch she had skirted was nowhere in sight. Squelching the threat of sudden panic, she whispered reassurance to herself, "This won't be a problem." Her almost inaudible words slicing into thick silence sent shivers crawling creepily over her skin. Ignoring an unsettling hint of foreboding she sauntered back toward the one highway linking her to civilization.

Checking her watch, her mood plummeted in despair. "I've been walking for hours!" She groaned to deaf surroundings. Her throat tightened. Her breaths came in quick choking gasps and she struggled to grasp hold of escalating fear.

"People have told me that if I ever get lost up here, all I have to do is walk in the opposite direction of the sunset. It is a no fail guide to the highway." She whispered encouragement to herself. Walking swiftly away from the sunset she listened hopefully for sounds of traffic even though she knew any noise would be muffled by the dense bush surrounding her.

Suddenly, all she wanted in the whole world was to find her way back to the very things she had been running away from. The fast pace of her walk was making her legs cramp from exertion. The moon was suspended in a faint shadow above her as an ominous warning of rapidly approaching darkness. Spending the night outdoors was not a welcome notion. She hated being without hot water, shampoo, perfume and all other fragrances capable of provoking animal attacks. One weekend of camping had been enough to last her a lifetime, and now she was facing the daunting likelihood of spending a night trapped under the stars.

"I was extremely mistaken in thinking this place is paradise." She grumbled angrily while kicking a small cluster of pine needles. Then, seeing a snowy patch, she quickened her pace to a near run. Instead of the gas station, she saw four more clusters of snow. Recognizing it as an unfamiliar landmark, she sat down on a log in defeat.

Exhaustion overtook every part of her body. Looking around herself she formed a plan. She piled rocks into a circle for a fire pit. She collected small kindling twigs for an easy start and larger logs to burn slowly. Next she made a mattress with mossy soil.

"My despised habit might save my life tonight. And if something saves your life once, it has paid for itself." She mumbled to the emptiness around her while flicking the flint of a lighter to start the fire and then lighting a cigarette from the fresh package she had purchased at the convenience store. She hadn't intended to smoke the cigarettes. She simply wanted to know she had them available.

"This fire is the only thing between me and the predators out here." She emphasized the importance of fire as a roundabout way to justify smoking the cigarette that was making her dizzy.

Diverting her thoughts from the agitation of her ongoing nicotine battle, she struggled to prepare herself for a night filled with eerie wolf howls. As usual, the more tired she became, the faster her imagination roared. Trying to ignore terrifying possibilities of animal attacks, Arista filled her lungs with smoke, and it made her cough. Several deep, and consecutive, smoke filled breaths made her dizzy, sent her stomach coiling nauseously, and caused her chest to burn. She threw the remainder of her cigarette into the fire.

A rustling sound jostled her skittish nerves and sent her leaping to her feet in readiness to scramble up the nearest tree. As the sound came closer, her heart lurched to her throat, and she blindly backed away. In an instant, a jackrabbit leapt through the clearing, spotted her and leapt back to the cover of brush.

"Oh." She slumped at the recoil of abrupt relief. "I definitely know why I hate camping." Feeling snow crunch under her feet, she scolded, "I know better than to venture onto this stuff." Stepping lightly, she cautiously walked toward solid ground.

The jackrabbit leapt bravely out of the brush, looked at her, and leapt away.

"Stupid rabbit!"

With a sigh she lifted her foot to take the final step to safety, and suddenly found herself hurtling downwards on some crazy super slide cushioned by snow. At times the ground seemed to fall away before she would land on another mound of snow hurtling her further and further downward.

Certain she was dead, Arista stared into solid blackness. Breaking into a hot sweat as pain seared up her leg, she moaned with the surety of being alive.

"It wouldn't hurt this much if I was dead." Moving into a sitting position sent sharp stabs through every part of her body. Cautiously moving her hand against the gritty feel of loose rock, she heard the result of her touch as pebbles went skidding down a slope hidden in darkness.

Warned by the sound, Arista crouched into an awkward position. On her hands and her feet, she tested each inch of ground as she moved with care.

Finally finding a solid floor of level earth, she staggered to her feet. Stiff muscles ached with each movement. Following a dim path of light, Arista let heavy eyelids droop in the warm humid air mingling with blanketing darkness. Feeling her balance teeter, she opened her eyes and saw a steep cliff dropping at the edge of her toes. Her heart skipped a beat before racing in rib pounding speed and she backed away from the ledge.

Ready to let bats nest in her hair, she was about to turn back into the cave when she noticed a small curl of smoke drifting skyward. Peeking over the edge, a new spurt of energy came to her at seeing a tiny house nestled in the trees below. Thinking it must be a mirage, or a miracle, she took a second and hard look. When it remained solidly intact instead of vanishing into nothingness, Arista's pulse leapt with excitement and she squealed, "I'm saved!"

Quickly searching for a way to get down the mountain, she strained her vision past the darkness and followed a strange shadow of hope dangling over the edge. She discovered a rope, complete with brakes, was securely tied to a brace fastened to the cave wall.

"Just because I have never repelled down a mountainside before is no reason to stop me from doing it now." Giving her jagged nerves a pep talk she grasped the hand brakes and let herself glide down over the edge.

Chapter 6

"Come 'ere Bud." Hauk patted his knee invitingly at the scruffy golden retriever/cross/mutt whining at the door. Despite concentrated interest with something outside, he immediately obeyed his master.

"What's wrong Old Boy?" Hauk ruffled the thick tufts of golden fur between ears perked in keen alertness. "You never get spooked. What's out there? Is there another dog? Maybe a cute little girl dog you like?" Leaning into plush padding, he slid his reclining armchair back. Hoping the dog would curl up comfortably on the floor beside him, Hauk flipped a hardcover book open where he had let it close over his thumb, and settled back into reading. The dog stood staring at the door.

When persistent whining changed to sharp barks broken by deep growls, Hauk abruptly closed his book. Getting up from the chair in one agitated movement, Hauk glowered at the animal. Bud rolled liquid brown eyes to him in a silent plea for Hauk to open the door.

"I don't know what you think is out there." Hauk jammed his arms through the sleeves of a lightweight jacket.

Bud wagged his tail frantically, yelped, and made frenzied attempts to dig his way under the door.

"Sometimes," Hauk lifted a disapproving brow at the animal, "you do the stupidest things."

Hauk put his hand on the doorknob. Bud folded his back legs like springs in readiness to leap.

"Bud!"

Bud whined at the reprimand in Hauk's voice.

Hauk commanded. "Heel!"

Turning sorrowful eyes to his master, Bud skulked unhappily to Hauk's heels.

"Thank you." Hauk looked at the animal straining for release from the command. He considered the hair standing on Bud's back, contemplated hooking Bud to a leash, and picked up a rifle instead.

Struggling to balance against the mountain, Arista groaned as she lost her footing. Wishing it was as easy to repel as it looked, she swung uncontrollably in midair. She regained some stability by lodging her feet into grooves on the mountainside. Straining weary muscles, she released one hand brake, and moved it down. Then, she followed with the second. Inching her way, she kept her movements as fluid as possible. There had been numerous slips sending her flailing wildly through the air. They were depleting her energy and slowing her progress.

Taking a deep breath, she thought of the house below and how desperately she wanted to be there. Forcing her body to respond, she moved another few inches down the rope. Carefully choosing footholds, her descent took on a rhythmic motion. After what felt like an eternity, she dared to look up. Seeing the distance to the cave above her, she smiled with relief and encouragingly thought the ground must be almost under her feet.

Looking down, she whispered, "I could almost jump the rest of the way."

She considered releasing the safety belt and free falling the short distance to the ground. Deciding the landing might be a bit hard, she chose to take the extra few minutes and go down properly. After an unexpected amount of time had lapsed, she realized just how high she had still been and how much a fast landing would have hurt. Glancing to the ground, her entire body relaxed at the sight of seeing it a few scant yards below.

The distraction swayed her into a reckless swing forcing her to struggle for a foothold. Then, she heard a low rumbling sound. Lodging her feet against rock sent small pebbles tumbling down. The sound of their short fall was the music of victory.

The low rumble intensified below her. Looking down, Arista froze in confusion. In the darkness of the night, eyes gleamed.

With only two choices available, in her exhausted state she was almost ready to take her chances with the wolves. A flow of tears rolled down her cheeks at facing the excruciating climb to safety. Doubting she still had the strength to make it, Arista began hauling herself up the rope. The encouragement of finding help was gone, and so was her determination. Stopping every inch, she hugged the rope to herself as tears mixed with sweat.

"You are rotten animals!" Screaming at the beasts below, she hurtled a handful of small stones at them. Her show of aggression did nothing to daunt

Epidemic

the stalkers, but it did send her flailing through the air. Dangling without a fight, she held onto the rope.

Alerted by the faint sound, Hauk stopped to listen. It had been too quiet to be distinctly heard over the crunching under his feet, and not hearing it again, Hauk looked to Bud for answers.

"What is out here Bud? Is it a person, or a cat?"

The sound of a wildcat often held an uncanny similarity to a human cry of distress. People rarely venture into this area, and he had never come across anyone out here at night. Sharpening his alertness, he braced for an encounter with an aggressive predator. He double checked the ammunition clip on his rifle, and released the safety in readiness.

Bud leapt exuberantly away from Hauk. Prancing with impatience to move ahead, Bud turned and waited expectantly. When Hauk almost caught up to him, the dog sprinted another short distance forward. Bud's fur shackled and he suddenly stopped, crouched low to the ground, and rumbled deep muffled growls in his throat. Hauk knew danger was within feet of them.

"Bud. Heel." Hauk whispered the command.

Bud's low growls throbbed in the night.

"What are we doing out here Bud? We don't usually look for trouble." Thinking he had been a complete idiot for following his dog's bizarre behaviour, Hauk decided it was time to pull rank and be the intelligent master. "C'mon Bud." Whispering, he turned back for the cottage. "Heel."

The words were still on his lips when Hauk's eyes locked with a pair of eyes glowing in front of him. Taking rapid aim, he saw the wolf leap, he fired, and the animal fell to a heap on the ground.

"Bud!" Hauk's growl rumbled lower than any of the beasts. "Why are you taking us into a pack of wolves?" Hauk took long, paced strides toward the house with hopes of getting back before his ammunition ran out. "Bud! Heel!" Without turning to look back, Hauk moved ahead with anger coiling in his bones.

"Help! Help me!"

Hearing the distressed cry, Hauk stopped and looked at Bud staying obediently behind him with his tail tucked between his legs.

"Bud?"

The animal whimpered in response.

Crouching beside the dog, he whispered, "Where Bud?"

Turning, Bud looked toward the mountain and his body trembled fearfully.

Feeling the vibration under his hand, Hauk patted the animal reassuringly. "You don't want to be out here any more than I do." Looking at the mountain, Hauk mumbled, "Man and beast. I guess we both do what we have to do."

Skirting the bushes, Hauk strained to see against the darkness. Hearing an abrupt frenzy of barking and growling, he cleared the bush in time to see her skidding down the rope above five snarling wolves. With no time to think, he sent a bullet hurtling against the mountain. Rocks flew, the bullet zinged in a wild ricochet, and the beasts scattered.

Swift as wind, Hauk was by Arista's side. Moving in front of her, he positioned his back to the mountain while keeping a keen watch. Almost dragging their bellies along the ground, each member of the motley pack scuffled in the dirt as intensifying growls rumbled warning of mounting aggression. Hauk saw the leader standing off to the side. The thick bulk of the animal was a sure indication of his age, but Hauk assumed the strength was there, and focused on the five slowly crawling toward them.

Puzzled furrows creased his brow as he studied one, and then another, until he had assessed the entire pack. Momentarily letting his guard lighten, he mumbled with a whistle, "They're a bunch of old dogs."

Bud's growl intensified.

Feeling the warmth of her breath on the back of his neck, Hauk heard the scolding, "Old or not, wolves are dangerous."

Positioning the rifle in preparation for immediate fire, Hauk glanced over his shoulder at the black haired beauty. He indulged in the pleasant sensation of being the popular choice for the moment. Her soft warmth pressed into his back, and the fearful vibration of Bud crushed fervently against his leg. He toyed with the ego appealing idea that they were drawn to his magnetic charisma. As enjoyable as the fleeting feeling was, he let it splutter out like a candle in a downpour while levelling the rifle he knew was the main attraction.

Without letting his attention flicker from the pack, he asked, "Are you badly hurt?"

"Me?"

He slumped with exasperation for the illogical question. "Who else is here?"

She stiffened at the insult.

He blinked slowly and in that second heard the single word, "Shoot!" Fingernails dug into his back. Hauk opened his eyes to the sight of blood thirsty fangs hurtling toward him.

A shot boomed in the night. Hostility fell dead at Hauk's feet. Pressing tightly against him, Arista's hot breath fanned over his back. Bud yelped and growled as he wedged himself tightly between Hauk and the sharp climb of rock behind them. In front of them, the pack slowly backed away into dark shadows where they became invisible.

Hauk grasped hold of Arista's hand. "Let's get to the cabin."

Setting a steady pace, not too slow, nor too fast, he led her in the direction of shelter. Bud followed nervously and closely behind them. Feeling eyes in the darkness, Hauk knew the creatures were never far from them. Still, he kept the pace steady, and the safety on his rifle remained unfastened until they reached the refuge of his house.

Hauk removed the ammunition clip from his rifle after securely closing the door behind them. It sent a sharp metal sound resounding through the cabin. Bud plopped down comfortably by the fire.

Arista looked around, saw nothing through the tears pooling in her eyes, struggled to swallow a well of emotion, and broke down in sobs.

Uncertain how to handle the situation, Hauk opened his mouth to say something reassuring, could think of nothing, and closed his mouth. He cleared his throat hoping it would somehow stop her flow of tears.

She stood trembling and sobbing.

Cautiously moving closer, he hesitated, decided there could be no harm in a friendly gesture, and placing his hand on her shoulder, he asked, "Is there anything I can do to help make you feel better?"

Sucking in a long shuddering breath she shook her head negatively.

Perplexed by the uncomfortable situation, he remained standing and watching her for long moments. Feeling the strain of the night, wanting to relax, he feebly asked, "Do you want to sit down."

Shaking her head in a negative response, she leant against his arm and sniffled.

Looking at her head rest awkwardly on his arm, and the hand he had on her shoulder, he felt perplexed. He was far to tired to stand in this position for any length of time. He wrapped his arms around her and pulled her into a hug.

Her shuddering sobs eased to quivering breaths.

He asked, "What happened?"

Staring up at him, she remained silent.

Searching the dampness on black lashes, tears pooling in burnt almond eyes, tiny scrapes on reddened cheeks, starkly pale skin, and red swollen lips, he impulsively wished to see her smile.

"I don't usually have strangers dropping in around here." He chuckled with light bantering that failed to cheer her.

The absence of electricity, heat, and all the other creature comforts in civilization, made the location repulsive for most. The few people undaunted by a lack of conveniences were quickly intimidated by the abundance of wildlife and the difficult trek. An ample number of areas offering better accommodations for tourists left Hauk undisturbed by intruders in this remote wilderness, until tonight.

He made another attempt at finding out why she was there, and easing her suffering. "What brought you into my neck of the woods?"

Silently staring at his lopsided grin and the lack of confidence in his eyes, Arista's mind swirled with confusion. Too many extreme events had attacked her in a few short hours to even begin explaining. Then, as if creating a diversion to protect itself, her mind became absorbed with exploring his appearance.

Over the familiarity of those comforting and protective shoulders, she now noticed the slight grey and pepper sprinkling in thick waves of coarse black hair, and the deep mystical lights of blue eyes a shade near black, under dark lush lashes.

Made nervous by her blatant inspection of him, he ran a wide palm through his hair.

Missing the warmth of his arms around her, too distraught to act bashful, she continued satisfying her curiosity. Beginning at the thick arch of his dark brows, her vision skimmed over his nose angling in a straight line. Underneath, his lips were distinctly defined. Her eyes lingered for a few seconds on the very kissable, without being excessive, full lips meeting in a decisively straight set suggesting strength of character. Yet, as strong and steadfast as the set of his mouth was, there was no trace of the pinched thinness usually accompanying a bitter personality. Slowly sweeping her eyes downward, she paused at his jaw. Like everything else about him, it ran in one clean, firm line. And the ruggedness of dark stubble enhanced his male vitality.

Watching her watching him, seeking to break her hypnosis, he brought his hand up and rubbed his chin hoping the movement would snap her back.

The sound of stubble bristling against the motion caused her stomach to lurch with primitive response and her eyes continued to roam. Scanning over wide shoulders and the appealing bulges of muscle encasing his arms made her yearn to step back into the soothing feel of them. Seeing the magnificent width narrow to sleek hips hugged in faded denim made her catch her breath.

When she looked back up at him, he saw through her eyes and into her soul. The night was untamed. Having been tested to the extreme, any inhibitions she may usually let rule were gone and consequence was of no concern. She would do anything he chose to ignite.

Seeing her eyes spark with raw emotion, his conscience commanded him to pacify the mood. "You are welcome to sleep here tonight." He pulled out the sofa bed, removed the bedding from it and brought fresh linens from the small closet nestled beside the bathroom. "Sorry about the lack of privacy." He shrugged his shoulders at the bachelor design of his one room kitchen, bedroom, and living room combination.

Sanity began returning, and her eyes fell on the room beside the closet. "Do you mind if I wash up?"

"Go ahead. Make yourself at home."

"Thank you." Once inside, with the door closed securely behind her, trembling inched through every fibre of her body and she braced against the wall for support. Glancing at the mirror hanging on the wall facing her, her heart plummeted at the sight it reflected. Her hair was almost grey with a thick film of dust clumping it into ugly mats. Dirt and blood were smeared on her cheeks. Removing her cloths for a complete inspection, she noticed tattered tears in every thread she was wearing. Underneath, she found small pebbles dug into her flesh everywhere. Rivers of tears poured down her cheeks.

In a few minutes a gentle knock sounded on the door and Hauk asked, "Are you all right?"

Sniffing loudly, struggling to find her voice, she finally sobbed, "No."

"Do you need help?"

"Yes." Engulfed in misery she flung the door open.

Immobilized with surprise, Hauk absorbed her form in one transfixed stare. Not even daring to blink, he finally saw her tears.

Through their blur, she stared back at him.

He slowly let his eyes drift downward and his mind raced to rescue him from the stupidity of male reaction. Irresistibly captivated by the softness of curves flaring and peaking to perfection, it took a few seconds for him to see the damage. "Oh. Ouch." He winced at the small, but numerous flesh wounds needing attention.

Violent trembling shook to her core as the stream of tears intensified. "Help me."

Every raw emotion rioted within him. One part of the man wanted the woman. Another surged with a need to help her. The two instincts mixed powerfully. Racing to the forefront was an almost panicked necessity to console her tears as he folded her into a hug with the pure intention of easing her anxiety.

She cried on his shoulder.

He instinctively moved his fingers through her hair. When they stuck in clumps of dirt, he grimaced at the mess.

"Let's get you into the shower." He eased her out of his arms.

Docile as a child, she waited quietly as he twisted taps. When the temperature met his approval, he told her to step into the spray of water, which she did. Uneasy with the blank glaze of her eyes he smeared an entire handful of shampoo into her hair. Unable to think of witty encouragement, he went about his task in silence. The shampoo refused to lather, so he rinsed it out and tried again. The second attempt almost produced suds. By the third application her hair was clean enough for the shampoo to work into a foamy froth. He gingerly patted the dirt off her skin with a soft cloth and shower gel.

"It smells nice."

Glancing from her to the plastic pump bottle in his hand, he looked back at her with a grin. "Thank you. It is the same scent as my after shave."

There was no response from her.

He didn't know what, but he had expected something. Taking her hand he led her out of the shower, wrapped her in a large bath sheet, and twisted the taps to stop the flow of water.

"Now," he opened the medicine cabinet, "it's time for the hard part."

Laden with cotton swabs, tweezers, and rubbing alcohol, he walked out of the bathroom. She followed without needing to be coaxed.

"If you lie down on the sofa, I'll get those pebbles out for you."

Dreading the pain it was sure to produce, her steps froze.

Tensing at her hesitation, he quickly put the supplies down on the table beside the sofa. "You might want to do it yourself." He backed away from his assumption of leadership with as much dignity as he could muster in avoidance of a dreaded female tangent about independence. "It might not hurt as much."

"No." She walked to the sofa where she plopped down on her stomach and gave in to the overwhelming heaviness of her eyelids, let them close, and took a deep sigh. "I'm much too tired."

"Are you sure?"

"Yes."

Obviously she was not going to tend to her wounds. He sat on the sofa beside her, and one at a time he began plucking the pebbles from her flesh. Each fresh opening was doused with alcohol.

To her relieve, after the first few painful extractions her skin numbed to the rest. A tiny pile of grains accumulated on the table. When he was unable to see any more he said, "You're going to have to roll over now so I can do the other side."

With a groan, she did as she was told.

"Are you going to tell me how you landed at the bottom of my mountain?"

"It's your mountain?" She half opened her eyes, and a smile finally toyed with her lips.

Looking at her, impulse throbbed into his veins. Struggling to contain his ill timed libido, his jaw squared, his eyes shadowed, and his smile dug notches at the sides of his mouth. He confirmed, "This is my mountain."

Recognizing his abrupt tension for what it was, Arista silently wondered why men always obsess with sex when women are least likely to respond. Deciding it must be something like irresistibly craving an entire chocolate cake layered with thick rich icing at the onset of a new diet, she persisted, "How did you become the owner of a mountain?"

He smiled with a spark of mischief, "I claimed it."

"How can I claim a mountain?" She goaded.

"It's mine because I'm here. Nobody else ever comes out this way." He looked at her sceptically, "Except you." He wiggled out a pebble deeply embedded in her shin. "Why did you climb up to the cave? I only use it as a watch station to look for possible threats like forest fires. Fortunately, my descents have always been easier than yours, and I don't usually choose to repel. It is easier to walk down."

Nothing he was saying was making sense to her. "How do you walk down?"

"The same way you went up. That is a gentle slope leading to the side opening of the cave. It would have been even easier to walk down than it was to walk up."

First, she realized he assumed she had gone to the cave by choice. Next, she wished she had known about the other way down the mountain. Then, she remembered the wolves. If she had been walking she wouldn't have had a chance. With a slight tremor running through her she stared at him. "You saved my life."

"You have to thank Bud for that."

They both looked at the animal. Bud perked his ears at the mention of his name. Hauk told her about Bud's persistence.

She recounted her story for him, starting at the beginning with her lousy work day.

She refrained from telling him about wanting to avoid Guy. Guy talked of love and marriage while his actions spoke of possession and selfishness. Wanting children and companionship, she was not about to discard the man she might be able to accomplish those goals with.

Like every woman, she had first been a girl. She had dreamt of being swept into the arms of her soul mate, and gliding down the isle in a perfectly fitted gown of white satin, and into the strong arms of her beloved. Childish thinking had guaranteed the happy ever after life that would follow with the wonderful man created especially for her. As a woman, she still wished for someone to share a special glow with, which on the odd occasion, flows from the eyes of one person to the eyes of another and back again. She longed for someone to hug whenever the urge tugged, and to hold onto when the storms of life rage. She wanted someone to coo with over a chubby faced baby, someone to laugh and tumble with under the blankets. The hankering for unfound warmth was accomplishing no feat other than to drill a frigid hole in her heart.

Neither did she tell him about the job she had ditched, or the career she was currently contemplating even though her entire being shuddered at the idea of pouring countless hours and thousands of dollars into improving herself in a profession giving her no satisfaction.

Afraid he would see her as a loser, and thinking she probably was one, she kept it a secret that her life was a mess and out of control.

Calmly doctoring her injuries, he quietly listened to her tell him about her work day, her stop for fast food, her pleasant drive to the mountain top, and the walk she had enjoyed for hours. When she told him about the crevice he stared at her in shocked silence.

"What is wrong?" She questioned his intent gaze with a nervous edge in her voice.

"Are you sure you slid down through the mountain?"

The exasperated look she gave him, ringing of sarcasm, made a distinct statement.

"Sorry." He promptly went about defending his doubts about what she had said. "You did take some rather mean knocks on your head."

Coolness intensified in her eyes.

Floundering to undo the damage, he resorted to his usual ploy of using humour with a cocky grin, "And some other areas I have been happy to tend to."

Alcohol relieved scrapes with tingling cleansing, and she confessed, "The pain has subsided wonderfully." Snuggling comfortably into the sofa, she smiled, "Thank you."

"You are welcome." He fastened the lid on the alcohol bottle. "Now, you need to get some sleep."

He got up, went to the closet, returned with an oversized flannel shirt she assumed was one of his pyjama tops, and left the room flinging over his shoulder, "I'm going to get firewood. You will have some private time to get comfortable without being disturbed."

Bud enthusiastically leapt and followed his master.

Fear constricted her breathing and she protested, "Those wolves might be out there."

One eyebrow arched and his cocky grin returned. "Bud would let me know if there were any wolves prowling about." He bent over and jostled Bud's ears, "He is the biggest coward of a dog you will ever meet."

The door closed behind them. She removed the bath sheet he had wrapped around her, and replaced it with the cozy warmth of soft, thick, flannel. Hauk's scent lingered subtly in the material smelling of fresh laundering. The scant intimacy of his pyjama shirt brushing over her skin filled her senses like a mild and calming drug.

Uneasy with being alone, Arista passed time by inspecting her surroundings. Looking at the fireplace built with pale stones carefully positioned and mortared, she sighed when the comforting sound of crackling logs failed to bring relaxation. Imagining Hauk hauling each stone in with Bud by his side brought a smile to her lips.

The rustic perfection of wood slatted flooring sanded to shimmering smoothness, and cupboards made to an exact match enhanced by thick butcher block countertops gave the appeal of warm welcome. The gleam of brass handles on the cupboard doors winked reassurance at her. How could anything go wrong in a place with such charm?

An antique oak dining table and chairs shone from regular polishing. A generator fed the building with electricity. Only the refrigerator was running. The room basked in a soft glow from two kerosene lanterns, and from logs burning in the fireplace. The utter tranquility of the atmosphere was unsuccessful at erasing her restless discomfort.

When Hauk walked back in, careful to keep his entrance soundless, she relaxed and took a deep breath.

Hearing it, he looked at her and smiled. "I thought you would be sleeping by now."

"No." She snuggled under his blanket and nestled her cheek against his pillow. The small movements caused his flannel nightshirt to softly caress her skin. Tiny tingles sparked through her. She loved his scent, his feel, and the peaceful comfort of his presence. On a sigh, she said, "I was waiting for you."

Teasing lights danced in his eyes. "There are no big bad wolves huffing and puffing at the house tonight."

"Good." Sleep fogged her senses blissfully as she watched Hauk toss a pillow and sleeping bag on the floor and then snuff out the lanterns.

Two hours later, she was still awake. The haze of sleep was some mysterious illusion hovering ever so close but not quite attainable. Seeing Bud curled into a ball by the fireplace, and Hauk sleeping on the floor just off to the side, Arista felt the irresistible urge of temptation. Desperate for rest, she decided her desire to feel his warmth and hear his heartbeat was strictly rational and completely prim under the circumstances.

Almost holding her breath in an effort not to waken either Hauk or Bud, especially Hauk, she picked her blankets up in a crumpled heap. Adding her pillow to the bundle made it necessary for her to squeeze tightly in order to get her arms around the bulk. Her toes caught in trailing material numerous times as she tiptoed gingerly across the room. The warmth from embers glowing in the fireplace brushed her skin like flecks of sunshine and moonlight flooding through the window waltzed with her movements.

Soundlessly, she wrapped the blankets around herself, slunk onto the floor behind Hauk, and wrestled her pillow under her head. Listening to the steadiness of his breaths, she thanked God for letting her succeed, and she resolved that she would return to her proper place before Hauk could awaken and discover that she had slept with him. She was asleep within seconds.

She didn't see the smile toy with Hauk's lips as he heard her breaths slip into tranquil rhythm. Neither did she hear the distant howling of wolves. He did. And only when he was confident she would remain asleep, did he let himself drift away from wakefulness.

Chapter 7

Day Thirteen - Saturday

Dreams swirled in chaotic succession. She was sweating over a pack of wolves one second, being held in strong arms the next, and suddenly she was inhaling the succulent aroma of bacon. Sleepiness slowly drifted to wakefulness and she blinked against bright sunshine streaming everywhere while frantically struggling to remember how she had come to her unfamiliar surroundings.

"Good morning Sleepyhead."

The cheery male voice quickened her mind with instant memory, and her veins chilled as she realized he had awakened to find her sleeping beside him. Mortification gave way to shame before surrendering to acute embarrassment. Horrified, she dared to sneak a quick glance at him. She was relieved to see him cracking eggs into a sizzling frying pan without any trace of annoyance. Bud perfected the scene with doleful and loving attentiveness showing in his huge brown eyes as he watched Hauk's every move.

Mesmerized by the quality of Hauk's life, Arista propped herself up on one elbow and watched. Warmth from flames greedily licking fresh logs in the fireplace drifted and enveloped her skin. Sunbeams cheerfully flitted into the windows occasionally bouncing off the chrome spatula and sending little circles of silver looping around the room as Hauk flipped eggs. It was a strange and comfortable zone compared to the empty hustle and bustle of her everyday life.

For the briefest second she wondered what the purpose was in her everyday choices, on the other side of the mountain, where she pushed to do things she hated doing only to gain the dissatisfaction of never attaining her goals, no matter how hard she tried. A very quiet thought, whispering at the back of her mind, suggested she was building on the wrong ideas, and in the wrong place.

"Breakfast is ready." He waited for her to join him at the table he had laden with orange juice, buttery toast, crisp bacon, scrambled eggs, and golden hash browns.

Mentally comparing his enthusiasm, and her reluctance to move away from his pillow, his blankets, and the warmth radiating from the fireplace, she said, "You're energetic this morning."

"I'm definitely a morning person." He beamed and his grin sailed straight to her heart.

Twisting and pushing up off the floor, triggered spasms of pain. Agony rippled through her body with a vengeance. Seeing her skin pale and her lips pinch to whiteness, Hauk put the plate he was carrying, heaped with cinnamon buns, down on the table. Alert watchfulness deepened the intense blueness of his eyes.

"Let me see where it hurts." Crouching beside her, he waited for her to show him the spot.

"Everything hurts." Easing back onto her pillow she moaned softly as she twisted onto her stomach. "This is the worst." She lifted the nightshirt and the action blazed her cheeks with hot embarrassment.

Her flustered discomposure was heightened by his gentle and thorough inspection of her buttocks. Her skin absorbed the warmth of his hands as he moved up the smooth slope of her hip. Stopping every few seconds, his hands performed probing nudges and his fingers worked over the specific areas causing her hip to throb with relentless pain.

"Ow!" A sudden stab of pain jolted a blazing path down her leg.

"You have some deep bruising." He eased down the hem of the flannel shirt, "The biggest problem is an inflammation caused by a patch of dirt still caught under your skin."

"It'll fix itself, right?"

"It will fester to push the dirt out, unless we clean it."

Dreading the guaranteed pain of more digging with the tweezers, and more stinging alcohol, her eyes darted away from him and she grasped the first escape her vision fell on. "Don't you want to eat breakfast first? It would be a shame to let your food get cold." She smiled with a surge of confidence. Coaxing him to eat breakfast might give her time to figure out a more comfortable cure for her problem.

"It will be better to do this while you have an empty stomach." He straightened onto his feet beside her. "It's going to hurt."

"Then you eat."

"I'll put the food in the oven to keep it warm." Heading toward the kitchen, he casually slid over his shoulder, "When the irritating particles are removed the pain should subside almost immediately." With a reassuring grin he added, "Then you will be ravenous after all the energy you spent yesterday." Dishes heaped with food were placed in the oven with speedy efficiency.

Fresh bursts of fire flaming from her hip made her stomach churn with nausea, and she doubted every word he said. Choosing to cooperate, she plastered a brave smile on her face.

He saw red blotches on her cheeks standing in stark contrast against the pale whiteness of her skin. His skin paled as her suffering seeped into him almost as though it were his own. He walked to the medicine cabinet where he fetched a pair of tweezers and a bottle of alcohol.

He gently worked at removing dirt from under her skin. Despite her extreme effort to be strong, tears streamed silently down her cheeks, and she hid them by pressing her face into the pillow she was tightly clutching with both fists.

"This is the last tiny sting."

She braced against the burn of alcohol.

"We are finished." The sound of him twisting the cap onto the bottle flooded her with relief. "Give it a couple of minutes."

He got to his feet, and she suddenly felt an incredible desire to ask, or beg if need be, for him to stay with her. Resisting the urge, she pulled the pillow tighter against her face. Drawing in a deep breath, she moved gingerly and waited for unbearable flames to stab through her leg.

"It should feel better soon."

Surprised that he was still at her side, a smile came naturally to her as she replied, "It already does."

Then he went and put away the tweezers and alcohol.

Moving slowly, she waited, and when no intense pain returned she rolled onto her feet.

Hauk came out of the bathroom and she grinned at him.

Seeing the success of his efforts, he chuckled, "I told you it would help."

"You were right." She brought a palm up and flattened it against her stomach as the nauseous rolling transformed to hungry grumbling. "I'm starving."

"Good." He flashed a cheerful grin. "I have a feast prepared for us."

Completely engrossed in her food she was puzzled when eating made her feel hungrier rather than filling the empty gnawing. Hauk ate at a slower pace and threw morsels to Bud, who greedily gulped down every crumb.

Three hours later, Arista drifted from a heavy sleep to wakefulness. Surfacing through a mist of disorientation, she glanced at the stillness in the log cabin and memory dawned. Hauk had taken Bud outside as soon as breakfast was cleaned up. Unable to resist the thick quilt bunched on the sofa, she had nestled into it and fallen asleep in seconds. Still enjoying the cozy warmth, she burrowed deeper under the quilt, and wondered what Hauk was doing outside for so long. She drifted back into a dream laden sleep.

Quietly walking through the door, Hauk stopped at the sound of muffled giggles. Arching one brow, he saw Arista laughing softly even though she was obviously sound asleep. She took a deep breath, laughed louder than before, and awoke at the sound of her voice. Changing mental dimensions did nothing to lighten the humour she saw in a source that was invisible to Hauk.

Rolling over with a merry giggle, her eyes suddenly locked with his. Realizing she had a small audience brought a blush to her cheeks. Unable to subdue the laughter bubbling from her, she had no options other than to explain, "I had the funniest dream."

Hauk watched a smile curve her lips and sparks dance in the depths of her rich brown eyes. The sight brought a smile to his own lips as he listened to her babble over nonsense.

"It was the funniest dream." She succumbed to another bout of laughter before breathlessly continuing, "This man was playing a guitar and it was about this big." She spread her fingers to a distance of two inches. "And it actually worked."

Hauk didn't see anything overly amusing about her story, but he watched her laugh until tears ran down her cheeks.

"It was so funny." She gasped for air between bouts of laughter. "I've never seen such a little guitar."

Hauk refrained from telling her she probably never would. His stomach growled, he walked to the fridge and took out a loaf of rye bread, a package of shaved corned beef, mustard, a tomato, a jug of milk, and a blueberry pie. Next, he opened an oversized drawer and took out a family size bag of potato chips.

Watching him, Arista sat up, hugged the blankets comfortably, and leaned onto an elbow she propped against the arm of the sofa. "What did you do all morning?"

Glancing up from the bread slices he was carefully laying on the butcher block counter, his brow arched as his mouth quirked in a lopsided grin. "I chopped some firewood. Then I sat down by the river and did some fishing."

"There's a river here?"

"It's more like a stream. It flows down and widens into the lake at the bottom of the mountain."

"There's a lake?"

"Yes." He chuckled. "There is a beautiful crystal clear lake."

"Did you catch any fish?"

"No." He slathered thick clumps of corned beef onto three slices of bread and doused them with mustard. "I should have gone a little closer to the lake. Maybe tomorrow I will take the canoe."

"You have a canoe?" Arista's eyes lit with anticipation.

He smiled, and he teased her by withholding the invitation he knew she was seeking. When her eyes clouded with uncertainty, he chuckled, "I even have a spare lifejacket you can use."

A spark of enthusiasm kindled in her eyes.

Misgivings shadowed his. "Have you ever been in a canoe?"

"Yes." The confidence in her voice exaggerated her previous excursions, which were maybe three or four.

Hanging his faded denim jacket on a hook, the subtle smell of leather reminded him, "Somebody is probably looking for you by now." He picked his cell phone, wrapped in a leather case, off the shelf beside him.

Spotting the phone in his hand brought Arista's mind back to the reality of her life. Her thoughts flashed through agitated customers, vehicles controlled by erratic drivers, stacks of overdue payments awaiting her, and nothing overly enjoyable to cushion any of it. She shrugged, "There won't be anyone looking for me."

Hauk lifted both brows in disbelief.

Ignoring him, Arista got up from the sofa, wandered over and looked out the window.

"Don't you have any parents or friends?"

"I'm not home much. Nobody will pay any attention to my phone going unanswered."

One dark brow quirked, he vaguely wondered what kept her so busy, and he couldn't resist teasing, "Do you slide down crevices often?"

"No." Her eyes widened at the deplorable idea. "Once is enough to last me a lifetime."

Hauk's stomach took an unexpected dive and his nerves prickled, which he knew was in expectation of hearing an unwanted answer to his next question, "Don't you have a boyfriend?"

Arista wrinkled her nose at an image of Guy piercing her thoughts. She reflected on his brown eyes, and decided she didn't like them. Neither did she like his mousy hair, his average height, his slumped posture, and his severely crippled attitude. There were no character traits she found admirable in the person she called her boyfriend.

"Does your silence mean, yes, no, or maybe?"

With a sigh of displeasure, she shrugged, "Maybe."

"Don't you think he might be worried?"

"Guy doesn't concern himself with much. He probably hasn't even noticed that I'm not home. Guy only thinks about Guy."

Nasty as it was, Hauk took his opening, "Does that mean Guy loves Guy?"

Hearing it, Arista giggled, and belated pangs of guilt prompted her to defend, "It's the way he was raised."

"He sounds extremely spoilt."

Arista's brows lifted, merriment bubbled in her, and she nodded agreement.

"It sounds like you might benefit from having a little space away from him."

"The universe might not have enough space to put between us."

His response was an affable chuckle that warmed her with an easy feeling and restless lust.

He teased, "I can't offer you a galaxy, but, if we go for a canoe ride, today instead of tomorrow, I will show you a world filled with freedom."

She loved the unconventional idea of being liberated from restrictions. She also knew the flimsy depiction of perfection was unlikely to survive harsh reality, so, with an arch of her brow she silently dared him to prove his statement.

Accurately reading her expression, confidence sparked in his eyes and his lips curved into a cocky grin.

The sexy notches his mood was producing at the sides of his mouth sent warm coils rippling through her stomach.

He saw that too. The notches deepened and his eyes shadowed with keen male watchfulness.

Feeling her muscles tighten in pure physical appeal to the electric currents running between them, Arista dodged the intensity of it by turning toward door and challenging, "Show me something new."

Hearing his chuckle, she instantly recognized her poor choice of wording, but she didn't miss a step in her waltz to the door. Reaching her goal, she realized her intention was to escape the seductive privacy of the cabin. Her plan was flawed. It was equally secluded for many miles around them.

Sudden awareness of him being a stranger slammed her with fear and she floundered with uncertainty. "You've already been out all morning." She glanced at the cell phone he had left on the table. It was her only link to civilization. "We don't have to go if you don't want to."

In reply he stepped behind her and swung the door open.

"Oh." Arista hesitated. "Are you sure?" She kept her eyes firmly hidden under lowered lashes.

"After the silent challenge you threw my way, I'm sure."

Without looking at him, she mumbled, "What challenge?"

"You have no idea what awaits you."

Almost ready to scream with mounting tension, she spun and faced him.

The intense distrust he saw in her eyes shot daggers through his heart. He let his hand drop away from the door.

Seeing carefree glints dissipate in blue depths, and puzzled creases etch between dark brows, and understanding dawn, Arista's heart plummeted with regret for her illogical bout of panic. She belatedly realized he had already had every convenient opportunity to be the villain if his intentions were tainted.

"Would you rather give your boyfriend a call and make arrangements to go home?" There was sadness glimmering in his eyes, but there was no trace of anger or resentment.

"No." Hoping he was still willing to accept her company, she smiled and almost begged, "We were going for a canoe ride." She tried coaxing further by cooing, "Remember?"

"First." He closed the door. "We need to discuss a few things." He walked to the table and pulled out one chair for her and another one for himself.

With a sinking feeling, Arista joined him.

"You should contact somebody to let people know where you are."

She lifted her chin haughtily, "I don't want to."

"I don't want trouble with the law if they come looking for you."

Her eyes twinkled and she brazenly lilted, "Are you a fugitive?" Wincing at visible anger building in his eyes, she regretted having made her second blunder in a few short minutes.

"No. I'm not a fugitive."

Knowing it was going to be her third inappropriate response didn't stop her from asking, "Then why are you hiding?"

Thunder intensified in his eyes, like she'd expected. For some daft reason the storm brewing in him quivered over her and she relished an exciting kind of anticipation. Her previous fear had transformed to impulsive lust.

Baffled by her behaviour, he scowled, picked up the telephone, got up, walked over to her, and plunked it down on the table in front of her. "Do you want to go canoeing, or don't you?" His scowl deepened, and her amusement heightened.

"Yes." She cooed at being once again invited on an excursion with him.

"Call someone to tell them you are all right first."

Wrinkling her nose with distaste for the task, she pressed numbers, and sent the call.

She listened to the shrill ring once, twice, three times, and closed her eyes with relief. Moving to disconnect the call, she swallowed caustic irritation when Guy answered. She barely said hello, and Guy barked, "Where are you?"

Glancing sheepishly at Hauk, Arista blushed and twisted the truth, "I'm at the lake with a friend."

She flashed a glimpse of Hauk as Guy bellowed, "I spent all yesterday evening looking for you!"

The loudness of his voice made it necessary for her to hold the phone away from her ear.

An arch of Hauk's brow silently chided, 'naughty of you not to call sooner'.

"I had all kinds of special things planned for us this weekend." Guy goaded with a lie. He hadn't had any plans, but he wanted to make her wish she had been home. In truth, he had been expecting to spend the weekend relaxing at her place, honouring her with his company, and letting her pamper him.

Arista scorned Guy's idea of 'special'. When, or if, he actually took part in any outings, they were repetitively designed to stage displays of flash and showy pomp in an effort to impress her friends and any other females happening across their path. Unfortunately his ploys were usually too successful. Arista deemed Guy to be a clown, and the women he attracted were delusional if they thought Guy was interested in them as anything other than ego food.

Hauk could not possibly be aware of those details, so, as usual, Guy was competently making her look like the one at fault.

Glad she had been spared from spending the weekend in Guy's company, and wanting to put an end to the conversation, Arista bluntly stated, "I'll call you when I get home."

"What?!" Guy's voice snarled through the receiver. "You aren't even going to apologize?"

"Mazey's waiting for me. I really have to go." Sneaking a glance at Hauk, Arista's blush deepened to a scorching crimson.

"Who's Mazey? Is she more important to you than me?" Sarcasm frosted across the line. Guy eventually filled the ensuing silence with, "Fine! Then don't bother calling me when you get back!"

Rolling her eyes at the redundancy of their quarrels, she compliantly agreed, "Ok. I won't call you."

"Arista?" His voice changed to a whimper.

"What?"

"You've never acted this way before."

Impatient with the whine in his voice, she innocently asked, "What am I doing that I have not done before?"

"You're acting like you don't care." He sniffled loudly.

Seeing Hauk holding back a bout of laughter, Arista clucked her tongue at the nonsense surrounding her. "We'll talk when I get back."

"If you are not back by tonight, there will be nothing to talk about." He snubbed, "I'm flying out in the morning." He added importantly, "I have business to tend to."

Easily picturing the haughty tilt of his chin, she rolled her eyes at memories of the conferences she had attended with him. They were all the same. Speeches were presented to an audience about millions of dollars available for the taking, and of the ultimate success each member would eventually enjoy. Arista scorned the false illusion. The entire operation was a legal pyramid scheme, and the top people were making a fortune, but the others, like Guy, were never likely to see their piece of the pie.

Still, the listeners, hoping for easy money, lapped up the enticing morsels they were thrown. Bra straps were showing on sloppy outfits, and negligently unzipped zippers were noticeable, in the crowd filled with clashing colours and fragrances. Each person did their best to feign important sophistication under the umbrella of delusion. The appeal of it was something Arista never quite grasped.

Less than pleased with herself for it, Arista knew she could be just as lofty and priggish as the next person when she put her mind to it. She saw it as a weakness in herself, and was striving to be honest.

"Are you still there?" Guy's voice gained strength. He was misinterpreting her silence. He believed she was regretting having placed their relationship in jeopardy, and she was afraid of losing him.

"Then there's nothing to talk about." She clicked the button that disconnected the call, and glared at Hauk. "There! Are you satisfied? Do you see why I did not want to call Guy?"

Hauk burst into laughter. "Now I understand why you said you 'maybe' have a boyfriend." He pushed his chair back with good spirits flicking in his eyes. "Let's go for our canoe ride."

Following him, Arista muttered a string of complaints ending with, ". . . just the stupidest thing." Twisting her mouth, she pitched her voice sarcastically, "Phone somebody."

Growing impatient with the conversation remaining focused on Guy, Hauk gently placed his hand on the small of her back, opened the door, and stopped when he realized, "You need better clothing than my flannel pyjama top."

Glancing down, her mouth trembled with a near onslaught of tears as she realized her shredded clothing was still lying in a dusty heap beside the bathroom door.

"This is an easy problem to fix." He walked over to his closet. "These won't make a fashion statement, but they should come close to fitting you." He pulled out fleece sweat pants and held them to her. "They shrank to half their original size the first time I washed them."

She took them from him and guessed that the elastic waist would be tight enough to keep them from falling down on her.

He continued sifting through his cloths.

As he was pushing hangers around, she spotted a cotton tank top appearing to have suffered equal shrinkage, and presumed Hauk was prone to throwing everything into the dryer on high heat for as long as the dryer would possibly run.

Quickly interrupting his rummage through the closet, she grabbed it, "Do you still wear this?"

Glowering at it as though it were the most despicable thing in the world, he shook his head and grumbled, "No. It shrank to a third of its original size. I don't know why they waste time making such garbage."

"Can I do anything I want with these cloths?"

"They're yours now." He shrugged indifference at the clothing he deemed worthless.

Locked in the bathroom, she inspected tiny red sores turning pink with healing, and went about her task.

When she stepped out, Hauk's first reaction was surprise, and then the narrowed watchfulness of a man suppressing sexual attraction.

Heat flushed her skin and her eyes lit. She had done her best with the clothing by rolling the ivory pants at the waist to bring the seat of them up from her thighs to where it belonged. The white shirt draping over the bulk had given her figure the appearance of a barrel with an extra wide girth in the middle, so she had taken a pair of scissors and cropped it a few inches below her bosom. It hugged her curves prettily, which suited her irrepressible urge to attract Hauk's attention to her femininity at every opportunity.

In silence, Hauk opened the door, waited for her to go through, made a motion at Bud to follow, picked up his rifle and ammunition, and closed the door behind them. Being unaccustomed to weapons, Arista's steps froze as she studied the metal barrel glistening in the sunlight.

Giving her a withered look, Hauk grumbled, "Fugitives carry guns."

"You're not a fugitive."

Remembering the wolves and imagining what else might be lurking in the shadows, she skittered to his side. He draped an arm over her shoulders. The companionable mood followed them into the canoe and down the stream.

"Look over there." Hauk slowly pulled the paddle backward to stop their motion.

Following his line of vision, she saw one of the wolves and considered it to be nothing more than a detestable predator.

"Why don't you shoot it?" She whispered an easy solution for the creepy feeling those animals gave her.

"Why?"

"They're mean and dangerous."

"They are what they are meant to be. You can't eliminate things just because you don't like them."

Her expression said he was the dimmest man on the planet, and she said, "They are just animals." On a further thought, she elaborated, "Wolves."

Giving her a look like one would give an erring child, he instructed, "Watch."

Nothing spectacular happened as they sat rocking soothingly on gentle waves. In a flash, a huge jackrabbit jumped from the brush. The wolf instantly became a moving mass of fur leaping left, then right, and back again as it followed the rabbit's frenzied flight. In seconds the prey fled to safety and the predator crumpled on the ground panting for breath.

"It's too old." Hauk concluded aloud.

"You should really put it out of its misery." Arista suggested, and received another withered look from him.

"You need to learn greater respect for life."

"I respect life just fine, especially mine, which explains why I would rather not have those beasts around."

"They were here first."

Scowling at the animal lying at the edge of the bush, she agreed, "I vividly remember the greeting they gave at my arrival."

He winced at the memories and thought hard in search of an answer to give her. Finally, he stated the facts at their simplest. "Life is what it is. I believe all forms and states of life are deserving of respect."

Lifting a paddle, he launched the canoe into motion. The wolf leapt, turned to the sudden splashing sound made by the paddle, growled, and ran off to hide in the shadows of the forest.

Hauk warned, "Brace yourself, we're coming up to some small rapids and it takes a bit of work to get through them."

In seconds the canoe was hurtling through frothy water. Seeing large rocks racing by, Arista paddled fervently to keep the back of the canoe from careening into a wild spin. In another instant they were on still water.

Dazed by the flurry of changes, Arista stared blankly at tiny diamonds of sunlight sparkling on glassy smooth water.

Chapter 8

"We've reached the mouth of the lake. It's easy going from here." Hauk's words rumbled into her thoughts and she turned her eyes toward him. It took another few minutes for her to notice the carefree grin playing at his lips. Thankful to be on still water, she lifted and dipped her paddle.

Matching his strokes to hers, Hauk observed, "You're being quiet."

With a shrug of her shoulder, she kept paddling.

"We are heading toward the middle of the lake."

Looking at where she was going, she angled her paddle to steer them closer to shore.

"Do you have any particular destination in mind?"

Holding her paddle motionless above the water, she watched tiny droplets fall from it and splash onto the lake and send ripples of disturbance over the glassy surface.

"Where are we going?"

"I don't know." She began rowing again.

"Maybe we should go the other way." Despite his suggestion, he rowed with her.

"Why?"

"There's a town on the other side."

"Oh." She continued paddling aimlessly.

Laying his paddle across his lap, he stopped helping her. The single sided push of her paddle turned the bow of the canoe around to face the opposite direction. Then, his strokes again matched hers.

"You really don't care which direction we take, do you?"

She continued to paddle in silent despondency. He lifted his paddle out of the water, put it down in the canoe and reached over to take the paddle from her hands. Not encountering any resistance from her, he eased her paddle to the floor of the canoe. They sat quietly in the canoe drifting on a gentle breeze. She stared blindly over the span of water surrounded by towering mountain peaks. He leant his chin on closed fists propped with elbows dug into his thighs, and he studied her with concern.

A pair of loons swooped onto the water nearby. The birds dove under the water, surfaced with graceful sleekness, and bobbed peacefully beside each other. Then Arista saw something she had never seen before. The pair peeped to each other in tones so soft she might have thought it was her imagination if it wasn't for the distinct movement of their beaks. Eventually one cried the famous call. They dove again and surfaced almost within touching distance from the canoe. Arista sat with Hauk in silent stillness. The pair dove, surfaced at a distance, and drifted further away.

Picking up their paddles, Arista and Hauk resumed rowing. Seeing a smile toy with her lips, he gently suggested, "Nature does wonders to heal the soul."

"Friendly birds do."

"Not big bad wolves?"

"No." She shuddered, "Not those."

Having expected a town with a noticeable population, Arista was surprised when they tied the canoe to a wobbly dock and strolled down a street lined with a few rickety old buildings. An aged two story with a sharply peaked roof had a humble panel of wood nailed to the side painted with the words, 'post office, groceries, liquor.' Judging by the severe sideways lean of the building, Arista assumed it generated a considerably inadequate income.

Walking past a small restaurant, she looked through the hazy glass window and she saw five empty tables adorned with bright red and white check tablecloths. The single story building had probably been perky when the white siding and red trim had been freshly painted. The white was now yellowed and the red was faded to a shade between rust and pink.

Two dilapidated bungalows lined the other side of the street. Set off a short distance down the road was a two story house attached to a single story hardware store posting the sale of fishing and hunting licenses. A sign hanging in the window read, "Gone to lunch. Be back soon."

Hauk informed her, "That sign has been there for a long time. I think he has been 'gone to lunch' for two years."

"That is a lengthy lunch. Has the store actually been closed all that time?"

"People phone him when they want something, and he opens the store for them." Looking at their surroundings, Hauk said, "That's probably the most efficient way to do business here. Everybody knows everybody, and they will call when they want something."

At the sound of an engine, Hauk took Arista's hand and they walked back to the dock. There he was given a parcel from the driver of a sporty boat with 'Water Taxi' painted on the side. Their exchange was brief, the boat left a churning wake behind in a speedy departure, and Hauk walked to where Arista stood waiting for him.

"You should use these before we go any further." He handed her a sturdy brown shopping bag.

Spreading it apart by the handles, she glanced inside. There was one pair of jeans, two ordinary tee shirts, two pairs of socks, one beige bra, some cute underwear, basic hygiene supplies, and one pair of white runners. "You don't like my outfit?" Remembering his smoky reaction to it, she grinned at him impishly.

"It's a little too noticeable." He struggled to explain, but simply stated, "I want to talk to Ben."

It gave her misgivings about Ben, and she asked, "Where should I change?"

"I'll show you." Taking her by the hand, he led her to a small square building by the docks.

She instantly recognized it as an outhouse.

Seeing her cringe with distaste at the prospect of going into it, he assured, "Nobody actually uses it anymore. It just hasn't been taken down. Let me check to make sure no rodents are inside."

Arista's skin crawled.

Holding the door open for her, Hauk assured, "It is safe."

Clenching her jaw, Arista embarked on her task. She was relieved to find the building vacant of four legged residents. Neither was there any foul odour. Still, Arista changed her clothing at a fervent pace and longed to get away from the confinement of the small and creepy building.

The jeans fit almost perfectly with only a little more room than was needed. The bra was a bit snug but it stretched generously. She chose the peach coloured tee shirt instead of the yellow one, and pulled it roughly over her head. She stuffed the cloths she had been wearing into the shopping bag.

To save time, she left the building bare foot, took a deep breath when she reached Hauk's side, and pulled the socks and shoes on. "How did you get this stuff?"

"I ordered it while we were in the canoe." Seeing that she was ready, he began walking toward town.

"Oh." Following him, she said, "I didn't notice."

"You were a bit glassy eyed. I think you were shocked by the rapids."

"Oh. Yes. I remember you making a phone call. I wasn't listening to what you were saying."

His eyes danced with fun, and he teased, "No wonder I didn't get a reaction when I guessed your weight."

Lifting her brows, she looked up at him.

He shrugged, and said, "Patti needed something to go by."

"Who is Patti?"

"She owns and operates the main clothing store in the area. I gave her a brief description of your figure and she picked the cloths." He did a sweeping glance over her selection, "She seems to have done all right. What do you think?"

Arista smiled agreeably. "Everything is stretchy." To show him, she pinched a piece of material up from her thigh and pulled the denim/spandex. "Patti made wise choices. I could be ten pounds above or below the size you suggested and these cloths would fit."

"Is that ok?"

"It's great. Thank you."

They turned off the main street onto a winding gravel road appearing to go nowhere. A one and a half story house became visible after the last bend in the road. Like the other buildings, the weather stained siding, which had once been white, was yellowed and pealing away.

Intensely curious about Hauk's purpose, Arista held her impulses in check and refrained from asking questions. Quietly walking beside him, she patiently waited to find out what he was doing here.

Finally, he stopped and said, "Ben lives here. He's a friend of mine."

"Oh."

"This is where I store my truck when I'm at my cottage."

Reeling as though she had just been dealt a physical blow, Arista fought for composure and her heart sank at what she knew was next.

"You need to get home so you can relax and rest." Instinct coiled against the logical action he was taking. As inexplicable as it was after knowing her for such a short time, the last thing Hauk wanted to do was bring her home, and that made it more important for him to do so. "You need to get back to familiar places and people. You took quite the fall, and it caused considerable stress on your body."

The shrill creaking of a screen door opening at the house drew their attention. Arista watched a tall, lanky man, with a chaotic mass of dark curly hair, walk toward them. His baggy overalls, once blue now faded grey and torn in numerous areas, lacked the slightest hint of style. His swagger was untamed and cheerful.

"Hello Hauk." He grinned as he closed the distance between them.

"Hi Ben." Hauk clenched his jaw in determination to complete his task despite the persistent urge to turn around and take Arista back to his cottage. "This lovely lady is lost. I will be bringing her home."

Ben's eyes lit with amusement as he guffawed, "Lost?!" Hearty laughter rumbled from his belly. "How'd ya find this place to ged lost in?" Ben was sure she was here on Hauk's invite, for lewd purposes, and Ben's interpretation of the situation was clearly visible in his expression as his gaze swept lustily over every curve now covered with ample material.

Arista surged with appreciation for Hauk having saved her from the error of her first outfit. Never did she want to entice Ben. Her impertinent actions were intended to arouse Hauk, and only Hauk.

Hauk gave Ben a stormy look.

Seeing his disadvantage, Ben put undue concentration into nudging the ground with the toe of his boot while asking, "I guess 'at means ye'll be wantin' yer truck?"

Hauk recognized the hint of trouble. Ignoring it, he pressed, "Yes, I need my truck. She lives-" stopping in the middle of his sentence, he felt immensely foolish for his oversight.

Arista named the city that lay on the other side of the mountain.

Ben whistled softly. "Ya've come a fair distance."

Keeping her thoughts silent, Arista figured her home was quite close via the shortcut through the mountain. The highway made a wide loop. It took a couple of hours to drive from one city to the other, but even that wasn't overly far away.

Being a stranger to shyness, mannerisms, or reservation of any kind, he instantly probed, "How'd ya ged all the way oud 'ere?"

"It's a long story." The sharp clip in Hauk's voice clearly told Ben he was not going to hear details.

Ben's attention and curiosity lingered on Arista for a few silent seconds. Then he looked at Hauk, and wittily suggested, "Wouldn' it be better to leave earlier in the day?"

"What did you do to my truck?"

Ben's eyes widened as he put an effort into looking innocent. "Nothin'. I'm just thinkin' it's a long drive. You're on holidays 'n' all."

Observing the two, Arista wondered what Hauk had meant when he had said he stores his truck here, and now Ben referred to Hauk as being on holidays. It made her curious to find out where Hauk was, and what he did, when he wasn't here on holidays.

Hauk repeated, "What did you do to my truck?"

Ben kicked at the dirt with the toe of his boot. "There were some wolves buggin' my dogs, so, me and Caleb went after them."

"You chased them down with my truck?"

"Ya. I guess we should've stopped at the ridge."

Hauk groaned low as he looked over to the ridge of rock cropping against sloping cliffs.

"It's not too bad." Ben grinned, "Just a couple of flat tires, and-"

Hauk interrupted, "Those were new tires."

"I know." Ben grimaced.

Relieved, and indebted to Ben for preventing her departure, Arista swallowed the urge to laugh.

Seeing her amusement, Hauk blinked slowly as he mustered patience for the situation, and he asked Ben, "What else?"

"The muffler shook itself a little loose."

Hauk diplomatically asked, "Is the muffler still on my truck?"

"Well." Ben dodged giving details.

Hauk's voice rumbled in the semblance of a growl, "How long will it take to fix?"

"I can ged it done in three days."

"Three days?"

"It might take longer."

"Why?"

Arista quietly studied the appeal of frustration tightening Hauk's expression and darkening his eyes, and her stomach jigged with electric attraction.

Ben's eyes flashed his lack of confidence before he dared a smile while admitting, "Me and Caleb's goin' fishin' tomorrow." A grin of anticipation broke, "We might'nt get back right away if the fish 'r bitin'."

Ben's pleasure-comes-before-all-else attitude drew a soft and spontaneous giggle from Arista.

For it, she was rewarded by a scowl from Hauk.

She almost laughed outright when Ben gave her a look of appreciation, and inching closer, Ben used her as a shield against Hauk's agitation.

Hauk simply stared at Ben, then Arista, and back at Ben. His glare settled on Ben. "Just fix my truck as soon as possible."

"You're supposed to be at the cottage for another two weeks." Ben made himself a comfortable berth of time. "It'll be just like you left it by then." He grinned confidently, "Only better, 'cause it'll have a spankin' new muffler." His attention riveted to something behind the pair, and he hollered, "Hi! Jack!" Amusement lit his eyes and he intentionally antagonized the other man by yelling louder, "Hi! Jack!"

Both Arista and Hauk glanced at the tense figure of a bulk of a man passing behind them and glowering at Ben.

When he was down the road and out of hearing, Ben chortled, "He's a little put out with me."

"So I've heard." Hauk lifted an accusing brow.

"He started it." Ben prickled defensively. "Who would swear at the minister's wife? Jack did that."

"The feud you have going with Jack is none of my business." Hauk chose to stand on neutral ground in the popular and growing animosity of the locals against Jack. "We need to get going." He took Arista's hand in his.

Living for the moment, in this incredible adventure she had accidentally fallen into, Arista walked by Hauk's side without concern for anything other than being with the man nestling her hand in his.

Chapter 9

Sliding the canoe off the dock, they paused when they noticed a short and plump woman with a cloud of cropped brunette curls walking swiftly toward them with an anxious expression. She was silently working her mouth trying to decide what to say.

"Hello Sofie." Hauk's smile radiated friendly assurance. After waiting a few minutes for her to tell him what was troubling her, Hauk took it on himself to broach the problem, "Is everything all right?"

"I hate to bother you." Dark brows worked nervously over brown eyes sunken under heavy and droopy lids. "Vinny has had a nagging cough for weeks now." She looked at Hauk pleadingly. "When I saw you here, I thought it would be good if you could take a look at him."

"Of course I will." He pulled the canoe back onto the dock, and took Arista's hand in his. They walked along the main street through town, and to the last house.

"It's probably nothing. I feel terrible about bothering you."

"It's no trouble for me." As always, Hauk's grin came with ease. "It will probably relieve your mind immensely."

A smile broke on Sofie's lips as she confessed, "I have been very worried about him."

Following her into her house, Hauk listened to her tell about Vinny's initial symptoms. It had begun as any ordinary cold, and had subsided before escalating to an aggressive cough. Hauk lifted the boy's eyelids, looked underneath, took his pulse, timed his breaths, and asked, "How long have you been sick?"

"One month." The boy moaned unhappily.

"Are you sure it's been a month?" Hauk grinned at what he suspected was a sure exaggeration.

Seeing Hauk's doubts, Sofie assured, "It might be a little longer."

It seemed odd, to Arista, that Hauk was checking Vinny. Why didn't Sofie take Vinny to the doctor? Assuming that friends help each other, Arista watched Hauk interact with Sofie and Vinny.

After a few thoughtful minutes, Hauk asked, "Has he had a fever?"

"No."

"Do you vomit or feel nauseous?"

"Sometimes I throw up when I cough."

"How long has that been happening?"

"I started throwing up yesterday."

"Do you cough hard?"

"Yes. I go down onto my knees because I can't breathe when I cough."

"How long have you been doing that?"

"I started doing that yesterday too."

"Do your eyes and nose get runny?"

"No."

"No?"

"After I cough, my throat gets yucky."

"Do you cough stuff up?"

"Yes! Lots!"

"Do you have sore joints or a sore throat?"

"No. My chest gets sore though."

"Where does it hurt?'

"Here." Vinny put his hand over his upper chest on the right side.

"Do you wheeze?"

"No."

"When did your chest start to hurt?"

"It started hurting today."

Looking at Sofie, Hauk asked, "Was there a lapse after the first cough?"

"Yes. I thought his cold was gone."

"I suspect this a second virus that is unrelated to the first." Hauk patted Vinny's knee and smiled reassurance at Sofie. "I don't think it's anything to worry about, but he should be seen by a doctor at the clinic."

"What do you think it is?" Sofie pressed for information.

"I can't say for certain. Make sure the doctor orders chest x-rays and a complete blood count." He studied Vinny thoughtfully and asked Sofie, "Have you noticed anything unusual about his cough?"

Confusion flooded Sofie's eyes, and she asked, "Unusual?"

"Does he make strange gasping sounds?"

Glancing at Hauk, Arista sombrely considered the implications of his unusual question. She decided she was being paranoid about an ordinary cold, and she let her suspicions slide away.

"No." Worry intensified in Sofie's eyes.

Seeing it, Hauk consoled, "I would like to write a note for you to bring along to the clinic."

"Oh thank you." She let out a sigh of relief. "If they know you are involved he will get the best care they can give him."

"They give their best to all their patients."

"Here you go." Sofie gave him a pen and paper with confident expectation beaming in her expression.

Hauk wrote the note.

Sofie telephoned the clinic.

Listening to the conversation, when she hung up he asked, "Did you get an appointment for today?"

"Yes." Sofie smiled as she dialled more numbers. "I'll call the water taxi right now."

While Sofie made the telephone call, Hauk smiled at Vinny and effectively erased Vinny's apprehensions by asking, "How is Sarg doing?"

"Great!" Vinny leapt from the chair in excitement. "Have you seen him?"

"No, I haven't."

"Hey! Sarg!" Vinny screeched at the top of his voice.

Arista, Hauk, and Sofie, all winced.

"Kids." Sofie mumbled with an apologetic smile.

A black bundle of fur sped through the room, crouched to the floor and squirmed gleefully at Vinny's feet.

Seeing a tiny puddle growing under the quivering puppy, Sofie marched across the room, twisted Sarg around, and scolded, "Look at this." She dipped the yelping pup's nose in the puddle, marched him outside, and returned with a mop and pail.

"Puppies." She again smiled apologetically.

"It was an accident." Looking mournfully at the door, Vinny defended his pet.

Sarg yelped and barked pleadingly at the other side of the door.

"I know." Sofie rinsed and wrung the mop before washing the floor for a second time. "He has to learn this belongs outside."

"He will." Vinny held his breath as he moved stealthily toward the door. Reaching it, he let his breath out, he turned the knob, and a remorseful Sarg slunk over to cower at Vinny's feet. Bursting into violent coughing, Vinny clutched his chest.

Concerned about Vinny, Hauk asked Sofie, "Do you still have my cell number?"

"Oh yes." Sofie assured fervently, "I wouldn't misplace anything of such great importance."

Arista paid close attention to Sofie's display of deep respect. Glancing at Hauk, Arista knew Sofie's high regard had to be due to Hauk's repetitive and reliably kind treatment of her.

"If you need any help, give me a call no matter what time it is."

"Oh." Sofie's brow creased as she stated earnestly, "I don't want to be a nuisance. It was awfully nice of you to take the time to come here today."

"Call me if he gets worse." Hauk repeated.

"I will." Her belief of having been bestowed with a great honour radiated on her face and in her voice.

Silently rowing along the shoreline of still water, Arista frankly stated, "Sofie certainly is taken with you."

"What do you mean?"

"Haven't you noticed the way she looks at you?" It was difficult to describe.

He nonchalantly shrugged, "She's Sofie."

"It's like she thinks the world revolves around you."

"She's Sofie." He angled the strokes of his paddle and moved them into the river.

Thinking Hauk was oblivious to Sofie's great respect for him, Arista pressed, "She looks at you as though she believes you are able to make the impossible happen."

"I have helped Sofie and Vinny out a few times. I guess she appreciates it."

Watching him closely, there was no trace of arrogance in Hauk's reaction. He was gorgeous, generous, compassionate, and humble. It was an amazing and refreshing combination of personality traits.

Struggling to put the needed pressure into her oar as they entered a current going against them, Arista no longer had time to rehash events. When Hauk turned the canoe toward shore, and then pushed the bow out of the water, Arista looked around nervously searching for lurking predators. Seeing none, she hoped Hauk would hurry with whatever he was doing and they would soon return to the safety of the water.

"This is where we portage."

Arista stared at him in shocked horror. Then she glared fearfully at the bush seeming to loom with potential death.

Hauk patiently stated the fact, "We can't possibly row up those rapids."

Staring at the frothy water ahead of them, she realized it was an obvious fact she had comfortably overlooked.

Lifting the shotgun in his hand he reminded her, "I still have this with me."

Fastening her trust on their single defence, she gingerly teetered to the front of the canoe rocking under her movements.

"Look at Bud." Hauk grinned at the animal romping in tall grass with carefree abandon. "He's the biggest coward of a dog you will ever see. If there were any wolves in the vicinity he would smell them, and you can be sure he would be hiding behind me with his tail tucked between his legs."

Remembering Bud hiding behind Hauk the night of her rescue, Arista actually felt her muscles relax. Only then did she realize how much she had tensed without being aware of the tautness setting in.

Hauk lifted the front end of the canoe. She took the back. They flipped it upside down, and carrying it over their heads they trekked along a well worn path, which she suspected was created by Hauk. In a short period of time, without falling prey to mishap, they slid the canoe back into the stream on the other side of the rapids.

Experience was teaching her that beasts were not lurking around every tree in readiness to pounce and devour her any more than bogie men were hiding under children's beds.

Chapter 10

A fire crackled as strums of Hauk's guitar drifted through the room. Watching him sit on the stone hearth, Arista basked in tranquility. The magic of his light hearted engrossment with the guitar swirling alongside the sweet smell of wood smoke brewed a mystical calmness able to dissolve the world away. The mood transformed his tiny cottage into a peaceful island of contentment amidst a scurrying planet set in a vast universe spinning with dynamic motion.

Thinking life couldn't get any better than it was at the moment, Arista snuggled into the cushy softness of Hauk's oversized armchair. Then the velvet depth of his voice filled the evening air with a gentle melody. What she had thought was perfection before, became enhanced as her senses beat to his rhythm. His words filled her with comfort and trepidation at the same time. His lyrics indicated a favourable absence of possessive traits and implied a daunting willingness to slip away from relationships without regret.

When he finished, a tiny and nervous giggle escaped her lips. Seeing his eyes cloud with a shadow of doubt, she prickled with guilt for her insensitivity and explained, "Your song sounded like a romantic send off to a female friend."

A grin quirked his lip, one brow arched, and he admitted, "It was, but she never heard it." With a shrug of his shoulder he added, "The phrases are perky, and I like the beat."

Detecting no remorse or longing for the past, she lowered her eyes to hide the insecurity it created for her. Oddly enough, the same element she was fretting over was causing another irresistible tug of attraction. She was unable to decipher whether she was being drawn to the challenge of his independent spirit, or if she felt safe with his lack of dictatorial pride, or if her femininity was tuning in to a sensitive side of him that she wanted to tap into.

He changed the beat and the words. His next song told of a legend from a different era. When he finished, he toyed with the strings, and then he looked at her and asked, "Who's your favourite hero?"

"King David."

Arching his brows over baffled eyes, Hauk asked, "From the Bible?"

Gently laughing at his surprise, she answered, "Yes."

Having expected a different answer, like perhaps the modern and fictitious version of Robin Hood, Hauk contemplated plausible reasons for her answer. Unable to determine any, he asked, "Why?"

The dreaminess of her romantic version waltzed in her eyes as she explained, "He was an epic warrior. His relationship with Bathsheba became one of the greatest love stories of all time, and his songs give his readers encouragement to this day." She grinned at Hauk.

Hauk arched an amused brow. "His life was worthy of admiration."

"I think so."

"His accomplishments would be hard to compete against."

"Impossible." She grinned cheerfully. "I think you better set your own path instead of trying to rival his."

"I can convey emotion." His brows creased sceptically as he once more strummed his guitar and launched into a song.

She reeled at his words. They were not about romance, but rather about life. Agony, darkness, and loss bled alongside hope, victory, and love.

When he finished, she conceded, "You have felt great emotion." Compared to the depths he sang, she was extremely shallow.

"The song is not about my personal pain." His brows arched over shadowed eyes. "It's what I've seen. My own life has not suffered many great tragedies." The guitar made gentle music at the touch of his fingers. "When it's all said and done, nothing in our life seems to be within our control."

She considered engaging in a debate, which would be easy to spin off his statement. The erratic events happening in her life were guaranteed to support his theory and give him the win. She relaxed against the softness of his chair and let philosophical thoughts slip away.

Far more interesting was the play of muscle rippling up his arm as he toyed with his guitar. Letting her eyes drift, she skimmed over the appeal of faded denim hugging him as he sat with the guitar resting on his thigh. When her vision shimmied naughtily where it shouldn't, she felt a blush heat her cheeks and she hoped he hadn't noticed. Her eyes suddenly riveted to his, and she knew he had seen.

The heat of her blush flamed to scorching.

His eyes challenged her for a brief second. He carefully placed his guitar in the case, snapped it closed, and asked, "Do you play cards?"

"Yes."

"What do you play?"

"I know most card games. You choose one."

His eyes sparked with humour. He got the cards, she hoped he wasn't planning on a betting game, and they sat on the floor by the fire. He dealt them each six cards and plunked the remainder face down between them.

Hoping she had the right game in mind, she chanced it, flipped two cards, and grinned when she revealed a wildcard.

He snarled at her card.

Bud was curled in his usual evening position by the fire.

The game required little thought, and lulling into their easy friendship, Arista said, "I never asked who your favourite hero is."

"Are you asking now?"

"Yes."

"Lancelot."

"Lancelot?" Sparks lit in her eyes and she envisioned armoured knights and glossy stallions. "Why?"

"He won the kingdom and the lady."

"Oh." Never having acquired a taste for history, Arista truthfully knew nothing about Lancelot, not even if the story was fact or fiction.

He grinned mischievously and teased, "You don't know anything about Lancelot, do you?"

She admitted, "No I don't."

"He was the bravest knight to sit at the round table. Lancelot is part of the Arthurian Legend. The Arthurian Legend is a collection of literature spun around King Arthur and his Knights with inspiration derived from chivalry, courage, unity, loyalty, and love. Parts of the legend are based on the history of King Arthur. Lancelot was implemented into the tales centuries after the first recorded myths." Hauk lit with enthusiasm. "I love literature. I used it to fill some art requirements at the university." With a cocky grin, he teased, "Do you want to hear about Chaucer?"

"No."

"Are you interested in Shakespeare?"

"No."

"Have you seen stories about the Holy Grail?"

"Yes." Unsure where the conversation was headed next, she watched him warily.

"It's part of the Arthurian Legend. You've heard of the magical sword Excalibur?"

"Yes."

"King Arthur's legendary sword is said to have been removable from the rock only by himself. Legend deems him to be an epic warrior."

"Then why isn't King Arthur your hero?"

"Lancelot won the lady and the kingdom." He grinned, "At least in some versions of the tale. You know what the best thing is about Lancelot?"

"What?"

"He's a legend. His story can be changed to become more suitable at will."

She grinned with freshly piqued interest. "How would you change Lancelot's story?"

"I would dress him in blue jeans. He would drive a racy car. Guinevere would not wear bulky robes draping from her neck to a flowing train trailing behind."

The lust whispering in the depth of his voice seeped into Arista and sent bursts of reaction warming the most fun places in her body. Her mind swirled with mini fantasies of the sexiest clothing she could think of. Her first thought was a playful lacy bra and a short full circle skirt and dangerously high stiletto heels. Amazing things could happen. Perhaps a delightfully sheer negligee would be fun, or fine silk clinging to every curve.

Seeing the direction of her mood in her eyes, and in the perky peaks of her breasts, Hauk silently watched her.

Blinking dreamily at the fire, Arista considered the possibility of it taking years to explore every arousing avenue with Hauk. The notion of 'years' was equally appealing. If they ever ran out of ideas, which she was sure they wouldn't, they could think up new ones. The extreme stimulation of his very presence would guarantee success. Snapping out of her fantasies, she asked huskily, "What would Guinevere wear?"

Her question, and the look in her eyes, effortlessly hurtled him into fleshy absorption. "She would wear," numerous tantalizingly revealing ideas flashed through his mind in rapid succession. All of them starred Arista playing the role of Guinevere. His imaginings quickly worked around to where there was no clothing, just nudity.

A shrill ring from his cell phone sliced the silence before he had a chance to give her a shameless answer. After a brief, and sober conversation, Hauk clicked the phone closed, turned to her, and stated, "I have to leave."

Fear raced through her veins and crawled over her skin. She didn't want to be alone, during the night, in this secluded place. As peaceful and wonderful as it is with Hauk, it would be quite the opposite without him.

Seeing her misgivings in her eyes, he suggested, "Would you like to come with me?"

"Yes." She got up, walked to her purse, clutched it tightly, pulled a comb through her hair, and began a search for the socks she knew she had discarded somewhere in the room. Then she thought of something just as unappealing as staying at the cottage by herself. "Are we going to take those rapids in the dark?"

"The rapids are too dangerous at this time of night."

She was glad to hear it, but, "How are we going to get out of here?"

A necessity to save time forced him to quickly explain, "There's a clearing out front. The hospital's helicopter will land there." He looked pointedly at her feet. "They'll be here in a few minutes and we want to be ready to leave as soon as they arrive."

Finding, and pulling on her socks, she wondered what was said over the phone. There was no sign of a threat. Still, there could be knowledge of an impending earthquake, or avalanche, or something. She anxiously blurted, "What kind of a disaster is expected to happen here?"

He was standing by the door waiting for her to join him. "They need me at the hospital." Placing his hand on the doorknob, he spurred her along, "The helicopter may be called for an emergency before it gets back. We don't want to keep them away any longer than absolutely necessary."

Hearing the drone of an approaching engine, Arista scrambled into her shoes and slung her tattered purse over her shoulder.

Chapter 11

Walking into the staff room after spending four gruelling hours working in the emergency unit, Hauk saw Arista sleeping in one of the six cushioned chairs surrounding a television set. On the screen, the news was reporting a hijack attempt made earlier in the day. Pausing to watch, Hauk unemotionally reflected on how events seem to go in waves. For the longest time there would be little or no such occurrences, and then for a stretch, like they had been seeing lately, they became almost daily happenings. He walked over and gently shook Arista.

"Huh?" She struggled to see him through the blur of waking.

"Let's go."

"Where are we going?" Her eyelids fluttered closed.

"I have a hotel room across the street for us." He looked at her twisted position in the small confines of the chair. "Beds will be very comfortable right now."

Motivated by the appeal of pillows, blankets, and a mattress, Arista struggled to her feet, wobbled with the imbalance of sleepiness, and vaguely began remembering the extreme respect she had been honoured with because she was with Hauk.

When she thought Hauk was a rugged bushman, with no real direction in his life other than enjoying solitude, he was unthreatening. Escape from social pressure was exactly what she wanted.

Discovering the truth of his life, and that his cottage is nothing more than a spot of temporary respite from everyday responsibilities, was giving her a sense of disorientation. Nestling her hand in the comfort of his, and walking to the hotel with him, she pondered the informative way staff members had showered her with kindness. Hauk was held in high regard by the people working with him, and that spoke volumes for his personality and work ethics.

Day Fourteen - Sunday

Three hours later, Arista woke to sounds of running water. Glancing at Hauk's bed and seeing it vacated, she decided to get up, gave into the temptation of snuggling into her blankets, and she drifted into a light doze. The bathroom door opened, and she waited to hear Hauk's mattress creak under his weight. The safety latch at the door clicked her from drowsy lethargy to alert wakefulness.

"Where are you going?"

"I have to get back to the hospital."

"You've only slept for three hours."

His grin sparked with an energy the fatigue in his eyes denied. "I'll be fine. There will be time to sleep later."

Heading out the door, Hauk considered the significance of the emergency meeting they had had a few hours earlier. Standard medications were in use to treat the exceptionally high number of people suffering with respiratory discomfort. Numerous doctors suspected they were dealing with a communicable disease. Dr. Monroe had dismissed the concern as rubbish, fought against straining the budget with what he considered to be unnecessary testing, and insisted that the influx of patients were suffering from asthma.

Arista remembered the last two nurses having taken a break in the lounge. They had discussed nine women in the maternity ward, all expected to deliver before morning. The emergency ward was overflowing with people suffering respiratory distress. Being in the lesser level of danger, victims of a bus accident were forced to wait for medical attention.

The bus passengers were relatively lucky as the worst injury sustained in the accident was a broken leg, which had been tended to immediately. It was remarkably good fortune considering the seriousness of the crisis. The bus had rounded a curve, come across an unexpected patch of snow that had slid down from higher on the mountain, lost control on the slippery road, careened along the sharp rock of the mountainside and tangled into steel mesh designed to protect the highway by catching falling rocks. The other side of the highway dropped over a sharp cliff. If the bus had slipped in that direction, the results would have been catastrophic.

Tossing restlessly, Arista rolled out of bed, slipped her jeans on, fastened a bra under the tee shirt she had used for pyjamas, and left for the hospital. When she got there, she began at the information desk, was referred to one station after another, and eventually, the head nurse in the children's ward sought Hauk's permission and, when it was granted, the nurse accepted Arista's offer to volunteer her services.

The nurse informed Arista that the shift change was due to happen in less than one hour, and there was still an overload of work to be done. The nurses were unable to give any care other than responding to immediate needs. Arista was given the task of sitting with one particularly ill and lonely little boy.

The nurse told her that his mother was at home looking after her other two children and his dad was at work. Being new residents in the country, they had no extended family or other network of support able to help. The father felt too insecure about his job to take time off. Their child was one of the sickest ones on the ward. Antibiotics were proving unsuccessful at treating his condition. His system was weakening noticeably from the constant strain. His doctor was expecting to place him in intensive care if his health continued to deteriorate.

A buzzer rang in a different room, and the nurse left to respond.

Looking down at the child placed in her care, Arista's heart twisted at the sight of his pale complexion. Sleeping on his stomach, his diapered bottom was lifted over bent knees. Deep black lashes fluttered over cheeks almost as white as the sheet. Then, he stopped breathing and alarms shrieked a warning.

Arista pressed the button for the nurse, and grabbed the child into her arms. When he took a loud gasp of breath, Arista released the breath she had been holding. Cautiously moving her hold on him without disturbing the intravenous tubes running into his arm, Arista positioned the screaming child soothingly against her shoulder.

A nurse raced into the room, quickly assessed monitors, and saw that the crisis had passed.

Arista explained, "He stopped breathing."

"He's been suffering interrupted breathing patterns." The nurse walked over and gently rubbed the child's head. "He is already on as heavy a dose of antibiotics as we can give him." Glancing at her watch the nurse apologized, "I'm sorry, but I have to go report to the morning shift and let them know what has been done and what still needs attention." Hesitating, she looked at the child, and then she assured Arista, "If he stops breathing again, one of the other nurses will respond." With a sigh, she left for her meeting.

Arista looked down at the child in her arms. Thick tufts of black hair curled in random sprigs over dark brown eyes. She saw the biggest, roundest, most trusting eyes, and she wished there was something she could do for him. His arms locked around her neck in a squeeze of a hug and her emotions dipped into a tailspin.

Sitting down in the rocking chair set in a corner, with the almost sleeping baby cradled at her shoulder, Arista's thoughts sank back in time. The reports she had prepared flashed through her mind as clearly as if she were reading them at this very moment. What she was thinking was impossible. Creating a diversion from her troublesome suspicions, she pressed a button on the remote control sending vivid colour and boisterous activity onto the television screen suspended from the ceiling by a metal apparatus.

Hauk walked in and caught the serenity of her mood. Standing quietly unnoticed he observed the scene.

Mulling over possible reasons for the child's respiratory distress, Arista read the hospital band on the child's wrist and saw the name David. Looking at the roundness of his mouth sucking his thumb, seeing him as positively adorable, she figured the name was perfect for him.

Having known her for only a couple of days, Hauk was amazed at her ability to roll with punches. He was certain she was the most easy going and content person he had ever met. He stood watching the beautiful woman rocking the sleeping child.

Her vision collided with his, he stiffened, and said, "You looked too comfortable to disturb."

She flashed him a spontaneous smile.

The warmth of it melted the exhaustion out of him.

"I didn't see you standing there." Arista got up and placed the sleeping child tenderly in the crib. "Are you finished?"

"Yes."

A nurse came bustling in with a beaming smile. "I would like you to meet Tracy. She's David's mother."

Tracy walked directly to the crib without paying heed to any of them. After ensuring that her son's health was no worse than when she had last seen him, she turned to the nurse, "He's looking a little better."

Everyone, including Tracy, knew there was no improvement in David's condition.

"He'll be fine." The professionally clad woman smiled with confident encouragement despite the difficulty they were having diagnosing and treating David's illness.

The mother leaned over and tucked blankets lovingly around her child. "I don't understand why he is not getting better."

Alertness kindled in his eyes, and Hauk walked over to the crib. He first inspected the chart, and then checked the child. "The worst of it should pass soon."

At her questioning look, he held his hand out in greeting and introduced, "I'm Dr. VanLiev."

She responded with a handshake and asked with refreshed hope, "You know what's wrong?"

Respectfully supporting his college, Hauk firmly replied, "He is in excellent hands with Dr. Braimer."

"I hope you are right." A doubtful quirk tugged at her lip.

"David will be fine." Hauk gave Tracy a reassuring smile and turned to Arista, "Are you ready to leave?"

"Yes."

As they were walking away, Arista heard the nurse telling Tracy about her having volunteered to help during their overloaded morning. Being a friend of Dr. VanLiev's was used as sound credential for the trustworthiness of Arista's character. Tracy replied by asking the nurse to thank Arista for her help.

Arista silently kept pace with Hauk. She had lost half a night's sleep, received no monetary gain for her effort, and there was no lofty prestige. Unlike ventures supplying tangible rewards, this one had given her the elusive treasures of fulfillment and satisfaction.

Chapter 12

Still being honoured with the sofa, an uncomfortable pang of guilt struck when Arista looked at Hauk sleeping on the flour. Even Bud was moving about with respectful silence.

Through the window, Arista saw the enticing glow of afternoon sunshine. Gaining confidence in the wolves having found better hunting grounds, she remembered the last sighting of them having been further downstream when she was canoeing with Hauk. Building her courage, she headed for the door. There she stopped, eyed the rifle, decided it must be simple to use if she needed it, and picked it up.

Bud whined softly and looked at her doubtfully.

Welcoming his protection, she patted her leg softly and whispered, "C'mon Bud."

Together, they went outside.

Nervous quivers instantly fluttered over her skin. Staying close to the safety of the cottage, she sat down on the steps by the door. There, boredom struck almost immediately. She quietly slipped back into the house, fetched her purse, went outside, and lit a cigarette. When she finished it without seeing any disturbances in the vicinity, she looked over at Bud. The animal was sniffing curiously around a nearby bush. His hair was flat, his ears were perked, and his tail was wagging gently. Seeing him fearlessly amusing himself, she decided to do the same.

Moving into a sunny clearing near the cottage, she placed the rifle on the ground beside her, squinted up at the clear blueness of the sky, and felt the warmth of the sun caress her skin. Daydreaming about Hauk, she imagined sultry fantasies revolving around the two of them, and developed an intense desire to make him as aware of her as she was of him.

Mulling over different possibilities, a suntan suddenly seemed to be just the thing to give her skin a healthy, sexy, glow. She slid her jeans off, and flounced her tee shirt over her head. Piling her cloths into a makeshift pillow, she laid back and enjoyed the sensation of sunshine waltzing warmth over her skin.

After half an hour she rolled onto her stomach to tan her backside. Looking around, she observed the utter privacy of isolation. Knowing Hauk would sleep for hours, she unfastened her bra. Squirming to smooth uncomfortable lumps of ground caused the loose straps to tangle around her arms. Impatient with the contraption, she added it to the pile of discarded clothing she was using for a pillow. Bud moved closer to her and flopped down in a lazy heap. She let herself drift into a comfortable doze.

Skipping over her skin, a playful breeze cooled the heat of the sun as insignificant dreams tripped over each other in her subconscious. "You're going to burn." Strange words vibrated through a skewed dream about green bologna. Her eyes fluttered open.

Seeing Hauk standing by her, she instinctively moved to scramble into a sitting position, remembered her state of undress, and sunk back onto her stomach. With scorching crimson flushing her cheeks, she babbled nervously, "I thought you were sleeping."

"I was." He sat down in front of her. "I got up to get a glass of water half an hour ago and saw you out here. I thought I should wake you before you burn."

"Half an hour is not long." She smiled with calm assurance. Her mind was speedily working at trying to figure out how she was going to correct her indecent state of undress.

Looking toward the trees, Bud rumbled a throaty growl and his shackles came up.

Fear overran her quest for prudence. Gathering the dusty bundle of cloths to her breasts, Arista stood up, "I think I will go inside now."

Allowing his eyes to linger on the breasts inadequately covered, he vividly remembered every detail of her. Noticing the anxiety in her eyes, he chuckled. "Bud is probably just harassing a mouse or a squirrel. Nothing is likely to bother you."

Doubting Hauk's words, Arista moved rapidly toward the house while asking, "Why not?"

"Animals don't like people." He shrugged. "Besides, I think they can smell the metal of guns, or the residue of gun powder." He picked up the rifle she had negligently left behind, and followed her. "Most animals don't make their presence known when I have a weapon with me." Performing a quick inspection of the rifle, he asked, "Do you know this is not loaded?"

She stopped and looked at him. "Why isn't it loaded?"

"I unload it for safety reasons. I only put ammunition in it when I expect to use it." An amused grin played on his lips.

A large sigh of exasperation for her oversight accompanied an exaggerated roll of her eyes.

"I store the bullets over the coat rack. Now you know where to find them."

She marched for the house with frustration evident in each movement. Intentionally lagging behind her, Hauk's vision lingered on the curvaceous lines of her back flaring into the soft curves of hips hypnotically swaying a turquoise lace thong and stretching down to enticing legs.

Containing his surging libido produced intense irritability, and in the two minutes it took to walk to the house his lips tightened with restraint digging one tight notch at each side.

Glancing over her shoulder as she turned the doorknob, Arista saw the lusty shadow in his eyes and the tense set of his mouth. It washed her under a warm tide threatening to sweep her legs out from under her. Walking through the door, she hid her reaction by keeping her back firmly turned to him.

Seeing her moving languidly away from him, his veins pulsed.

Arista slipped into the privacy of the bathroom and closed the door gently and firmly.

Staring at the closed door, Hauk ran a wide palm through his hair.

Arista leant back against the door, took a deep breath and let it slowly glide out. None of her plans were working. The field of her chosen profession had spun out from under her. The flow of circumstance had her working in a bank and dating Guy. Guy was a black hole on the planet sucking her into his abyss. Another bizarre twist had landed her in this confusing and lustful paradise.

With a groan, she rubbed her temple.

"Did you say something?" Hauk's question drifted through the door.

The sound of his voice swam through the liquidity of her reactive body. Rubbing her temple harder, she answered, "No." Her natural reaction to him had all the coolness of flames leaping to gasoline. "I was just clearing my throat." She coughed twice to make the excuse believable.

After putting her cloths on, she walked out of the room with staunch determination to hide her chaotic attraction to him. She plastered on a fake, but believable, smile. Seeing the drawn pallor of his complexion, she accurately guessed the cause, and her practiced, reliable, perfect, plastic smile, drooped with a lopsided tilt.

Lifting a brow at the torture of sweet tension between them, Hauk knew he should offer to take her to a bus station and get her home. Instead he suggested, "Let's take the canoe upstream. There is a fantastic swimming hole not far from here." He grinned, "You have to see it to believe it."

Embracing the idea of cold water stinging away the pooling heat within her, she clutched her purse, headed for the door, and waited for Hauk to join her.

"I'll interpret that as a yes." He followed, and opened the door.

They pulled the canoe ashore, turned it upside down by a cluster of trees, and secured their oars and life jackets underneath. Hauk took her by the hand and led her the few feet to their destination.

Arista stood in a clearing staring at the beauty of nature. She spotted a thin thread of sulphur water gently trickling down the mountain, into a cavity eroded into the ground, and overflowing into the stream. On the other side of the valley a thunderous waterfall tumbled down a lush green mountainside.

"Wow!" Arista walked to the pool of warm water. About to dip her hand in, she hesitated uncertainly. "Is it safe?"

"Yes." Hauk squatted next to her at the edge of the natural tub. Proving it, he put his hand into the water. "It's always the same temperature."

Testing it, she discovered that it was neither hot nor cold, but a pleasing degree just slightly warmer than her own skin. Seeing uneven erosion on a submerged rock formation she wondered if it was as convenient as it looked, and asked, "Those mounds of rock under the water, are they comfortable to sit on?"

"Yes." Anticipation danced in his eyes, he grinned and said, "Let me show you something."

Walking beside him, she realized he was aiming for the waterfall. It had appeared to be a short distance away. After walking for more than fifteen minutes, she guessed they had covered about one mile, and they were only halfway there.

He told her that bears and cougars are sighted in the area from time to time, and buffalo occasionally wander in from a nearby wildlife preserve.

She chided, "You are trying to make me nervous to keep me close to you."

He flashed a teasing grin, draped an arm over her shoulders, and pulled her tightly against his side. Then, his expression sobered and he told her, "It is important for you to know how to defend yourself. Never play dead, run, or scream. If you encounter a bear, stand still and let it determine that you are human. It will probably leave you alone. If it attacks, attack in return. Do the same with a cougar. Put your arms above your head to add to your size and look intimidating. Pick up a stick or any other large object you can find. If the animal doesn't leave, you have to fight back. Buffalo will come close, don't spook them, and they will probably ignore you. If a bear, or a buffalo, are in the mood for a fight, look for the nearest tree to climb."

Remembering the wolves, she shuddered, put her arm around his back, and drew tightly against him.

They stopped talking as the growing rumble of the waterfall drowned their words. A narrow path led up to a wide grassy ledge behind the fall. Only a few steps into the entrance, Arista found herself standing behind the cascading water. It was breathtakingly beautiful. Uncountable water droplets flashed by with all the colours of the rainbow.

"Do you notice anything different?" Hauk's voice whispered.

Awestruck, she stated, "Everything?"

"It is quiet on this side."

Listening to the silence, it was surprising to realize that she would probably have missed the distinct and obvious detail if it had not been pointed out to her.

"Let's go this way."

Walking out on the other side, Spray misted up and coated their skin with glistening coolness.

"This is gorgeous."

"There's something else to see here."

Following him back behind the falls, she stopped at the middle, watched the display of coloured water droplets, and said, "You are living in paradise."

Hearing her words, his opportunity for career advancement swiftly pierced to his core, and his stomach twisted with acidic tension.

Sensing the abrupt change in his mood, Arista looked and saw a faraway gaze in his eyes. She expected it to lapse, but it didn't, so she asked, "What's wrong?"

"There's nothing wrong. I was just thinking that this is possibly the best place in the world." Gently tugging her hand, he reminded, "I was going to show you something. Look over there." He pointed down at the bottom of the fall.

Standing at the narrow entrance of the cave, she saw a slender stream of runoff from the fall lace underneath a rock formation. Hauk climbed up the rocks, she followed, and at the top she looked down. Below them was a glistening blue pond, fed by the waterfall, and spilling its excess into a small band headed for lower ground.

"This is where some of the water goes." He flashed a boyish grin. "It makes a great swimming hole."

Looking up to the crest of snow at the mountaintop, she assumed it was creating the flow of water by thawing, and she shuddered, "It must be freezing."

"The temperature is perfect." He clambered down the slope to the water's edge.

She made her way down at a slower pace.

"Sulphur springs keep it warm." He pointed out three thin threads of steamy water trickling down the mountain.

"Life really doesn't get any better than this, does it." Her statement had no hint of a question attached to it. Having complimented his choice of lifestyle, she was at a loss as to why his eyes again took on a haunted look.

Her concern disappeared when he asked, "Are you ready for a swim?"

Unsure, she walked to the pool and dipped her hand in the water. The temperature was invitingly cool without being cold, but, "How deep is it?"

"It's not." He grinned at her cautious approach. "The deepest it gets is to my waist, so," he skimmed a glance over her, "it might be a little higher on you."

A mood of carefree fun swept her along and made the pool irresistible. After rapidly considering how many cloths she would remove, she grinned, slid her jeans off, and made a dash for the water.

Lagging behind with dashed hopes of her deciding on a nude dip, he brushed off disappointed anticipation, dropped his jeans in a heap, and followed her into the pond. She laughed at the sight of his loose fitting yellow tee shirt overlapping red and black plaid boxer shorts.

He splashed a spray of water at her, and demanded, "What's so funny?"

She backed away from his splashing with a full bout of laughter. Then, feeling warmth move beneath her feet she let out a terrified scream and scrambled to get away from whatever it was.

He laughed heartily.

Staring at him, she pointed to the spot, made a hasty retreat for shore, and warned, "There is something there."

Amusement dancing in his eyes was the last reaction she expected to see. Staring at him, she stated, "It is warm, and it is moving!"

"I know." He moved to her side, circled an arm around her waist, and sauntered, with her in tow, back toward the middle of the pool. "It's a natural spring coming up from the ground."

"I don't think so." Stiffly following his lead she squirmed around to the other side of him positioning them so he would be the first to step on the spot.

He grinned, placed a hand on either side of her waist, lifted her, and swung her onto the spot.

Wrapping her arms around his neck in a death grip, she waited for one of the dreadful fates her imagination was sketching in rapid succession. When nothing happened, she cautiously eased her hold on him and let one foot move slowly toward the ground. Feeling the movement of loose pebbles with her toes, she let her foot rest over the movement. Releasing her grip on him, she stood still, and finally believed the movement was warm water filtering into the pool.

"This is marvellous."

"I told you." He sent a teasing splash of water her way, and the war was on.

After madly flailing water at each other, they engaged in swimming contests, dunked each other numerous times, and eventually flopped down beside one another on the shore. She welcomed the breather. He appeared to be every bit as vigorous as he had been at the onset. Closing her eyes, Arista vaguely wondered why men always seem to have so much more energy than women.

"Don't move." Hauk suddenly commanded.

Seeing his keen alertness fastened on something beside her, she automatically obeyed while whispering, "Why?"

He slowly got to his feet without his eyes flickering from whatever he was watching.

Looking in the direction, Arista saw nothing.

"Come over this way."

She did, looked again, and still saw nothing.

"It must be dead." He picked a stick off the ground. When he jostled the limp carcass, Arista's skin crawled creepily. "It's just a small one." He plucked the motionless snake up onto the stick and carried it farther away from the pond.

Shuddering, and already knowing the detestable answer, she asked, "There are snakes here?"

"They don't usually cross to this side of the stream. But you do have to be alert, especially when you step over small clusters of shrubs."

Her hatred for snakes slithered goose bumps over her flesh.

Later, they soaked in the warm, almost hot, pool by the stream. Going with the current, the canoe ride was easy. By the time they were in the cottage she was pleasantly tired, starving, and relaxed. Never had she imagined the possibility of living a life so full of priceless treasure.

Chapter 13

Hauk placed two thick steaks in a frying pan spattering with hot butter. Arista asked for ingredients. Hauk got them for her. She mixed dough for baking powder biscuits, placed the dough on the countertop, pushed it to the desired thickness with her hands, pressed out circles with a glass, placed them on a cookie sheet, sprinkled salt over them and put them in the preheated oven. She sliced leftover potatoes, and boiled eggs, added salad dressing, mustard, salt and pepper, and mixed it into potato salad. Moving from the fridge to the counter with a small bag of white mushrooms, Hauk paused, pinched flour between his fingers, and flung it at her. In return, she did likewise to him. When he moved to brush the white smudge from her cheek, their eyes met.

Looking into the blue oceans of his eyes, the world disappeared under a tide pulling her into his soul. His gaze lowered and lingered on the saucy succulence of her lips. Time pulsed and their hearts merged to one beat. The gentle parting of her lips flipped him into the pounding realm of ancient instinct. He lowered his mouth to hers and slowly tasted her warm sweetness. Playfully nibbling at each other's lips, they toyed with age old rituals. Then his mouth plundered hers with welcome savagery. In unison their lips parted, closed, parted again and tongues twisting around each other danced in and out of primitive tangles while the coarse stubble of his skin gently raking over the softness of hers drummed a primal beat.

"Ow!" She quickly stepped back from the sizzling steak spitting hot fat at them. Wishing the interruption hadn't happened, she rubbed tiny burn spots on her arm.

Turning the heat of the element down, Hauk appeared to be concentrating on the meal they were preparing. Hating to do it, he finally broached the subject he dreaded, "Where do you work?"

"I work as a teller at a bank." She frowned at the area of her skin responsible for this change of atmosphere.

"When do you have to be back?"

Leaning against the counter in a sudden gloom of dejection, she thought of returning to her mundane routine.

"There is a bus leaving for your city tonight."

Her skin chilled. She had the most incredibly strong and intensely irrational urge to stomp her feet and scream in frustration. Instead, she folded her arms over her waist and obstinately decided on finding a way to dodge catching any bus. "What time does it leave?"

"At nine thirty."

Glancing at her watch, she wished she had more than five hours to think up a master plan. Needing details, she asked, "How long will it take us to get to the bus?"

"If we use the canoe, we will be there in a couple of hours." Dusting seasoning over the steaks, he hid his aversion to her leaving. "If we leave by six thirty, we will have plenty of time to get there."

Her first plan was to delay their departure.

To her chagrin, they were seated in the canoe by six forty five with her meagre belongings tidily packed in a plastic bag on the floor by her feet.

She scowled over his successfully having thwarted her subtle ploys of feigning a sprained wrist after intentionally tripping over a mat on the floor, bitterly complaining of a throbbing headache due to the pain in her wrist, and pleading nausea from the trauma. Obstinately looking at the tensor bandage wrapped around her wrist, she was determined to do better with her next tactic.

She stuck to the story of suffering agonizing pain with her wrist, and he cleared the mini rapids by himself. For it, she received numerous looks of vexation from him. Fifteen minutes away from the mouth of the river, while the shoreline was still relatively close, she picked up a paddle.

"What are you doing?"

Flinching at the agitation in his voice, she answered, "Helping you row."

"Your wrist is too sore." Sarcasm rumbled in his words.

"It's better now." Her nose angled haughtily.

He looked at her with distrust.

She let her paddle slip, quickly reached to retrieve it, and the stupid canoe refused to capsize. The paddle drifted out of reach, her eyes widened with true surprise, and she looked at Hauk. Seeing the stiff tautness of his posture, she realized he had effectively countered her sabotage.

When he remained motionless, staring at her with obvious impatience, she arched a brow at him. "Shouldn't you do something to get the paddle?"

Silently dipping the oar he moved the canoe alongside the paddle and retrieved it from the water. Gently placing it on the floor of the canoe, he put his down beside it, studied her quietly, and asked, "What are you doing?"

Lowering her eyes to hide sudden intimidation, she took a few steadying breaths. Turning large and innocent eyes at him, she cooed, "Me?"

Clouds of agitation shadowed his eyes. "First you fake a sprained wrist. I'm a doctor able to accurately diagnose a sprain." He let a few seconds of silence emphasize what he was saying. "Now, you tried to tip the canoe."

Nervous under the steady scrutiny of his direct attention, she lowered her eyes and struggled to find a logical excuse capable of protecting the secret of her true motive.

"Let's narrow this down. Why do you want the bus to leave without you?"

Hearing the bluntly accurate translation of her actions, she floundered under a flood of humiliation. Meeting his eyes, she blurted, "Why would I want to miss the bus?"

In response, his eyes filled with a brewing mixture of emotion. The frailty of hope laced itself through threads of vanity and pleasure.

Angered by the arrogance sparking at the surface, Arista grabbed an oar. She plunged it into the water with a hard tug pushing them forward.

Reaching over he placed his hand on her arm, "Please stop rowing."

"No." She dug her oar into the water.

He removed his hand from her as the water taxi raced past. "Let's turn into the wake coming at us."

Refusing to cooperate with him, she put her oar across her lap, "You do it."

He gave her a menacing look, clenched his lips, dug his oar into the water, and the first wave slammed the side of the canoe making them teeter dangerously. Hauk worked fervently with the oar, but the second wave came too soon and it rocked them into the third, which flipped them into the water.

Bobbing in their lifejackets, Hauk arched a brow over smouldering eyes, "Are you happy?"

Looking at him, and then at the overturned canoe, the entire situation turned incredibly funny and hearty laughter bubbled from her.

Swimming over to it, he grabbed hold and looked at her, "Are you going to help me?"

Enjoying fate's unexpected help in delaying her departure, she swam over with giddy movements made tediously slow by the encumbrance of her lifejacket.

With little help from her, he got the canoe up and over. "If we both climb in at exactly the same time and on the opposite sides, this will work."

The first attempt was clumsy and sent them plunging back into the water. The second effort worked perfectly.

Seated in the upright canoe, Arista glanced at her watch, beamed at Hauk, and boasted, "It's still working." Studying it, she squirmed at the realization of having lost less than half an hour in the incident.

Reading her thoughts, he confirmed, "We will still be able to make it in time for you to catch the bus. Unless," his eyebrow arched as he dared, "you would rather not."

Staring at him, she deliberated. Plunging an oar into the water, she flashed him a sidelong glance speaking volumes. The male-female-stand-off began. Knowing she was feeding on pride, and he was doing likewise, he pushed his oar through the water in rhythm with hers. Stubborn determination goaded them into moving closer to what neither of them wanted.

A strange crack penetrated the air and pulled a deep groan from Hauk.

The feel of water pooling at her toes prompted her to look down. There, on the floor, she saw a tear running through the middle of the canoe. "Is this where the noise came from?" Looking at Hauk, she hoped he had a simple solution for this, like he had for everything else.

"Yes." He grimaced. "This happens sometimes. Taking canoes over the rapids eventually tears them apart." He scowled at the water seeping in. "There's usually some warning. I've never had one let me down in the middle of the lake before."

Arista visually assessed the distance between them and the shore. "What do we do now?"

"I'll row." Lifting both oars, Hauk placed one on each side of the boat and launched powerful strokes toward shore. "You scoop out as much water as you can."

"What should I use?"

"I don't know."

Searching for something, all she found were, "Shoes?"

"It's probably the best we have."

Gently taking off one shoe, and then filling it with water and poring it into the lake, she soon realized her actions were going to have to improve if she wanted to keep up to the leak. Using both shoes, she filled them and dumped them. It was still too slow. Instead of filling them, she used them to scoop the water up and over the side of the canoe. Regardless of her frenzied efforts, the rising water was now almost up to her knees and the shore was still a distance away.

The weight of the water was bogging down the canoe and making Hauk's progress slow despite pushing the paddles hard and fast. When he suddenly stopped rowing, Arista gave the shore a longing glance and waited for Hauk to resume moving them to safety. Wondering why he wasn't, she gave him a quizzical look.

He silently secured the paddles into metal fasteners. Familiar with many aspects of her personality, he knew it was better to wait for her to accept unexpected conditions in her own time rather than to try forcing issues on her. He had learned trying to get an instant reaction from her almost always brought reckless abandon instead of calm intelligence. At the moment, he preferred the later.

"We are already wet." Wringing water out of the bottom of her shirt, she shrugged dismally. "I guess it will be easier to swim the rest of the way."

"You should put your shoes on first."

His suggestion sounded ludicrous since it was easier to swim without them and her look told him as much.

"You will need them when we get to shore."

It startled her to realize she had neglected to think past the current problem of having to swim. She silently tied her shoes onto her feet. "This is going to be very uncomfortable." Every nerve in her body protested against swimming fully clothed.

"If you like, you can tie them to one of the rods inside the boat we are going to try to get this thing ashore with us."

She groaned at the idea of being encumbered by the boat. Their lifejackets were going to slow them down enough without the added burden.

"It's got a number of advantages." He smiled reassurance. "If we get cold or tired we can always take a break by climbing onto it."

"Ok." She removed her shoes and fastened them around one of the side ribs in the boat. Her desire for comfort won in a second and she squirmed out of her jeans. She tied them beside her shoes. "There." She grinned brazenly. "This will make it a bit easier."

Losing precious time with the frigid lake temperature licking over them, he prompted, "Ready?"

She glanced hopelessly at water lapping against the upper rim inside the canoe, arched her brows, curled an artificial smile on her lips, and showing false bravado, cheered, "Let's go." Seeing him ready to follow her lead, she slid over the edge and into the lake.

They were both blue lipped and shivering by the time they had the canoe pulled ashore. Cold and wet cloths were removed instantly and they stood in sunshine rubbing warmth back into their flesh. Finally their goose bumped skin smoothed back to normal and the pink glow of health returned.

"Wow!" Staring at the lake, Arista stated the obvious. "That was cold."

Hauk growled and flashed an antagonized glance at the canoe as he picked up the clothing he had randomly thrown off in his hurry to get the coldness of it away from his skin.

Retrieving her tee shirt from the ground where she had dropped it, Arista grimaced at the dirt and pine needles clinging to it. Looking at the water, she shuddered at the thought of touching it for even the few seconds it would take to rinse the mess away, and like Hauk, she hung it on a branch to dry. Unlike Hauk, the filthy state of it nagged in her mind, and she plucked it from the branch, and marched down to the water, and rinsed it clean, and hung it back on the branch.

Watching her, Hauk chuckled at her deep disposition for orderly procedures. He had no doubt she would be motivated to create a comfort zone for herself, and, he could quickly become accustomed to sharing the lifestyle her personality traits were sure to generate.

Stunned at the direction his thoughts had taken, he sat down on the loosest patch of dirt he could find just so it would cling to him in an unsightly mess. It was irrational rebellion against the threatening feel of willingly sabotaging the life he had competently built by himself and for himself. Glancing at her through the thunderous mood mounting in him, he saw her very attractive backside bent over deliciously as she smoothed a grassy patch to sit on. His mind instantly blanked, and he found himself sitting at her side.

They sat in warm sunshine. A gentle breeze rapidly dried their clothing, including Arista's shoes, which Hauk had salvaged from the canoe and hung on a branch. Still recovering from the chilly swim, they didn't say much, and when Hauk broke the silence it was to tell her they were relatively far from any inkling of civilization, and he suggested they start walking. He secured the canoe, upside down, between two trees and placed their lifejackets underneath.

Making their way back to his cottage, they talked about everything and nothing. Hauk made small detours to show her some of the beautiful secrets surrounding them. She saw magnificent clusters of grand white blossoms lifting on long stems adorning craggy nooks in lush shrubbery. Tumbling waterfalls lavishly laced the distant background. Tucked in nature's crannies, she discovered the richest landscape splendours imaginable.

Hoping to soon reach the rapids, as an indication they were nearing their goal, Arista walked with determination.

Slowing his pace, Hauk suggested pitching a makeshift camp for the night.

Without hesitation, she stated her preference to continue walking through the night, or for however long it would take to get them to the safe haven of his cottage.

He flatly refused. He dodged informing her of the dangers accompanying nightfall.

Forced to spend a night outdoors, she sulked by the fire he built.

He went to the water in search of food. When he returned, he had two fish fillets pierced through with one stick. He criss-crossed two sticks at opposite sides of the fire, and rested the roasting stick on them with the fish over the fire.

Watching him, she pondered his survival skills. The only tools he had along were matches, an exceptionally sharp and oversized knife, ammunition and his rifle. He told her he always carried the supplies in a waterproof emergency survival kit fastened securely inside the canoe.

Keeping the suspicion to herself, she thought his preparations seemed to be based on experience. She wondered how often he had made the trek home by foot. Her stomach rolled nauseously when the fire spluttered as he pitched cut chunks of the fish head and innards into the flames.

With ever increasing agitation she grumbled, "Why are you throwing that in the fire? It's gross."

"We can't leave these lying around. They might attract unwelcome guests."

She stared with wide eyes. He shrugged as though it were the most natural thing in the world to find oneself in this predicament. They slumped into silence. He laid back and closed his eyes enjoying harmony with his surroundings. She sat with her knees bent up hugging them tightly to her chest, and wishing the entire experience would pass quickly.

They ate the fish. She discovered it to be tasty. Stars winked in the sky. The air smelt of crisp pine and sweet smoke. Sitting by the warmth of the fire, Arista's vision wandered to a small portable water container, which made her laugh softly. It was more like a plastic bag with a spout, and was another item from Hauk's emergency kit. It sat off to the side filled with cold stream water.

"You shouldn't laugh. My jug is saving you from having to make a trip to the stream every time you get thirsty."

Faking a sigh of relief, she grinned at his exaggeration. The stream was less than ten feet away.

Glad her mood was lightening and she was finally relaxing in her surroundings, Hauk eased them into light conversation. They talked about favourite foods, colours, activities, and anything else entering their minds. When he mentioned, without the slightest complaint, his love for relaxing by his fireplace with his guitar on quiet evenings like this one, she felt incredibly selfish.

She realized they were equally inconvenienced by the situation. Unlike her, he had been doing everything he could to make things as comfortable for them as possible. The enlightenment had a strange effect. Recognizing his strength, and her weakness, and his patience with her shortcomings, her attraction to him took one giant step into affection. She longed for a way to makeup to him for having wronged him, even if he didn't seem to care.

A full moon gracing the star gilded sky, and a fire crackling its warmth, sparked magical contentment into the night. Arista drifted into the crook of Hauk's arm. Sleepily snuggling beside him, she squirmed at the hardness of the thick tree trunk they were leaning against. Their conversation wandered aimlessly, until it landed on Guy.

With a lazy yawn, Arista grumbled, "Guy." Her jaw automatically tightened. "He is an idiot."

Hauk lifted a highly inquisitive brow. "Why do you insult him? He's your boyfriend."

"He does stupid things." She cuddled closer to Hauk's side.

He gently and firmly squeezed her to him with the arm he had draped over her shoulder, and he wished they could stay exactly the way they were for a very long time. Too tired to analyze his emotions, or feel threatened by them, he let his head bend over her crop of silken curls, and he watched the fire through heavy lids. He expected the two large logs would burn through the night. If they burned out, he would add more.

"What does he do wrong?" He wanted to know what actions antagonized her, so he could avoid making mistakes.

Stifling another yawn, she complained, "He says I'm fat."

Running a finger over her side, Hauk argued, "Fat? I can feel your ribs."

"It tickles." Soft giggles escaped as she curled herself almost on top of him to get away from the irritation of his finger brushing her ribs.

Frowning with concern, Hauk wondered why Guy would suggest such a thing to her, except to undermine her confidence and gain power over her. In truth, she should gain a few pounds. "You are not fat."

"I know."

It was a relief to him to hear her disagree with Guy's criticism of her. Hauk echoed her sentiments, "Guy is an idiot."

A gentle smile lifted her lips, and she drifted asleep enveloped in the warmth of Hauk's arms and their growing friendship.

Chapter 14

Day Fifteen - Monday

Skipping through the door, Arista basked in the sheen of polished wood and closed her eyes with pure joy for finally being home. Tears leapt with her abrupt remembrance of her real home.

Watching her shoulders slump as though the weight of the world had just fallen on them, Hauk's brow furrowed, "What happened? You were so happy to get here a minute ago."

"I am happy to be here." She smiled through the mist of unshed tears. Wanting to treasure every pleasant moment available, she pushed negative thinking to the furthest corner of her mind.

There was one detail in need of immediate attention. "I have to call work."

"Use my phone." He handed her the cell phone from the shelf. Fortunately it had been forgotten when they set out the day before, otherwise it would probably have been destroyed by water.

When the connection was made a receptionist's singsong voice greeted Arista, and promptly transferred her call to the appropriate person.

Listening to Arista admirably feigning laryngitis and an agonizing cough, Hauk was once again uncomfortable with her deceptive tactics. He regularly chose to believe people. Some of his associates scoff at his trust in his fellow human beings, some even deem it to be a weakness and use his trust to take advantage of him. But generally, to his way of thinking, unwarranted suspicion closes too many doors.

With her coolly flat voice, the manager accepted the excuse that Arista had taken ill at a friend's place. Arista was granted one week of holiday time.

"There!" Passing the phone to Hauk she beamed. "May I spend my holidays here?" Her smile drooped when he hesitated. She had expected him to welcome the idea as much as she did.

Tantalizing moments of the last few days flashed through his mind and produced a cocky grin. "Yes."

Leaping against him she wrapped her arms around him and hugged him with gleeful abandon. "Thank you." Just as quickly, she relinquished her hold and turned for the bathroom. "I'm going to take a shower. I feel grossly dirty."

She blew out of the room like a small tornado. He plopped himself down in his favourite armchair and worked at sorting out the tangling details of his life.

Feeling warmth on his thigh, he looked down, "Hi Bud." Ruffling the golden curls of fur, Hauk mumbled, "I don't believe this. I actually forgot about you." He puzzled over why Bud had kept himself so cautiously out of the way, until now, instead of greeting him with the usual frenzy of excited yelping.

Chuckling, Hauk looked at doleful brown eyes. "We're getting confused by all the commotion around here." Hauk restlessly wandered to the kitchen.

Prancing out of the bathroom, wearing the altered tee shirt and sweat pants she had devised from Hauk's handed down clothing, Arista's steps faltered at the scene of utter tranquility meeting her. Hauk was preparing a fresh pot of coffee, and Bud was standing beside him with a gently wagging tail. The moment consumed her with a burning hunger to become part of Hauk's life.

Turning, he caught the intensity darkening her almond eyes making them almost black. Baffled by why a shower would create such a powerful mood in her, he arched a brow and chose to keep things simple by asking, "Would you like a cup of coffee?"

"Yes. Please."

He prepared two cups for them, brought them to the sitting area, sat by the fire, and silently studied Arista.

Blushing under his scrutiny, she giggled nervously and asked, "What?"

"You should write a song for me to play."

An instant sweat filmed skin chilling with nervous recoil. Pressing a tense hand to her throat, she pleaded, "I couldn't. I have no talent." Intimidated by her lack of creativity she launched into a tirade of babbling. "I'm a painfully boring person. I only know how to do stuffy things like counting money." Considering the dilemma of her personal finances she added, "I'm not good at managing money."

Aware of the unflattering description she was giving herself, her stomach twisted. The quick flight she had made from her previous life haunted. Now she was running from her new life. Each break away was triggering another like a crazy merry-go-round she was unable to escape.

Thinking about it, she hated to admit how easily she was letting circumstance spin her around. Someone always seemed to stepping in the way of whatever grand plan she was out to accomplish. Even feeble Guy had easily walked into and over her life.

"I don't see you as a boring person." Arching his brow, he chuckled, "You are quite the opposite."

She suddenly wanted to rival the strongest women in history. It would be marvellous to have the stunning beauty of Cleopatra, the lusty sex appeal of Lady Guinevere, and the adventurous spirit of Calamity Jane. Determination took hold as she aimed at transforming her lukewarm existence.

Her first step was aimed at pouring a brazen pool of molten tantalization. Catching the sly look she threw his way, Hauk's breath jerked and he hoped whatever cockamamie plan she was forming would prove to match the fiery promise smouldering in her eyes.

She suggested, "Don't you want to take a shower after sleeping on the ground and trekking through the bush for two days?"

Glancing down, Hauk saw that his clothing was coated by a thick layer of dust and matted with small clusters of twigs and pine needles.

Gulping down the last of his coffee, he got up from the comfort of his armchair. "I need it, don't I?" He placed his mug in the sink, gathered clean clothing, and disappeared into the bathroom.

Rummaging through Hauk's closet, she found a threadbare cotton shirt with a button up front. She removed her tee shirt and bra, put on the oversized shirt, rolled up the sleeves, left the buttons undone, folded the hem up and tied it together in a knot at her waist. Ample folds of material closed together covering the gaping openness of it, until she moved. Next, she pulled out a deep green muscle shirt. Folding the top half into the bottom half, seam facing seam, with the armholes positioned to be hidden by the outside layer, she created a makeshift miniskirt.

Hearing the shower stop running, she quickly tidied the dishevelment of clothing she had scattered around herself. Confronted with the opportune circumstances for her ploys, her courage suddenly fled. Schemes, she was discovering, were considerably easier to conjure than to act upon. Needing to escape the anxiety she was creating for herself, she made a dash out of the cabin to hide the results of her impulsive actions from Hauk.

Hauk stood in the bathroom doorway watching Bud as the animal looked quizzically from Hauk to the entrance door and back again. Arching his brow, he asked, "Where did she go?"

Whining his answer, Bud lumbered to the door where he patiently waited for his master.

Following Bud's lead, it was only seconds before Hauk was quietly standing in the shadows trying to figure out what she was doing.

Frustrated with the fold in the makeshift skirt clumsily rearranging itself every time she moved, Arista was preoccupied with correcting the problem.

Hauk's breath caught when she yanked the shirt-cum-skirt off and revealed a pink thong throwing sparks of glittering sunshine from appliqués.

Holding the shirt with the neckline hanging downwards, she stepped one foot through each armhole, and yanked it straight up until the hem reached clear over the top of her head.

Deep laughter rumbled from Hauk.

A shriek erupted behind the material, she turned while pulling it down from over her eyes, and she stared speechlessly at him.

"You look goofy." He teased, but his throbbing libido gave his mouth a harsh set causing him to fall seriously short of appearing humorous. As silly as her antics were, she was incredibly sexy. Enslaving his attention, the green shoulder straps of his tank top were seductively hugging her inner thighs. The sexual tension she was instigating, on regular intervals, was driving him out of his mind.

Seeing tight notches straining at the sides of his mouth, Arista misinterpreted his tension as rebuke. She defended, "I was trying to make myself somewhat fashionable." Positive she was rapidly becoming an unpleasant imposition for him, large tears rolled down her cheeks. She timidly folded the shirt into a skirt and fervently hoped it would stay properly in place long enough for her to get back to the cottage where she could change into pants.

Seeing his vision wandering over her bosom snapped her into awareness of yet another problem. With a groan she remembered leaving her shirt unfastened in readiness for a provocative game of peek-a-boo. He had happened on her at the most inopportune time, and tipped her plan to maintain control of the situation. The resulting display of gaping undress was hardly the enticing tease of allurement she had hoped to stage. With an annoyed huff she roughly pushed the buttons through the holes and angled her chin haughtily.

Lifting her nose even higher as a silent snub, she moved to storm past him. He smoothly stepped up beside her and matched his strides to hers. Stopping, she turned and glared at him with seething frustration. Blue eyes clashed with burnt almond, and sky blue hazed to ice grey with the torrential speed of a raging sea. Transfixed by the raw strength emanating from him, Arista stood staring in utter fascination.

Swept along the rising flood of infatuation flowing from her, Hauk's intelligence submerged under a rush of passion. In a breath her lips were pliant and moving under the husky demands of his. Her breaths quickened as sizzling waves of hunger pulsed from him to her. The steely warmth of his arms tightened around her.

Enslaved by the spectacular series of explosions he could so easily ignite in her, she teased his lips between hers, and wrestled his tongue with hers. She believed the situation was under perfect restraint and she would rein it to a halt within proper boundaries. She just wanted one more kiss. The craving flashed into a consuming blaze roaring to a throbbing tempo.

Growling snarls vibrated into Hauk's senses. Seeing Bud's fur shackled, Hauk visually skimmed the area, saw no immediate threats, and suggested, "We should go inside."

Arista made herself comfortable on the sofa. Hauk joined her. They talked quietly, exhaustion caught up to them, and they fell asleep snuggled together on the sofa.

A couple of hours later, Hauk awoke. He positioned her more comfortably on the sofa, put a pillow under her head, and covered her with a blanket. He made his bed on the floor.

Chapter 15

Day Sixteen - Tuesday

Lazily anticipating a quaint, quiet, and sleepy, village, Arista sighed as Hauk secured his boat to the dock. The morning began by fully living up to Arista's expectations. A strange thing, she had the desire to soar high as a kite and sing a song of joy from the clouds. She temporarily wondered why such an odd hankering would make its presence felt when it is impossible to accomplish the feat. She was reading way too much into Hauk's invitation to attend his friend's sister's wedding with him.

In her world it was an unusual day for a wedding. Here it appeared to be accepted as normal. Snapping from the reverie, her heart leapt to her throat and she stared at the wide, low to the ground, furry black tail disappearing around a rickety fence surrounding a dirt arena commonly used for amateur rodeo events staged and attended by the local people. Within seconds the sharp nose of the creature peeped back around the fence followed by its black body, which was clearly identified by a thick white stripe running down the center of its back.

Preparing to flee, Arista took a few stiff steps backward. Quickly searching the surroundings, dismay swept through her when she saw how far they would have to run to reach the nearest building. Taking deep breaths in preparation for the physical exertion of the race, her eyes widened when she noticed Hauk watching the animal waddle behind a wire fence dividing the schoolyard from the street they were standing on.

Arista's eyebrows quirked and she realized her instincts would have steered her in the same direction that the detestable critter was moving in. Their best escape was to keep going forward. When the animal was parallel with them, Hauk resumed his step with agonizingly casual slowness.

About to ask why he was showing so little concern, Arista clamped her mouth shut as she realized the skunk was showing no signs of being aggressive or rabid. Arista contented herself with the slow pace, and glanced back to insure the menace was still walking away from them.

Seeing the tautness of her body, the alertness in her eyes, and the firm set of her mouth, Hauk grinned with appreciation for her high spirits. She could leap from relaxed, to tantalizingly feisty, to a tempest, to the survivor ready for battle, and land back at subdued as fast as one could blink an eye. She radiated constant unpredictability. Although many people would find the quality nerve wracking beyond durability, for him it compared with his beloved retreat. Like her, his mountainous alcove flashed a mesh of peace, chaos, strength, power, and tranquility, it was always alive and always undergoing change.

Each lost in their own thoughts, the distance to their destination closed. Looking at the weathered building, Arista decided it was in worse condition than the buildings she had previously seen in the area.

Gingerly walking through the door Hauk was holding open for her, she saw his eyes glow with pleasure as he introduced her to another of the familiar, and treasured, places in his world. Arista was unable to see anything appealing in the dank entrance facing a long narrow stairway going up.

An older woman bobbing down the stairs in a flurry of polyester and smiles bellowed, "Hauk!" Then, she smothered him in heavy fragrance and a bear hug.

When the woman turned to her, Arista stiffened against a possible assault of friendliness, and relaxed gratefully when she received no more than a hardy handshake. "You must be Arista."

"Yes." Smiling politely, Arista silently wondered how this woman knew who she was.

"I'm Doris." She turned and began climbing the stairway. Obviously expecting them to follow, she flung over her shoulder an apologetic, "Please pardon the smoke smell. Those young fellows upstairs are human chimneys."

After having been away from the smell of smoke for a length of time, she did find the smell repulsive. All the same, she craved a cigarette instantly.

Doris explained, "This building is a combination. The sanctuary is downstairs. The upper level was built by the community to accommodate social gatherings. Unfortunately there is some controversy about how and when rules extend from one structure to the other."

At the top of the rickety stairway, an old door opened soundlessly to her touch. Doris stood at the entrance and waited for the other two to precede her. Arista walked through first, and looked around a single open room. The only furnishings were long tables surrounded by wooden chairs. The thick, darkly stained, wooden furniture was as aged as everything else about the building.

The three of them stood indecisively in a small walkway divided from the main room by a low spindle railing made of the same wood, design, and colour, as the tables and chairs. Arista quickly assessed the two obvious choices. She could either enter the main room, or follow the walkway to another narrow flight of stairs descending to a closed door leading to the sanctuary visible through windows lining the wall below. Feeling intimidated by the notion of conspicuously entering the lower level, she chose the more secluded upstairs.

Unable to find a way through the barrier, Arista stepped over the low railing. Her action produced a chorus of chuckles from the spatter of adolescent boys in the room. One of them walked over to the railing, indicated the gate set into it, and opening it, said, "You just have to lift the latch."

"Oh." Arista mumbled as she made her way to the nearest chair. The curious eyes following her made her she squirm nervously. To her dismay, she looked down at the sanctuary and saw that even the minister was looking at her. Agitated and embarrassed by the excessive attention, she silently scorned that guests must be rare amongst these people. Realizing the truth of her thought, which was born from sarcasm, her defensive inclination to brew hostility shifted to placid tolerance.

The pianist abruptly switched tunes, all eyes focused on the back of the church, and Arista got her chance to discreetly observe the people surrounding her. Almost everything about the culture of the area was different from what she was accustomed to. Most of the male guests were dressed in blue jeans and plaid shirts. The minister was surprisingly young, probably in his late twenties, well built, and had thick dark hair.

The first bridesmaid stepped to the front of the church with her escort. The second pair joined them in a few moments, and then the maid of honour and the best man completed the line of wedding attendants. Mauve dresses shimmered on one side, and impeccable grey tuxedos lined the other.

Signalling synchronization, the pianist changed the tune to the traditional wedding march. The minister made a request for all guests to stand. In a cloud of white satin and glittering beads the bride gracefully walked beside her groom with her arm daintily entwined in the crook of his elbow. Her black curls were elegantly piled over a short veil and around a sparkling Tierra. His blond hair was cropped short. He was tall. She was average height. He was bulky. She was willowy. His black tuxedo stood in stark contrast against the frothy whiteness of her gown. When they reached the front of the church, where decorations of white blossoms overflowed white containers and spiralled down white pillars, the bride handed her bouquet of white roses to the maid of honour. Spontaneously, the bride turned and flashed her groom a radiant smile. Lowering his eyes, he looked into hers with adoration.

Witnessing the absolute beauty of a unity so uniquely reserved for the love of a man and a woman, Arista wished for the same. Guy hazed through her thoughts. He was a far cry from the glamorous picture she carried in her imagination. Wondering if she could tolerate, much less find happiness, being married to him, a sudden barrage of daggers shot through her being. Paralysis overtook her entire body, her breaths raced in jags, her cheeks tingled, and when she tried to get Hauk's attention she found herself unable to speak.

Sensing a problem, Hauk glanced over, stopped, and frowned. "What's wrong?"

Frantically trying to tell him, she would have screamed if she could, but sound refused to leave her lips. With a slight gasp her breath returned, she brought her hand up to the tingling sensation in her cheek, and her limbs unlocked. Confused by the ordeal, she whispered the physical details to Hauk.

"It sounds like severe anxiety." He placed his fingers around her wrist and timed her pulse. "What triggered it?"

"I don't know." She shrugged and tried to look nonchalant. He saw her tension.

Looking into her eyes, wisdom and compassion radiated from the depths of his ocean blue eyes. "Only you know what was on your mind, but, perhaps, whatever you were thinking about is not good for you." Hauk glanced down at the wedding party, back at her, and silently wondered if she was severely afraid of commitment. It occurred to him that she may have a broken marriage in her past. He suddenly realized how little he knew about her.

One of the boys in the room lit a cigarette. The others did likewise. Although she still considered herself to be a smoker, Arista swallowed a dislike for the lack of respect she thought it displayed for the ceremony.

Downstairs, an overweight, middle aged, woman challenged by a mental disability, stepped up behind the bride and groom, and stood watching the ceremony with avid intensity. The bridesmaids and groomsmen looked at each other with baffled confusion. Each hoped the other would take charge and tactfully resolve the situation. Flustered by the unexpected intrusion, the minister's words faltered and he knocked his papers off the pulpit. The bride and groom remained blissfully oblivious to the disruption happening behind them. Seeing the bridal couple remaining unaware of the problem, the minister smiled at them, picked up his notes, and continued with his sermon.

The woman's sister quietly moved to her side, and engaged in persuading Klarissa to return to her seat. After listening to the request whispered very softly into her ear, Klarissa shook her head in vehement refusal and stubbornly stayed where she was. Her sister then made a second attempt at coaxing her to her seat. In reply, Klarissa's eyes sparked wildly as she edged toward indulging in one of the many temper tantrums she was prone to. Next, she was promised an entire ice cream cake, later, if she returned to her seat quietly. After only a brief hesitation, Klarissa sat down in the pew.

Attention returned to the wedding couple only to discover that the vows were already said, the rings were exchanged, and the minister was concluding the service missed by everyone except the bride and groom. They signed the register at a small table beside them, and lit the unity candle. The minister pronounced them husband and wife. The bridal party swiftly walked down the isle and exited the church in a flurry of chiffon and smiles.

Without warning the air exploded with a glass shattering blast and a strange whooshing sound of air being sliced. The minister, followed by a handful of hardy men dressed in blue jeans and cowboy boots, erupted with instant action. Violent curses flew in accusation of a well known local named Khalikan. Anger growled as engines roared to life and four by four vehicles revved in full pursuit of the man.

Struggling with disorientation, Arista absorbed changes she hadn't seen taking place. Only women and old men remained in the building. Some were sitting. Others were pacing.

"Don't go fainting on us Dearie."

Glancing in the direction of the voice, Arista saw Doris' cheeks bunched around her always present smile. For some strange reason, Doris' continuous smile was inexplicably grating on Arista's nerves. Wanting to be left alone, Arista hoped to display antisocial behaviour by crossing her arms on the table and burying her face in them. She silently cheered her success when nobody disturbed her.

It was the same position she had awakened in. Amazingly, she had remained propped against the table without tumbling over. Unlike sleeping, fainting had lapsed minutes into a void where there was no sensation of time having passed. The only indication of having lost consciousness was the visible change in her surroundings. Now she was in a bizarre zone of sedate wakefulness where she felt completely incapable of concentration.

Within the hour, the men returned to the church in an uproar over Khalikan having erroneously sent a bullet flying through the church window when, in a state of intoxication, he fired at a deer, missed, and the bullet ricocheted off a rock hurtling it into the building.

Arista heard Hauk's voice in the distance. Hearing a female respond, she assumed he was talking to Doris. At the feel of his hand on her shoulder she lifted her head. He was the only person on Earth she wanted to acknowledge at the moment.

Brushing his finger over the raw flesh at her temple, concern shadowed his eyes. Does it hurt?"

"Does what hurt?"

"This." Cautiously placing a gentle finger on the injury, he waited.

"No." Pushing his hand away she rubbed hers over the area to feel whatever was there and found a slightly sensitive area. "Should it?"

He placed one hand on each side of her face, tilted it up to his, and studied her intently. One hand moved to her wrist and found her pulse, which he timed. Next he pulled her eyelids up, then the bottom ones down, carefully examining each one.

Too confused by his behaviour to protest, she allowed him to do what he wanted, and finally asked, "What are you looking for?"

"The skin on your temple is injured. What happened?"

"I don't know."

"Have you ever fainted before?"

"No."

"The bullet sank into the wall just behind where you were sitting." Ice chilled his veins. "I thought it might have grazed your temple on the way past." One brow arched, "Now, I think you bumped the table when you fainted."

His face broke into a grin and Arista's stomach flipped in reaction to the sexy notches digging deep grooves beside his lips.

"You probably just need something to eat. Let's go home." He took her hand in his.

The action came naturally to him, and it went straight to her heart. Doris' blue eyes watched intently from across the room.

Chapter 16

Sitting quietly on the steps leading down from the front door of the cottage, Arista relaxed with a cup of freshly brewed coffee.

Hearing scuffling twigs, she watched a squirrel scurry into the clearing, stop, look at her, and scoot up a tree. Smiling at the pure bliss of her present environment, she squinted up at a patch of intense blueness in the cloudless sky and wished her life could always be this carefree.

Feeling the oddest sensation of jitters, she blamed it on nerves. Rotating her shoulders, she tried to ease her shakiness. When it persisted, she thought it might be hunger. About to lift the cup sitting beside her, she saw tiny circles rippling in the liquid. One by one, round ripples quivered toward the center of her coffee where they disappeared only to be continuously replaced. Regardless of knowing it was safer outside, she looked up the sharp incline of the mountain and, welcoming a false sense of security, hurried into the shelter of the cabin.

Hauk looked over at the abruptness of her entry, and saw stark paleness in her complexion. "What happened?"

Creases worked her brows, "I think we are experiencing tremors."

"Tremors?"

"The coffee is rippling in my cup."

"Tiny tremors happen often here." He flashed a grin of assurance. "The way the plates are positioned under the ground they move just enough to create small gaps, so the earth trembles as it shuffles."

"If," Arista took a moment to organize her thoughts before voicing the speculation, "this area is prone to tremors than it must be susceptible to earthquakes." The mountainside looming beside them suddenly took on the image of a dangerous foe, and she discovered the first snag in this blissful retreat.

"No major disturbances have been recorded in this area for hundreds of years." Mischief lit blue eyes, "The hot springs imply a possibility of volcanic activity."

From the corner of her eyes, she slid him an annoyed look. He acknowledged it with hearty laughter.

"Come on." He took her hand in his. "Let's go enjoy some of the potential disasters around us."

Throwing him a shadowed look meant to be seen as exasperation, he saw the glints shimmering in burnt almond eyes saying she was in agreement with him.

Warmly tightening his grip on her hand, he swung her around to the door. When he opened it for them, they both saw the sudden and scurried movements of a wolf. It tucked its tail between its legs, laid its ears flat, turned squinting eyes at them, rumbled a throaty growl, the shackles on the back of its neck bristled, and it dashed away into the bush, all in the flash of a few seconds.

Closing the door, Hauk studied the worry etching itself on Arista's face.

Staring at the door keeping out, what Arista again deciphered to be, vicious wilderness on the other side, she mumbled, "This is the first time I have seen that one."

Hauk arched a dark brow. From his expression, she supposed it was the first time he had noticed it as well. "He is most likely a lone wolf enticed into the area by the female. She is much younger than the pack."

"If a new wolf is invading their territory, what will the pack do?"

"The alpha male will probably challenge the new one. By rule of nature, I assume the younger one will prove to be predominantly stronger and the alpha female will join him. In which case she will become his mate, produce a litter of pups, and they will build a new pack."

"Here." He handed her a can, which resembled a small fire extinguisher, and instructed, "This is bear repellent, better known as pepper spray. Be careful never to spray it against wind, it will blow back at you. A heavy wind or rain may make it ineffective." He picked up the shotgun and opened the door for them.

"I'm not going out there." Arista folded her arms in stubborn determination.

"The wolf will be long gone by now."

"How do you know?"

"Wild animals don't like people."

"Then why was it here by the cabin?"

"Wolves are opportunists by nature." Hauk guessed, "It was probably drawn to the smell of food." Taking her hand, he led her out the door.

Whether the wolf was gone or not, it kept its presence undetectable when they left the cabin. They rowed the canoe upstream and sunshine glistened on the water like diamonds. A rumble resembling steady thunder filled the air and dust billowed into the heavens. They both looked in the direction, and then at each other.

"What is that?"

"I'm not sure." Hauk rowed toward the disturbance. Curiosity won over fear, and Arista moved her oars in unison with his. After bringing the canoe as close as possible, they hauled it ashore, walked through a dense patch of evergreens and into a clearing where they could see dust still swirling amidst a pile of rocks at the bottom of a mountain.

"It was a rock slide."

Looking up the mountain, Arista wondered aloud, "What caused it?"

"They happen for no apparent reason." He turned them back in the direction they had come from. "They cause the ground to tremble. Perhaps it was something like this that made the ground quiver earlier."

Pondering over the previous ripples in her water, she kept her thoughts to herself. Blaming this incident on an episode of earth tremors might sound crazy, or paranoid. Instead of following Hauk's lead, she went in the opposite direction, toward a little flower with a single miniature purple blossom sprouting over a scraggly stem.

Stepping up behind her, Hauk asked, "What are you looking at?"

"This." She gently toyed at it with her finger. "It is so cute." Completely enchanted by the petite creation, she smiled as mauve petals fluttered in the breeze.

Watching, Hauk was captivated by her genuine pleasure with the tiny wildflower.

The mood of content relaxation shattered when a distressed whine sliced the air. In a breath Arista was up and clinging to Hauk's arm.

"Wait here." Prying her hands away, he took slow purposeful steps in the direction of the sound. She timidly followed at a distance. "Careful." At the warning, she looked in the direction Hauk was watching with alert concentration. Trapped under a fallen tree, the bulky wolf appeared unthreatening.

"Is it the one we saw by the cottage?"

"It might be."

Holding her breath with hopes of being right, she asked, "The pack must not be close by, right?"

"I don't know. It might be."

"If he's here, the pack should want to keep a distance, right?"

"Probably, still, one never knows." Although it was unlikely, he did want her to be on the lookout while he worked at freeing the trapped animal. "Do you know how to shoot?"

Glancing at the shotgun in his hand, she winced, "Kind of."

"Here." Before handing it to her he clicked the safety off. "It's ready to go. Shoot straight up in the air if you see anything."

Plastering a brave smile onto a face paled by fear, she took the rifle from him.

Cringing at their predicament, he turned to the wolf. "You need to cooperate with me."

As though understanding what had been said, the animal laid its ears back, pressed his sharp muzzle to the ground, and pawed in Hauk's direction.

With a grin, Hauk explained to Arista, "For a wolf, those are signs of submission." Inching closer, he held the pepper spray in one hand while lifting the tree with the other. The animal crept out from under the encumbrance, and kept its belly close to the ground, its ears back, and it slunk away giving them one last look before leaping into the cover of evergreens. As vague as a shadow, there was a glimpse of something else slipping alongside him.

Still staring at the spot, Arista mumbled, "I never expected to see something so weird."

"I think he may have enticed the female away from her pack."

Stuck on her previous thoughts, Hauk's observation fell on deaf ears and she continued, "The way he obeyed you. It was like he understood. It was strange."

"Animals usually respect people. It's an instinct."

"They know they will die if they challenge us."

"It keeps the natural order in balance." With a chuckle he wrapped his arm around the indent of her back. "Are you ready to go home?"

His use of the word 'home' sang in her heart.

Chapter 17

Looking at Hauk, over the brim of her cup, Arista belatedly replied to a previous topic, "Why do you think the female has left her pack?"

"What?"

"When the wolf was skulking away, you said you thought he had taken the female from the pack."

"Oh." Hauk chuckled at her, "That was a delayed response."

"I had other things on my mind before." Meeting silence and an amused grin, she read a distinct joke at her expense in his expression. Scowling at him she brought her coffee cup to her lips, and looked away to the cozy fire lazily licking logs and reflecting in the shined polish of wooden floors.

Hauk asked, "Did you see the movement beside him as he was leaving?"

Trying to remember details, she said, "There was a shadow." Thinking about it, she realized it may have been another animal. "You think it was the female?"

"He has likely wooed her to be with him."

"Then what will happen to the pack?"

"Those are all old wolves, and she was the only female." He shrugged, "It will probably die off. It's romantic in its own way."

She stared at Hauk, considered the wolves, and burst out laughing.

"What's so funny?"

"How can wolves be romantic?" Laughter continued to bubble as she fervently tried to envision the predator being given to strong feelings of warmth and passion rather than savage survival instincts.

With a shrug, he defended his description, "He very likely captured her attention with superior hunting capabilities. After all, he is accustomed to surviving without the help of a pack."

"Her pack wouldn't be much competition with their hunting skills." Scorn bristled over the pack she detested, and she hoped the arrival of competition would become its end. "Remember how the rabbit scrambled to safety in seconds and the old wolf fell down panting for air."

Seeing malice in her eyes, Hauk commented, "You really do hate those wolves, don't you?"

"Yes." Her chin squared, "They would have killed me."

"It's their nature."

Aggravated with his acceptance of the creatures for what they are, she angled her chin haughtily, "It's my nature to despise them."

"Do you know why you feel the way you do?"

"Yes." Her look said, 'you are being a chowder-head,' and her mouth said, "They wanted to tear me apart."

"Did you ever think your hatred for them might be triggered by fear of them?"

"Of course I'm afraid of them."

"Would you care enough to hate them, if they posed no physical threat?"

"Facts are what they are, and those animals are creepy."

"You're mistaken."

Glaring at him, she refused to join him when he walked to the door and threw over his shoulder, "Are you coming?"

"Why?"

"I want to show you what happens when fear is removed."

His was a statement worth testing. She was positive he would not possibly be able to make her unafraid of wolves.

Hawk was lining up pine cones for the tenth time, and hiding vexation for her slow progress in learning to use a gun. He decided this was going to be the last go at trying to teach her. Agitation gave way to alert tension at the sound of a quietly throaty growl. Backing away from it, he stopped when a second growl rumbled behind him.

"Hauk?" Arista's voice floated in steady calm contradicting the terror slamming her heart into her throat.

Assessing the nearest tree and determining how quickly he could climb it, he calmly replied, "Back slowly to the cabin. If they attack, shoot."

A deeper, more aggressive growl, rolled eerily. In reply the alpha male made himself as large and threatening as possible by raising his tail, perking his ears forward, snarling, and lifting the shackles on its back. The larger, blacker, lone wolf entered the clearing showing the same display of challenge.

"Keep backing away from them at a steady pace with as little movement as possible." Hauk whispered to Arista. Seeing stark terror in her eyes, his breath caught. "Stay calm. Don't panic."

Trembling, she quietly moved as he did.

In a frenzy of fur, the two animals meshed in battle.

Hauk moved slightly faster, and he breathed with relief when Arista did likewise.

"We're almost there." He glanced behind him. "If we have to, we can close the distance at a run before they will be able to catch us."

"Should we?" Her heart leapt with excitement at the prospect of reaching safety.

"No." Then he saw the female with her shackles bristled off to the side of them. She was too close to outrun. "Move slowly and steadily." Glancing at Arista, he slid his arm close to her with one languid movement. "Pass me the rifle."

"Why?" Fright iced her voice as she cautiously transferred the rifle to him. When the task was completed, she let her arm fall to her side in a quick and jerky motion. A slight shuffle accompanied a muffled growl at close proximity. Arista felt every muscle in her body quiver with terror as they continued backing away.

Evil eyes squinted at them suspiciously. Shackles lifted, her tail lifted, and then, unknown to Hauk and Arista, she recognized them. Her tail tucked between her legs and her ears pressed flat to her head as an indication of submission rather than aggression.

Frowning at the odd behaviour, Hauk took Arista's hand and they continued moving for the cottage. Finally, they were backing up the steps, he opened the door, they slipped inside, and Hauk secured the door barricading them away from the predators outside.

Arista crumpled into a crying and shaking heap. Bracing against the wall, she accused, "You knew they were out there!"

Hauk numbed, and he tried to make sense of why she would blame him for purposefully endangering them. There was no way he could have known the wolves were by his cabin. His goal had been to teach her proper use of firearms. He thought she would lose her fear of the wolves if she was confident in being able to defend herself against them.

Misinterpreting his silence as agreement and admission, her anger fuelled to fury, "You said you were going to teach me not to be afraid." Grabbing her purse and slinging it across one shoulder, she plucked ammunition from the shelf and jostled it into her pocket, and then grabbed the shotgun. "Well, guess what." She spat, "I'm not afraid." And marching out the door she slammed it hard behind herself.

Seeing the furry beasts still there engaging in combat with each other, she fired a shot into the air. The only reaction it triggered was to make them back away from each other with fangs bared in snarls of readiness to once again lunge at each other. She shot into the air two more times. The beasts paused long enough to grumble at each other one last time, and ran for safety.

"This makes me so mad! Never, have I been subjected to anything so stupid!" Muttering her agitation to nobody, she marched for the stream. "So! I'm not afraid of the stupid wolves anymore! I'm just mad!" Grumbling to nobody, she was spurred forward by a surplus of adrenalin surging in her veins.

Watching from the window, Hauk thought it was wise to give her a marginal head start. A sudden burst of flame flashed down the chimney, and Hauk's blood ran cold. Uncoiling the hose hooked up for emergencies, he turned the water on, raced up a ladder, and doused the chimney and roof. The entire disaster, caused by a squirrel having stuffed nuts in his chimney, only lasted a few moments. However, when Hauk was finished assessing the damage, and was certain the fire would not reignite, the only way to catch up to Arista was to intercept her by taking a shortcut.

Breaking through thick bush, she saw the rapids. Hauk hadn't bothered coming after her, and that hurt. In her anger his concern for her wasn't something she had expected nor wanted. Now that she was calmer, it seemed to her that he could have tried talking to her. It might have stopped her from getting herself into this predicament. Tears streamed down her cheeks and she kept walking.

When the flow of water twisted into a band rushing over pebbly ground, she waded in, splashed the film of sweat off her skin, and cupping her hands she brought water to her mouth. Assessing her situation, she realized it was one of the few spots with a relatively shallow depth, and it was a good place to get across. Carefully choosing her footing and testing the depth as she went, she crossed. Clambering onto the opposite shore, she aimed for the only town she knew how to find.

Wanting to reach town before nightfall, she increased her pace to a slow jog and appreciated the steady decline she was moving along. Another hour brought her to the mouth of the river. There, she sat down to rest. Tears fell again as she longed for the safety of shelter and the comfort of food. For the first time in a long time, she desperately craved a cigarette. If nothing else, the deep desire for nicotine gave her motivation.

In another hour she walked into town with her tee shirt clinging to sweat dampened skin, her face smudged with dirt, and her hair hanging in matted clumps. Stopping at the grocery store, she unloaded the shotgun, leant it against the outside wall, went in, and bought a package of cigarettes. Outside she lit one, and it burnt her throat. She was amazed to discover how her body had lost its previous tolerance for the substance. She sucked another dose of smoke into her lungs. It made her dizzy and her stomach rolled queasily. Squashing the cigarette under her shoe, she forgot about the shotgun, and went into the restaurant where she seated herself at a square table beside a hazy window and observed her surroundings.

The floor was covered with faded linoleum having dulled long ago. Walls painted pale beige were heavily filmed with yellow smoke stains. Seeing it reminded her of the habit and she pulled a cigarette out. Prepared for discomfort she inhaled a small breath of smoke. It smoothly slid into her lungs, then trailed out, and soothed her nerves with welcome tranquility. Unnatural or not, she liked it, wanted more, and filled her lungs again.

Almost giddy with the dizzying sensation of satisfying an ignored addiction, she smiled easily when a short, plump woman came and stood beside her table. "Would you like a menu?"

"Yes." Arista smiled at her. "May I please have a glass of water?"

"Sure." Hesitant to leave, the woman studied her and asked, "Are you in some kind of trouble?"

"No." Rubbing a hand over her forehead, feeling grit under her fingers, she realized, "I've been hiking."

A relieved smile broke across thin lips and friendly eyes warmed. "I hope you've had a good day out there."

"I covered miles, but," she grinned sheepishly, "I will want to take the water taxi from here. Is there a phone I can use?"

"There's one on the counter." A podgy finger pointed in the general direction.

Looking, Arista was surprised to see an old, black, rotary dial telephone sitting on the counter by the cash register.

"You must be starving?"

"I will be. Right now my stomach is still crimped from walking. Do you have soup?"

"We have homemade Chicken Noodle soup, and, there is tuna salad left from our lunch special. If you like, I'll make you a sandwich."

"Chicken Noodle soup and a sandwich would be great." Quickly looking around she saw no signs, so asked, "Do you have a washroom?"

"It's the first door to your left." A quirk of her head brought Arista's attention to a dank greyed hallway.

"Thank you."

The stout woman disappeared into the kitchen, and Arista went into the bathroom. Cringing at the dusty and dishevelled person staring back from a foggy and cracked mirror, she wished she had access to a shower, soap, shampoo, a blow dryer, curling iron, hairspray, perfume and cosmetics. The small room held a white porcelain toilet tank and bowl with an age yellowed seat, a toilet paper holder with a new roll, a soap dispenser full of thick blue liquid and mounted on the wall by a small stained porcelain sink, and a paper towel dispenser.

Substituting paper towelling for wash cloths, she cleaned her face, her arms, her legs, and her torso. Seven plastic teeth flew from her comb when she pulled it through her hair, which did little to loosen the layer of dust clinging to the matted mess. Blinking through the mist of building tears, she patiently worked the comb through her hair. Using a damp comb, the clinging dust did the job of hairspray and backcombing, and she shaped her hair into a rugged and tame style. She imagined Hauk sitting by his fireplace contentedly strumming his guitar without sparing a thought for her.

Frustrated with her irrational emotions, she knew full well there was no reason for him to be thinking about her. Being inattentive had landed her in a dangerous situation. Hauk came to her rescue, doctored her injuries, fed her, sheltered her, and shared his world with her. In return, she had done nothing. She hadn't even thanked him. She just left in a huff. Why would he give her a second thought?

Hauk was dangling his legs over a branch he was straddling. Relaxing against the thick trunk behind him, he glanced at the irritating brute snorting below. Sooner or later the beast was sure to move onto easier prey. Squinting at the blue sky, Hauk glowered at the ill fate of a grizzly encounter. It did happen, on rare occasions. Pushing buttons on his cell phone, he fumed over this day, of all days, being one of those occasions.

"Hello."

The sound of a familiar voice was music to his ears. "Hi Mady. I need some help." Glowering down he growled, "A grizzly has me up a tree."

"What?" Alarm pounded Mady's heart into her ribs and tightened her voice to a squeak, "Are you all right? I will send somebody to help you."

Pacing chaotic zigzags reflecting the dither she was working herself into, she frantically asked, "Where are you?"

"I'm fine. There is no reason to send anyone yet. It should tire of me and move on soon." Hauk scowled at the brute. It snorted in return.

"Are you sure?"

"If this drags on for too long, or if you don't hear from me in the next little while, then send someone." Pushing at the tree trunk with its front paws, the shaggy creature bellowed with frustration. "If this doesn't let up soon there is going to be one dead bear out here."

Hearing anger rumble in Hauk's threat, Mady smiled with admiration, and she cooed, "You could probably take that animal down with your bare hands."

He doubted it. Arching a brow at his small rifle, he decided it was better than nothing, but he wished it was higher calibre. He asked, "Have you seen Arista?"

Being a sparsely populated area, Arista's previous visit to the town had been the main conversation. Assuming her unfamiliar guest was Arista, she said, "She came in a few minutes ago."

"Would you do me a favour?"

"I will do anything for you." And she sincerely meant, anything, as lewd thoughts tickled her imagination.

Pausing at the inviting undertows in her voice, he frowned and chose to ignore it. "I don't expect to get there before Arista leaves, so, will you find out where she is going?"

"I'll try." Puckering her lips with obstinate stubbornness, Mady considered asking a few questions, and saying she did her best. For certain, there was no way she was going to put an honest effort into helping Hauk keep Arista around.

Knowing it, he hoped to inspire cooperation from her by praising, "You have the best investigative skills in the area. It will be a cinch for you."

Grinning at the compliment, she lilted, "Thank you." Almost saying his name, she stopped herself. The last thing she wanted was to have Arista overhear the conversation and learn of Hauk's concern. Arista was leaving, which meant there must be some huge misunderstanding, otherwise, as far as Mady was concerned, no woman would ever walk away from Hauk.

For a fleeting moment, Mady felt a strong tug to win Hauk's approval by proving her investigative skills. Ranking higher was her wish to see Arista disappear. Inspecting Arista under lowered lids, she wondered what attracted

Hauk to her. Planning to find out, and use the same techniques on him herself, Mady watched Arista with intense curiosity.

In the extended silence stretching over the telephone, Hauk had a good idea of the conflicting interests distracting Mady. Pique churned in him for her longstanding adoration. Exasperated with the brute snorting below him, Hauk clicked the 'end call' button, fought an impulsive urge to throw the phone at the bear, and pushed it safely into his pocket. Growling down at the beast, he crossed his arms over his chest and prepared to endure the annoying nuisance.

The bear growled back. Hauk rolled his eyes heavenwards. The beast pushed on the tree with his front paws. Hauk growled again. And so it went, until Hauk realized his nonsense was deterring the animal's departure. Hauk took to ignoring the creature below. Finally, two and a half hours later, the beast shook his head to and fro, stood on his hind legs, bellowed, dropped to four legs and lumbered away.

After waiting just long enough to make sure it was not going to come back, Hauk clambered down the tree. No longer hurrying to detain Arista, he walked for a leisurely ten minutes, kicked a stone lying in his path, cursed, and swung through the door into Mady's restaurant.

Mady lit like a Christmas tree. Seeing it, Hauk's stomach plunged. He liked Mady, and remembered the day her mother had brought her home from the hospital as a newborn baby. They were neighbours at that time. His mother and her mother were friends. He had been dragged kicking all the way, because he had wanted to keep playing with Ben, to see Mady. He still remembered being awestruck with the perfection of such a tiny human being, and the terror of touching someone so incredibly fragile. He had stood back watching her from a safe distance. At the time, he never would have imagined such a delicate little person growing into the boisterous and assertive woman Mady had become.

"Hauk!" With a squeal she flung herself against him and wrapped her arms around his neck like a boa constrictor. "I was so worried about you." Easing away from him, she intentionally brushed her ample bosom against him and smiled unabashedly.

Creating distance, he walked around the counter to the coffee pot, took a clean mug from the tray beside it, and poured himself a steamy cup of coffee. "It's never a good thing when there is a grizzly in the area." Turning he saw her blush as her eyes lifted from their inspection of the faded denim, complete with spots wearing too thin, snuggled over his buttocks. Closing his eyes against the aggravation of it, he asked, "What did Arista have to say?"

"I wasn't able to get any significant information."

Turning his back to her, he cringed at the unattractive face she was making by trying to pout sexily. "What did she tell you?"

"Well." Filling a cup with coffee for herself, she informed, "She was expecting to catch a bus this evening." Mady seated herself across from Hauk, at a table positioned cheerily in front of a window and decorated with a faded red and white checked cloth.

"I know where she is going, but, it's a large city and it would be difficult to find someone. I was expecting her to stay for a few more days. I didn't even get her last name." Heat scorched his cheeks and he fiercely hoped he wasn't blushing.

Seeing the hue of embarrassment, Mady chuckled.

Aggravation took hold, and drinking from his coffee he fumed.

Hoping to impress him, Mady blurted, "Her last name is Zinger."

Mady wisely refrained from telling him she had come across the information by telling Arista she was going to become Mady VanLiev. It had caused Arista to joke about her name, Arista Zinger. She said she had been subjected to endless taunts that were especially merciless during junior high school. Despite Arista's friendliness and easy smile, Mady gloated to herself that she had won a marvellous victory. Unshed tears of defeat had misted Arista's eyes when Mady had told her she was in a longstanding relationship with Hauk and they were presently in the midst of a lover's quarrel.

"Her name is Zinger?"

"Yes."

"How many people can be listed with the name Zinger?" Thinking his work was going to be easy, he sat back and relaxed. An abrupt surge of tiredness filled his lungs with a hardy yawn.

Turning to a piercing squeak of the door, they watched Ben walk in. Stopping, he looked at them watching him, gave Hauk an empty glance, and his vision fell on Mady. "Hi." He flashed a grin. "These hinges need oiling. Do you want me to look after it for you?"

Hiding his reaction by lowering his head, Hauk arched an inquisitive brow at hearing Ben speak proper English rather than his usual slang. The last thing Ben ever concerned himself with was what other people might think of him. Amazingly, Ben had not been employed at a real job a day in his life, and his finances always came around for him. His house was inherited along with a mediocre amount of money having the potential of lasting a lifetime in Ben's hands. Small chores, like the one he was doing, kept Ben going.

Hauk watched Ben fix the hinges on Mady's door. In exchange Mady would allow Ben to choose anything he wanted from the menu free of charge.

The lifestyle was in perfect accord with Ben's priorities. The only thing missing was the materialization of the sexiest woman in the world. By Ben's definition, the perfect woman should have frizzed and sun bleached brunette hair billowing from under a baseball cap, and she should enjoy fishing, hunting, and sex. Although she was proving impossibly difficult for him to find, Ben seemed content with his lot.

Ben loved the earth, the smell of it, the feel of it, and every bountiful gift springing from it. Money had little value to him. Equally trivial to him was prestige or any other form of public distinction whether it was good or bad. All Ben wanted was to fish, hunt, explore the great earth, and acknowledge the present, as he lived it, without wasting time looking to the future or the past. It was simple.

In some ways Hauk envied Ben's happy-go-lucky ease. In other ways the going was difficult for Ben. He occasionally voiced his dream of getting married and establishing a family. He doubted it would happen for him. It would mean exchanging his hunting and fishing for a job that would provide an acceptable lifestyle. Especially, since children were cruelly ridiculed over anything less than normal, even in an area as remote as this.

Hauk glanced at Mady, who was bending over and wiggling her ample rump with more gusto than was required to wipe tables. Then he looked at Ben diligently repairing the door with unruly hair spiralling around his head like millions of crimped wires. The two seemed to be perfectly suited, and completely oblivious to each other.

"How is this?" Ben spoke loudly to draw attention from both Mady and Hauk. When they looked, he swung the door soundlessly on its hinges.

"Great." Mady praised the job.

Pure satisfaction shone on Ben's face.

Mady's smile widened.

As always, when Ben did something, whether the task was large or small, it was done properly.

Watching the interaction, Hauk considered the conflict in Ben's character. Ben was decidedly the strangest perfectionist anyone could ever come to know. Ben lived in a house built by hand in the pioneer days. Though it was earthy, it was decorated with unusual pizzazz. The interior walls were finished with well fitted planks of wood, cut from his property. His wooden sofa was handmade and covered with layers of treated hides – leather. Tables and chairs, likewise, were handmade from trees felled on his property. The wood in Ben's house was smoothed, stained, varnished, and polished to perfection. Although he did have electricity, he preferred the soft glow of lanterns. Rather than wasting time, as he put it, watching television, he read from countless books. Hard cover books, new, antique, famous, and never heard of, filled wooden shelves lining his sitting area. Ben's living room was in fact a well kept library. He insisted on using his feet for travel rather than purchasing a vehicle.

He readily used and damaged Hauk's truck when it was available, which reminded Hauk, "How are the repairs going on my truck?"

"Come take a look."

Seeing confidence in the smile lighting Ben's face and eyes, guilt nudged Hauk into suggesting, "Let's go after you finish your meal."

"It's right outside." Ben grinned accommodatingly.

Having assumed the truck was at Ben's house, Hauk arched a brow at the bold way Ben helped himself to it. Knowing it was pointless to bring it to Ben's attention, since he didn't have the slightest clue he was doing anything wrong, Hauk complied, "Ok. Let's go take a look."

As usual, the repairs were excellently done and Ben was returning the vehicle in better condition than it had been in when it was left with him. Hauk supposed it was Ben's consistent display of respect for other people's belongings that kept him in good enough standing with everyone to gain him almost unconditional access to borrowing anything he wanted.

"I think it might really be something to live in a big city. It sure would be different than living here. How do you feel about city life?"

Hauk stared at Ben for a few speechless moments and vexation churned over the breach of privacy. The only people informed about his career change were the administrators at the hospital, and they were supposed to be trustworthy with confidentiality. "Nothing was supposed to be said. What have you heard?"

"Huh?" It was Ben's turn to stare with blank confusion.

Sensing a misunderstanding, Hauk quirked a brow, and brought the subject back around, "Why are you asking me about big cities?"

Ben blinked at Hauk with annoyance, and then explained, "There were two men at my place today." Ben took a deep breath. "They were fine looking people with expensive suites and articulate speech. Maybe I've been making a mistake here." Pinching his lips he shuffled dirt under his boot. "I'm not too old to change and build a real life for myself."

"Build a real life?" Hauk arched both brows and stared at him. Despite the odds against him, Ben successfully customized a lifestyle ideally suited to his likes and dislikes. Hauk figured it was as real as it gets.

"Maybe I should get an education, a career, a wife and some kids." Staring at craggy mountains, he squinted up to the sky, and then looked at Hauk. "I could keep my place here and come back from time to time." He shrugged with a sigh. "Women don't go for this kind of life."

Hauk refrained from saying Ben's time would be crimped if he found what he was suggesting, and frequent returns might fall by the wayside. Judging by the forlorn shadows in Ben's eyes, Ben was aware of possible contradictions in what he was saying. Ben's life should not logically work the way it does now either, so, who knows?

"You think you might enjoy living in a city?" It was impossible to imagine Ben donning a suite, going to work regularly, studying for a degree, paying attention to bills, or any of the other demands his plan entailed.

"Those two men made it look good today."

Recovering from the shock of hearing Ben, who was always the same from one day to the next, contemplating change, Hauk acknowledged the next peculiar occurrence in the day's events. "Why were they here?"

"They are scientists exploring some radical and rare ground movement they claim we will be experiencing over the next few weeks as plates shift."

Still adjusting to this new Ben, and his sudden show of intelligence, it took a few minutes for Hauk to register what had been said. "Plates are shifting?"

Ben nodded, "They say this area is the closest to the center of the activity, so we are going to feel the brunt of it."

"How long are those men going to be here?"

"They plan on spending at least two weeks in the area."

"If they are sticking around the threat must be minimal." Numerous recent events became suspicious in light of this new information. "Have you noticed any peculiar changes in the landscape lately?"

"Hate to say it, but, odd things have been going on. Sometimes the birds all fly up squawking at the same time without any noticeable reason. It gives me the spooks." Ben locked eyes with Hauk, "It just ain't right."

Hauk bent his head to hide a warm grin for hearing the familiar slang return to Ben's lips. It made things feel right again. Hauk admired the instinct in his friend. Ben had a feel for the land. He was almost one with it. It was something nobody could ever be taught. It was a gift.

They made their way back into the restaurant, and to their seats, while they spoke.

"Animals have been getting skittish without provocation. Sometimes, especially at night when I lie in bed, I feel small trembles and my skin wants to jump from me to make the ground still itself. The earth's grieved lately. I hope her wounds heal quietly, but, she will do whatever needs doing to mend her affliction."

Walking past in time to catch his comparison of the land to a woman, Mady gave him a backhand against the arm producing a loud smack and she berated, "You really don't get out much do you?"

"Not enough." Ben grimaced at her. "I should be out right now. It would be pleasanter than it is in here."

"Pleasanter is not a word."

"Don' ged in my face Mady."

Chuckling at the increasing use of slang, Hauk got up from the table. "I'll be taking my truck back tonight."

Both Ben and Mady looked up at hearing his announcement.

"Are you heading back to town?" Mady's smile drooped to a pout she hoped was alluring.

Turning from the annoyance of it, he asked Ben, "Do you want a ride home?"

Ben flashed perfect teeth and grinned arrogantly, "Since when do I need a ride? I have my feet."

"Have you met up with the grizzly hanging around here yet?"

"There's a grizzly?"

"It kept me up a tree for hours."

Deflated at having the grizzly discovered by someone other than himself, he confessed, "I haven't come across any signs of a grizzly hangin' 'round these parts."

"Don't take it too hard." Hauk grinned and Ben gave him a withered look. "It might not have been around for long, and," he hoped, "it might just keep moving."

"It will probably stick around a bit. Unwanted pests are usually hard to get rid of."

"Ya." Standing up, Mady stacked dishes to clear off the table while flinging over her shoulder, "Like you."

Ben thought about the men at his house, thought about the real life he was thinking about, and decided to give sophistication a try. "If you don't want me here, then I will leave." Pinning her under an intense stare, he waited for her to reply.

Fidgeting nervously, Mady angled her chin and oozed with sarcasm, "Where would a guy like you possibly have to go?"

Thunder built over his mood and across his expression. He took reign of it, and steered it into a charming smile. The smile fell short of reaching his eyes. "You haven't said that you want me to leave." He fastened a hypnotic gaze on her that challenged her to try a new approach, and a watchfulness to see what she might come up with.

Excited butterflies danced in Mady's stomach. She hated herself for her unwelcome attraction to the new side Ben was showing today.

Both men saw the feminine response soften Mady's eyes and brush her cheeks with heightened colour.

Ben stood with a transfixed stare. He had never seen Mady act like a normal woman for even a second. He liked what he was seeing.

"I will leave you two to sort out this confusion." Hauk turned his back to them and both pairs of eyes riveted to him.

Hauk let the door close behind him, and hoped the pair would get together. It seemed to him to be the perfect solution for ridding him of Mady's infatuation, and for keeping Ben settled here where he belongs.

Driving slowly along winding gravel roads, he looped his way to the main highway with his thoughts twisting more than the roads. He contemplated the best way to go about finding Arista, how to present himself when he did, and exactly what direction he wanted their relationship to take from there. Reluctant to jump into commitments, especially with anyone as talented at deception as Arista, he knew caution would be necessary when he found her. Whatever the outcome may be, he knew he had to find her.

Chapter 18

Curling her legs underneath her, and nestled into the cushioned seat, Arista stared blindly out the side window of the highway bus she was riding. Huge tears welled in almond eyes. She blew her nose, and suffered a sudden and hostile bout of coughing afflicted by harsh gasps between coughs.

Other passengers looked at her from the corner of their eyes. Assessing her, deciding she wasn't a threat to them, they promptly did their best ignore her. She was grateful for the callous society promoting isolation even when they were packed together in the close confines of a bus.

Unconcerned with the discomfort she was inflicting on the other passengers, Arista continued torturing herself by replaying every moment she had spent with Hauk. Nothing, and nobody, could ever match Hauk, from his heady, musky scent, to the mixture of sparks and shadows waltzing from his eyes and skipping to her. He was the only man in the entire world able to bring all her senses to life at once. It created an odd mixture of emotion and placed a strange weight on her heart.

Without Hauk having entered her life, she wouldn't even know those feelings could coexist. No matter how difficult it was going to be to accept his absence, she had gained a treasure. As with anything worth having, it brought a potentially high cost and she might never again be willing to settle for less.

Emotionally drained, she fell asleep with tears soaking her cheeks. In her sleep the tears kept flowing and she dreamt short successive dreams alternating from playing with Hauk one minute to being utterly alone the next. Shuddering at the fear of spending the rest of her life alone, she was jolted to wakefulness as the bus slid into its assigned parking spot.

The driver flipped switches, swung the door open, got up, went out of the bus and waited to assist passengers down the stairs. Merging with the others, Arista walked off the bus and into the depot where a too thin, hyperactive, middle aged man, blocked her path waving an open box of chocolates, "Do you want a chocolate?"

Covering her mouth with her upper arm, she coughed, and then answered, "No thank you." Cautiously avoiding attracting unwanted attention from him, and at the same time striving to sooth any offence he might take, she curved her lips into a friendly smile. Watching him pop a candy into his mouth as he walked away without concern, she realized she needn't have wasted her energy keeping the situation calm since it had never been volatile.

Stepping onto the concrete sidewalk, Arista stretched crimps out of her neck. She took a cleansing breath of fresh air sweeping away the stifling gloom from the stuffy depot crowded with too many different lifestyles. Turning to the sound of a muffled voice, Arista saw a heavy woman with brunette hair matted in dirty clumps, wearing soiled and torn clothing, talking to her.

"I beg your pardon?" Trying to swallow against an annoying tickle in her throat, Arista hoped the woman would soon go away and leave her to the coughing spell hanging in her chest.

The woman repeated herself.

Arista didn't know if she was speaking a foreign language or suffering from a speech impediment. Whichever it was, Arista was unable to understand what she was trying to say. Requests for cigarettes were common on the street, so Arista handed one to the woman.

"No. No. No." Taking the cigarette, the woman shook her head negatively.

Money was the next most popular request. Arista dug into her purse and pulled out two dollars. "Here." She handed her the money. Unable to restrain, Arista coughed against her upper arm.

Clutching the money in her hand, the woman again shook her head, "No. No. No."

It seemed to be the only word she could pronounce properly. Looking at her, Arista could not think of anything else to offer, so she took back the cigarette and the money.

The woman gave her a dumbfounded look.

Arista shrugged, walked away, and gave in to a vicious attack of coughing.

Chapter 19

Day Seventeen - Wednesday

Along with the sunrise, traffic noise invaded her apartment with tireless consistency. Instead of blending into a tolerable rhythm of sound, tires droned over the paved street, followed by intervals of silence, and then the annoying sound of rubber rushing over cement would prevail again. The odd broken muffler added frustration to Arista's already unbearable intolerance of a society racing in spastic chaos and seeming to go nowhere.

Agitation popped her nerves as she rolled out of bed. Just then, the neighbour's overly zealous washing machine bounced into the wall and promptly threatened to hurl Arista's framed pictures to destruction as they vibrated to the tempo of a hearty spin.

Stretched nerves snapped into fury and Arista pounded against the wall.

"Sorry." A female voice filtered through the wall along with the scraping sound of her machine being tugged.

Arista rubbed the tension out of her temples with small circular motions of her fingers. "What is the matter with me?"

Searching for contentment, Arista pressed the power button on her remote control. The television screen flicked to life. Finding a light comedy, she pressed the volume button to reduce the sound. The neighbour's lawn mower roared to life. Every muscle in Arista's body tensed.

Above the racket made by the traffic and the lawn mower, she heard the chirps of birds. Angry about everything, Arista's thoughts flashed back to the prevalent peace at Hauk's cottage.

A second lawn mower joined the commotion. The picture on her television slowly merged into a horizontal white line running through the middle of her screen. When she hit both sides of the television, the line once again expanded into a picture. Pain throbbed in her head. Needing to escape, she filled her bathtub with apricot scented beads and sank into the fragrant warmth. There, her thoughts drifted to Hauk. Rivers of tears streamed down her cheeks.

She deducted that the good things in life compare to an apple. It comes home from the store shiny, red, and fresh. Within days, unless it is eaten, it begins to brown from the center. Either way, it is quickly gone.

She got out of the tub, dressed in a comfy tee shirt and denim jeans, and headed for her den. The entire time her mind remained submerged in despair. She ached for the ideal mirage she had glimpsed just long enough to tantalize her to the brink of insanity. At Hauk's side, in his life, she had found a niche. It was a place she felt fitted to. And it disappeared, leaving her aching and longing for what it had teased it could be.

Three quiet knocks at the door forewarned, and Sherry hollered, "Hi! Arista? Are you home?"

Walking out of her den, closing the door on the bills scattered over her desk, she moved into the openness of her main living area, and greeted the petite brunette standing by the door.

A smile spread and Sherry bubbled, "I needed to get out for a while and I was hoping you would have time for a visit."

"Your timing is perfect." Arista grinned with sincere welcome. "I'm bored," she shrugged, "and could use some company."

"Oh good!" Slipping her shoes off, Sherry's smile widened. "I snuck out while Glen was getting breakfast for Linzy and Nat. He has the day off today, and we will do something later."

Arista set a fresh pot of coffee to brew for them, and Sherry grumbled about the tedious chores of picking up behind children all day long. Despite her complaints, contentment radiated on Sherry's expression.

Hiding a sudden threat of tears, Arista busily took two mugs from the cupboard, two spoons from the drawer, filled a creamer, and got out the sugar bowl.

Sherry yakked about everything and anything without taking a break until, "Listen to me." She grinned sheepishly. "You know how those people who never get out of the house talk for hours without letting anyone else say a word because they don't see other people often enough." She giggled nervously. "I'm turning into one of them."

"I prefer to listen, so talk away." Arista placed two cups of coffee on the table for them.

Sherry's peach glossed lips curved in a smile as she lifted the white ceramic cup, edged with blue trim, to her lips and gently blew steam off the surface of its contents. "What's been happening with you lately? I haven't been able to catch you at home for days." When her question met silence, Sherry studied Arista with close scrutiny. "You have been up to something!" Curiosity jumped to life creating an avid interest in listening.

The events retold sounded outlandish even to Arista. It was hardly surprising when Sherry levelled a disgusted look on her and said, "If you don't want to tell me the truth, don't. You don't have to make up a story."

"It's all true." Needing a confidante, she lifted the hem of a pant leg to reveal wounds healing where pebbles had penetrated her skin, "Look."

Finally believing her, Sherry chimed, "You found a whole loaf."

"No." Arista shook her head. "I told you. We parted on nasty terms."

"You will make up with each other."

"What makes you think so?"

"You two sound made for each other."

"How do you figure?" They were worlds apart. He was smart, successful, and steadfast. She was always at loose ends.

"The speed you connected at must mean something."

Faking a carefree grin, Arista asked, "What if the whole thing was no more than a lustful interlude for us?"

"Was it fun?" Merry dimples dug beside her lips.

Memories danced in Arista's eyes as she sought words.

Sherry teased, "There was a real connection between you two."

Sherry's faith in people made Arista long for an optimistic disposition.

Sherry asked, "What if he is the one for you?"

Intense desire invisibly ripped Arista's emotional state apart in a second. The storm raged inside. With a cool facade, Arista flippantly replied, "If we are meant to be, then, somehow we will be."

"I made my interest in Glen very clear." Sherry cooed as she moved her left hand and sparks of light danced from the diamonds snuggled on her finger. "Otherwise," she shrugged, "who knows." She arched a dark brow at Arista silently suggesting she should follow her example.

"Was Glen standoffish?"

"Glen!" Sherry giggled and pink hues flushing her cheeks told of Glen's pursuits. "No."

"Hauk is thoughtful and cautious. It would be fair for me to see if he will make a move."

"Why would you leave it to him?"

Lifting her cup to her lips, Arista arched a brow, "He knows exactly what he wants and is capable of pursuing it, if he chooses to." Certain he would prefer not to, she clenched her cup hard in an effort to stop the slight tremble in her hand.

Seeing the tremor, Sherry used care in selecting her words. "What makes you think he is any good at deciphering his emotions? Men are usually daft about feelings."

"Hauk is different. He's a doctor. He's above average in intelligence, patience, kindness, charisma, charm, and appearance." Arista sighed, "He is absolutely perfect."

"Is he? Perhaps your feelings for him are painting a glossed image in your mind?"

"Love is blind?"

"If you ask me, I think you might be letting pride get in the way."

Arista weighed what was said. "If I do decide to contact him," she gave Sherry a look that emphasized the possibility of deciding not to contact him, "the worst thing that could happen is that he would tell me to leave him alone. Right?" Abruptly changing the conversation, Arista informed Sherry, "I've been offered a promotion."

"Congratulations." Sherry easily slid into the different topic. "Where does this put you on the career ladder?"

"My salary will provide a decent living. It also means relocating."

They shared the sadness of losing their close proximity to each other, vowed to stay in touch, and decided the mosquitoes couldn't be as troublesome as people said. The prairie winters, they were sure, were also highly exaggerated.

"There is no purpose in hankering over a relationship with Hauk if I'm about to move one thousand miles away."

"You might be right." Contrary to her words, Sherry's look clearly stated she believed Arista was about to make the biggest mistake of her life, even if she might never know it.

A shrill chime from the doorbell sliced the air.

"Are you expecting company?" Sherry quickly picked up her cup and deposited it in the sink as she prepared for a rapid departure.

"No. It's probably my landlord with some dumb complaint. I was giving Sally a hard time about her washing machine before."

"Again?" Sherry plucked her cup out of the sink, rinsed it, and refilled it as she waited for Arista to return to their conversation.

When Arista opened the door, she was clutched in an unwelcome bear hug, "Hi Hon!"

Staring at Guy in speechless surprise, she eased distance between them.

"What's wrong?" His smile wavered slightly as the tiniest doubt crept in and he momentarily suspected her unenthusiastic greeting might be sincere. Then, his usual arrogant grin twisted, and his silent pride sent a fresh flare of confidence leaping to the forefront.

"Why are you here?"

"I better go home and help Glen." Guy's presence made Sherry distinctly uncomfortable.

Guy waited quietly until Sherry left before continuing, "You don't look happy to see me."

Frowning at him she grumbled, "I thought we had agreed to end this relationship."

"Did you think I was serious on the phone?"

Fury built in Arista. Judging by his cocky grin he didn't believe she could be anything less than thrilled over his presence. He walked past her and opened her refrigerator. Turning her back to him, she fluffed the cushions on her couch, and searched her mind for a way to approach the situation politely.

Letting out a long sigh to dramatize the pretence of being heavily burdened, he complained, "It was quite the convention. Let me tell you."

His grumbling slid past her. She focused on watching him spread a thick layer of salad dressing on a piece of bread. Next he layered the bread with shaved ham, tomato slices, three slices of cheese, more salad dressing, and slapped on a second piece of bread. The way he used her belongings as though they were his made her furious.

"There were three meetings a day plus appointments with potential customers. For all my trouble I didn't land one contract." He blew a loud sigh to emphasize his undue belief in his own importance. "It was a complete waste of time."

Watching Guy lean forward looking soberly thoughtful, Arista's attention to him perked as she wondered if he was finally seeing a glimmer of reality and thinking about changing his life.

Her spark of hope sputtered out when he enthusiastically gushed, "Next time will be better." Flashing a grin, he boasted, "Things must have been boring around here for you."

Egotistical glints sparking in his eyes said he believed her world revolved around him and his absence had assuredly heightened her awareness of it, which clearly stated he had not noticed her having been away for the extended time.

She knew Guy was selfishly blind to most things other than Guy, and delusional enough to believe the rest of the world was fascinated with Guy and only Guy. Being so completely clueless to the changes happening in her life, and with their relationship, was radical. His ego was tedious and tiresome to the point of intolerable.

Arista scowled and her heart launched her mouth into an attack aimed at ending their relationship. "Guy, things have changed while you were away."

Suspicion flickered in his eyes for only the briefest moment before his smug grin returned.

Seeing him looking as though he were indulging a child, and waiting out a petty tantrum, accelerated her fury to pure hatred. She bluntly announced, "I'm moving next month."

"What?" He was on his feet in an instant. Remaining silent she watched him pace the room for tense minutes. Then, Guy sat down on the sofa and asked, "Why?"

She pretended to perk, plastered a plastic smile on her face, and babbled, "The bank has offered me a position as an assistant manager. I am obligated to acquire a few degrees, but I will be able to do that while I am doing the job."

"Where will this leave us?" He looked taken aback for a second, and then angled his chin haughtily, "There's this hot chic. She's a friend of-"

"Hot chic?" Arista interrupted.

He spared a second to give her a look saying she was a ninny for not understanding and then patiently explained, "Well if you are not going to be here, what do you expect me to do?"

Instead of pleading with him the way he assumed she would, Arista scorned, "You go get yourself that hot chic." She glowered at him as she rose to her feet. Her breath caught and released in violent coughing. Pausing with fleeting knowledge that the attacks were unusual and easy to ignore, due to the long lapses of normality between coughing spells, she mentally denied that there was anything seriously amiss. She regained her breath, and refastened her attention on loathing Guy.

He moved his mouth as if he was about to argue, then changed his mind, got to his feet, angled his chin, quirked a brow, and spat, "Maybe I will."

Desperately wanting his share of her good fortune, and increased income, Guy thanked his lucky stars for having been asked by a friend to hold a ring in safekeeping until the weekend. Plucking the small velvet box from his pocket, he flipped it opened, displayed the sparkle of diamonds cradled in gold, snapped it closed, thrust it back into his pocket and spat, "When you come to your senses, you know where to find me." Certain she would chase after him and beg him to marry her he confidently swaggered from her apartment in an arrogant flap.

Closing the door behind him, Arista hoped the split would remain intact without any more uncomfortable encounters. The diamond ring highly indicated otherwise. One week earlier she would have jumped at the chance of marriage. That was a scary thought.

Chapter 20

Day Eighteen - Thursday

First thing in the morning she walked into the bank and spoke with her boss. Previous arrangements were already in place, the apartment was empty, and the branch she was transferring to was straining with a staff shortage. They were able to move the date ahead to accommodate her. She swallowed continuously to battle the annoying itch in her throat, and managed to hold back from coughing until she reached the privacy of her car.

When she got home she contacted an auctioneer. After assessing her belongings, in the comfort of her apartment, they settled on an amount, and he wrote her a cheque. Within the hour his employees were loading her possessions, now his, onto a truck that would take his purchase to his storage buildings for a future sale.

She packed her remaining items into two suitcases. An acquaintance was called, and her apartment was sublet to him for the remaining three months of her lease.

Taking the two suitcases holding all of her worldly belongings, she went to the airport, boarded a jet, and left her problems behind.

Finally, he saw the address. Parking his car, he cursed the grizzly for having complicated what should have been a simple interception of Arista's departure. It was going to be extremely difficult to coax forgiveness from her after giving her anger time to root. His longing to see her, even if he was in her bad graces, was stronger than the trepidation of having to apologize. He walked to the door and rang her doorbell.

When the door handle twisted, Hauk smiled and warmth crept into his eyes in anticipation of seeing Arista. The door swung open to a bulk of a man with a thick crop of dark hair and work stained calloused hands. Reeling with shock, Hauk stared speechlessly, and he frantically thought of explanations for this man to be here. Maybe he was a relative. Worse, this man could be Guy, although, he didn't fit the description. Thinking it over, Hauk remembered how regularly Arista had lied.

"Can I help you?"

"Yes." Having regained his composure, Hauk asked, "Is this where Arista lives?"

A wide grin broke on the man's face. "She did, until today. Now, I live here."

Struck with the possibility of Arista having been violated in any way by this man, Hauk's anger simmered under the surface, and he calmly asked, "Do you know where she is?"

Spastically jerking his shoulders, his wide and floppy lips twisted down. "No." His shoulders jiggled again. "I never thought to ask where she was going. If you contact Sherry, she will know how to get in touch with Arista. I'll get a piece of paper and write down Sherry's phone number for you."

Arista was busy checking out her luxurious, and empty, two bedroom apartment. Her life was in the midst of absolute change - again. The new job title was giving her a spacious office with her name engraved in a polished brass door plaque, a decent paycheque, and prominent connections in the banking industry.

No matter how fast she moved, keeping pace with her was the ever present cloud of discontentment shadowing her life. None of her achievements held the treasures she craved. Even knowing there were oodles of people striving for, and failing to reach her status, which was a sure indication of the difficulty it presented, did nothing to ease her restless discomfort.

Arista decided life is infuriatingly weird. The greatest desire of one's heart, whatever it may be, seems to be the hardest goal to achieve. For some it is the acquisition of money. For others it is love. It only took moments to think of valiant causes such as freedom, equality, human rights, and an endless list of honourable and unattainable ambitions. Worse, when hopes are realized they seem to shift and new aspirations take hold.

She unpacked her laptop computer, plugged it in, turned her wireless network on, searched the news and saw, "An earthquake registering 7.4 forcefully shook the Canadian Rocky Mountains. The effects were felt in Alberta,

British Columbia, and Montana. There are no injuries. One mountain peak avalanched into a remote valley. After performing a routine air search, rescue crews have reported the area as uninhabited with no indication of human casualties."

Clicking appropriate icons, Arista found a map of the affected area. It appeared to have broken away along the same path she had fallen through. Using her cell phone, she dialled Hauk's number got a recorded announcement telling her he was away from his phone.

After paying an outrageous price for her ticket, she was seated in a 747 flying west. In a few hours she was bobbing with the waves and staring at the scenery from her rented canoe. Tears streamed down her cheeks. The creek was gone. Only a small inlet followed the shoreline, and the lake lapped where the mountain stream had once gurgled. Worse, from where she was, she could see half a mountain of boulders piled onto what had been her version of paradise. It was utterly and irreparably destroyed.

Squelching rising fear, she told herself people knew of Hauk's cottage. They would be searching for him if he had been there, and the news had said there were no people in the affected area.

Angling the oars, she turned the canoe around to make her way back. It felt like an immeasurably long time before she was finally walking into the main entrance at the hospital. Keeping her posture rigidly straight she put an effort into presenting a calm appearance despite the anxiety almost knocking her legs out from under her.

Interrupting her swirl of thoughts, a woman at the information counter asked loudly, "Can I help you?"

Arista swallowed a lump of dread. "Yes." She cleared her throat. "May I please speak with Dr. VanLiev?"

"I'm afraid he's not available."

Fear clutched Arista's stomach as possibilities raced through her mind. Losing her composure, she blurted, "Do you know if he was at his cottage when the earthquake struck?"

"I don't know anything about a cottage. Today is my first day working here."

"Arista?"

Arista clenched her teeth, turned to the direction of the beckon, and saw Doris barrelling down on her from across the entrance.

"What are you doing here?" Doris' ever present smile broadened.

"I heard about the earthquake."

Arista took a breath in preparation to ask about Hauk.

Doris plunged into describing, "It was the most terrifying thing. I was in the basement when it started. Try running up stairs when they are going like this." Doris moved her hands from side to side. "There was so much noise." Her eyes widened, "At first it was like a very loud train. When the mountain fell," she clucked her tongue, "I have never heard anything like it."

Grasping the first moment between words, Arista blurted, "Have you seen Hauk?"

"Not since this morning."

Panicky vibrations began in her stomach and worked their way to every limb. "How can I find him?"

"I'll give you his number." After rummaging in her purse, Doris pulled out a paper and pen, "And his new address." After writing down the information she handed it to Arista.

Staring at it, the ground tilted and she realized she was forgetting to breathe. Correcting the problem, she took a deep breath. "Are you positive he wasn't at his cottage?"

"Of course I am, he's my son." Doris' smile drooped for the first time. "Didn't he tell you?"

"I'm sorry. No he didn't." It seemed Arista's own importance had just crashed to nothingness. Hauk hadn't even put enough significance on their relationship to tell her that Doris is his mother. Daring to glance up, she saw hurt clouding Doris' eyes as well.

"Perhaps he is ashamed of me." Doris hid her eyes behind lowered lids. "Sons are sometimes strange about their mother, especially when a beautiful young woman is involved." Her smile indicated humble acceptance.

"He likely just thought it was unimportant because he knew I was leaving."

"You are keeping in touch with each other though, aren't you?"

"No."

As a keen glint, very definitely resembling happiness, lit in Doris' eyes, Arista regretted having bothered feeling bad when Doris had appeared hurt by Hauk's oversight.

"Maybe I should take back the information I gave you." Doris' hand snaked toward the paper.

Arista crumpled it into a ball in her palm and closed her fingers tightly and protectively over it.

"I thought you would be keeping in touch. He said he was going to stop in to talk with you at your place."

"How does he know where I live?" Stiffening, Arista looked at the woman with suspicion.

Intimidated, Doris stammered, "I don't know. He said something about a woman named Cher."

"Sherry?"

"Yes." The familiar smile returned.

Arista's breath caught. Red flags warning of dangerous stalking blazed through her mind. Then, typical stupid female reaction won and she embraced the information of Hauk being in search of her.

Needing to make absolutely certain, Arista asked, "He was not near the cottage when the earthquake hit?"

"Oh! No!" Her face paled. "If Hauk had been at his cottage, it would have been terrible! Do you know half the mountain fell into the valley?"

"Yes. I saw it on the internet, and came here as soon as I could."

Heavy grey brows creased, "It just happened today."

"I know. I caught the first available flight."

At hearing the intensity of Arista's feelings, Doris recognized the signs, and her heart became heavily burdened with facing another unknown twist in life's road. In her younger days, when nature chose to streak her hair with fiery red highlights instead of grey ribbons and her waistline had known where it belonged, she had believed she would be able to handle every situation with calm confidence by the time she reached this age. She had been mistaken. Things were just as scary now as they had been when she was young. It was infinitely easier to become a daughter-in-law than a mother-in-law. The label, 'mother-in-law', and all the jokes associated with it held about as much appeal as the bubonic plaque.

Doris commented, "You look pale. Have you had something to eat?"

The mention of food brought an awareness of the raw emptiness gnawing at her stomach and she shook her head.

Doris' smile brightened. "I haven't had supper this evening. Should we go get something to eat?" Meeting stunned silence, Doris coaxed, "I really would like to get to know you better."

"I am starving."

"I know just the place."

She led Arista from the hospital to a tiny, faded restaurant, with a narrow entrance. Inside, the walls were decorated with sections of orange and brown striped wallpaper framed in wooden borders and surrounded with a weaving of variegated golden colours resulting from special painting techniques.

Sitting on a brown vinyl bench at a brown table and flipping open an orange menu smudged with grease, Doris' smile reached her eyes. "They serve the world's best hamburgers, and their french fries are smothered in generous portions of rich gravy."

Staring at her own menu, Arista contemplated Doris' girth and her own low fat diet. Instead of healthy heart choices, she discovered the menu consisted of single, double, or triple patty hamburgers, french fries, pastries, deep fried breaded fish, deep fried chicken, and deep fried battered shrimp. The only salad choices were spread at the salad bar, and she quickly rejected the idea of making any selections there as she watched a sloppy couple use soiled utensils to refill used plates.

"Are you ready to order?" A plump blond waitress with short spiked hair smiled down at them and poised her pencil over a notepad. "Do you need a few more minutes?"

"I know what I want." Doris' ever present smile widened. "I'll have a hamburger with cheese, tomato, and bacon." A pencil scratching across the paper kept pace with Doris. "French fries with gravy." Clasping podgy hands in anticipation, she added, "And a piece of cheesecake with cherry topping for desert."

When the waitress looked at her expectantly, Arista asked, "Do you have soup?"

"Yes we do. Today's selection is either Cream of Mushroom, or Beef Vegetable."

A relieved smile curved glossed lips, "I'll have the beef vegetable and a tomato sandwich with no mayo on dry toast please."

Doris' smile turned almost completely upside down. "Are you trying to lose weight?"

"No." Arista assured as she shuddered over being the cause of sufficient negative emotion to erase the smile from Doris' face.

"Good." With a cluck of her tongue she bluntly stated, "You are already as thin as a rail."

Arista laughed at the outspoken frankness, and shook her head as she argued, "My last boyfriend was always telling me I was gaining weight."

Two salt and peppered brows arched high in surprise. "Why would anyone say such a thing to you?"

Silently, Arista thought about Guy, and her unpleasant memories of him.

Reading the veiled thoughts racing through Arista's mind, Doris loathed Guy without having to meet him, and she assured, "You are not heavy by any standard."

With a giggle Arista spontaneously blurted, "I wish everyone was like you."

"Why?" Doris' eyes lit from the compliment.

"I would be singing," she put a melody in her voice, "bring on the pizza, and the french fries, and the chocolate shakes." Soft laughter rippled as she indulged in a food frenzy fantasy.

The waitress placed soup and a sandwich in front of Arista, and the hamburger platter by Doris. "Is there anything else I can get for you ladies?"

"Yes." A chipper smile played at Doris' lips. "We would like to add one small mushroom pizza and two chocolate milkshakes, please."

When the waitress left, Doris assured Arista, "You don't have to eat any of it if you don't want to." She winked merrily. "It sounded good when you said those things."

Arista highly suspected Doris considered her to be too thin and was out to fix what she perceived to be a problem. For the moment, Arista nudged vanity into the background and placed her priority on enjoying this lunch with Doris as she bubbled, "I'll eat some."

"Now," Doris carefully flattened a paper serviette onto her lap, "Tell me about your former," she put distinct emphasis on 'former', "boyfriend."

Taking a sip of her ice water, Arista wished to wash down sudden discomfort. "He has a home based business." Gulping more water, she almost retched at hearing her imitate the same pompous pretences Guy uses when describing his useless existence and making it sound grand. "I guess one would call him a businessman." Her stomach tightened painfully.

"Had you been seeing each other for a long time?"

"It was a while."

"Oh." For the second time, Doris lost her smile. "Do you love him?" Ocean blue eyes, for the first time Arista noticed them to be the same colour as Hauk's, shadowed with accusation daring Arista to say she was in love with someone other than Hauk.

"No."

Blue eyes lit. "You will know when the right man comes along." Doris believed Hauk was the 'right man'.

"How does one know?" Creases worked between Arista's brows. "I mean, I thought I was in love with Guy. What if I had married him? Or, what if I marry someone else and later realize I don't love him at all, and it is a huge mistake."

Doris chuckled, "Then you get a divorce."

"No!" Arista protested. "When I get married, I want it to last for the rest of my life."

Doris smiled with approval. Then, tears misted in her eyes despite the smile on her face. "My husband passed away when I was forty three."

"Oh." Arista felt her muscles tense, and she searched her mind for something wise to say. As always, she couldn't think of anything, so she remained silent. Nervously looking up, she saw there was no need to reply. Doris was staring blindly at thoughts churning in her mind. Grateful the conversation was being interrupted, Arista watched the waitress place their pizza in the middle of the table.

"Doesn't this look good?" Doris' smile made a rebound and she lifted a piece, waited for Arista to hold her plate up, and slid the pizza onto Arista's plate. Doris then took a piece for herself.

Discomforted by the additional exercise it would take to burn off the pizza, Arista performed a quick tally in her head, came out with the count of about three hundred calories for the pizza, and figured jogging for three miles should burn it off. All in all, she concluded it was a reasonably small effort for the friendship she was building. The arrival of chocolate milkshakes increased the treadmill distance by another four miles.

Later they were walking along the lakeshore. With placid reminiscing, Doris told stories of Hauk's childhood. She told of the walks they took, and how they had enjoyed crunching leaves under their feet in the fall. Talking worked its way to telling of battles with the education system over a serious speech impediment Hauk was encumbered with as a child. They eventually realized he needed his tongue clipped to correct the problem. Until a proper diagnosis was made, hurtful setbacks directly caused by the impediment were part of his everyday life.

Even though his school work was always done to perfection, the professionals staunchly judged his inarticulate speech to be caused by intellectual disability. Their evaluation was based solely on his incorrect pronunciations. However, the problem was corrected when his tongue was clipped and he could communicate clearly. When others were able to understand his words, they finally had no choice but to notice the intelligence spinning in his mind. Deeply grateful to the doctor who corrected his speech by performing minor surgery, Hauk decided, with determination, to become a doctor. He wanted to be equipped with skills enabling him to have a profound and beneficial impact on people.

Sharing details while they talked, Doris painted a picture in Arista's mind of a small, curly dark haired, child, suffering painful and undeserved humiliation. Instead of nurturing bitterness over the unfairness dealt to him, he chose to develop perseverance and character. Having found the help he needed, he now wanted to give the same to others. Hauk, Arista concluded, was the ultimate in admirable.

Thinking of the man Hauk had become, and envisioning, someday, having a small, curly dark haired, child of her own she dreamily said, "Children really are worth making sacrifices for, aren't they?"

"It depends." Blue eyes held the hint of a wisdom Arista was unable to grasp. "There is generally less money for frivolous spending. And, of course, the relationship between the parents will undergo various levels of strain at different times." Sadness glimmered in her eyes despite the smile on her lips. "Love is what brings it all together. Love overpowers the wrongs family members deal to each other. When all is said and done the family basks in the warmth of love. But, without love, I don't know where it goes."

They walked a distance in thoughtful silence.

"It is so wonderful to be young and in love." Pure innocence radiated as Doris reflected, "I remember my wedding day as though it were yesterday." She grinned at Arista. "I was terrified. I didn't know how I was going to make a promise expected to last for the rest of my life." She envisioned cherished memories. "When I got to the church and saw Jed, everything was right and I knew I would be able to keep all the promises I was about to make. I loved him more than I would have thought it was possible to love another person." She grinned at Arista. "The love kept growing even after we were married. It was wonderful." Her smile never faded, neither did her step waver, and one large tear slid down each cheek. "I'm so sorry." Regret filled blue eyes. "You know what they say. Cry and you cry alone."

"Everybody has to cry sometimes." Arista entwined her arm into the crook of Doris' elbow.

"When are you going home?"

"I plan on leaving tomorrow."

"Do you have a place to stay tonight?"

"No. I still have to find a hotel room."

"It's getting very late." Doris absolutely beamed. "You can stay with me. It has been such a long time since I have had overnight company, and my big house gets lonely."

Arista agreed, and Doris brought her to a massive log house, with a private beach, sizeable boat house, and large speed boat tied to her private dock. Bud bound to them with excited yelps, stopped politely at Arista's feet, and looked up at her with his loving doleful eyes.

"Hi Bud!" Arista ruffled his furry throat. "What are you doing here?"

"Hauk always leaves him here when he is away from his cottage. We share Bud."

Bud's tail wagged furiously at the sound of his name.

"It's a shame his cottage is gone. He spent all of yesterday locking it down and preparing it for a lengthy absence. He loved that cottage, and today, he said it was one less thing for him to have to worry about. Sometimes I don't understand my son."

Doris led Arista through the front door of the house, and they stepped onto luxurious marble tiles. The open floor plan flowed into a large and elegant living area. Arista removed her shoes and followed her hostess onto plush carpet. Doris' walls were filled with pictures of all sizes, frame types, and eras. Large portraits of Doris' ancestors, dating as far back as the early nineteen hundreds, graced the room in handmade wooden frames. Small family pictures were coddled in cluster frames. Doris had been incredibly thin in her younger days. Arista paused to inspect a picture of Hauk wearing a graduation gown and cap.

"The picture you're looking at was Sebastian's high school graduation." Doris volunteered. "This one," she pointed to another, "is his graduation from university. It took one year longer than it should have. I'm afraid I made quite a nuisance of myself when Jed was taken away from me. Sebastian came home and helped me."

Cautious with the emotionally charged area of Doris' life, Arista chose to remain silent rather than chance saying something wrong.

"Would you like a cup of tea?"

Arista quickly adjusted to the change in conversation. "Yes. Please."

In the kitchen, Doris lavished a silver tray with a china teapot, two china cups with saucers, a china creamer and sugar bowl, a china plate piled with sliced cheese and crackers, and two sterling silver teaspoons. The china was all bone china decorated with a matching flowery pattern and winking gold accents.

Carrying it into the living room for her, Arista carefully placed it on a lace scarf draped protectively over a cherry wood coffee table surrounded by two oversized armchairs and a sofa, all of which snuggled around a fireplace stretching its masonry chimney upward through a two story high maze of cedar beams in the open ceiling above them. On the other side, above the kitchen, the second floor was developed as living space.

The evident luxury in Doris' lifestyle made Arista intensely curious about what Jed had done for a living when he was alive. Not daring to ask, she commented, "You have a beautiful home."

"Thank you." A wan smile and haunted eyes said it had been more of a home in days gone by, and Doris invited, "Would you like to come upstairs with me and see the guest room. It has a private bath and patio. I hope you will find it comfortable."

Thrilled with the prospect of a private bathroom, and excited about having a patio off her bedroom, Arista plastered on her practiced expression showing no more than a polite smile. She hid bubbly excitement behind a calm mask as Doris led her into a room decorated with rich blues and neutral greys brightened with splashes of pink, and furnished with a king size sled bed, triple oak dresser, and high back wing chair.

Spotting grand glass garden doors leading to a cedar patio with white wicker furniture, she forgot herself, smiled, and gushed, "This is gorgeous." Scanning all the small details, right down to tiny pink soaps in a blue dish, she discovered every article to be in perfect harmony with each component of the room. Arching her brow at Doris' meticulous attention to detail, she complimented, "You are very talented with colours."

"Thank you."

"I could never decorate like you do." Arista grinned sheepishly, and she confessed, "I use a hodgepodge of colours and styles to make everything chaotic enough to work."

Heading back to the living room, Doris shared, "I took interior decorating courses when I was younger." Her brow furrowed. "It was useful for my own personal enjoyment. At the time I thought it was enough. And, it was. It's just," she shrugged, "I don't quite know how to make myself useful anymore. After spending so many years knowing my place as a wife and mother, I haven't stopped floundering with being alone."

Listening, Arista silently vowed never to lose her identity, if she was ever lucky enough to find her identity.

Seeing vying emotions flash over Arista's features, Doris smiled with the confidence of experience as contentment settled in her eyes. "I loved the stage of my life when it was easy to see my purpose on this planet and bask in satisfaction from the tasks filling my days. These days I'm finding myself at loose ends."

Doris refilled her cup with tea, held the pot over Arista's cup and waited. When Arista shook her head, Doris put the pot back down. "Spending all my time doing nothing more than looking after myself and my house is leaving me feeling rather useless in the overall scheme of things."

Doris looked at Arista and pondered sharing her dream. Deciding she wanted someone to discuss it with, she feigned more courage than she felt, and despite the vulnerability of honesty, she boldly stated, "I've been thinking about going back to school." Squaring her shoulders, she asked, "Do you think I'm too old?"

"No!" Arista's eyes widened. "Nobody is ever too old to pursue their interests."

Arista's declaration made her dilemma sound much simpler. Relaxing, her shoulders eased and she chuckled, "I'm fifty years old."

"What do you want to take?"

Blushing profusely, Doris admitted, "It's very different from anything I have ever done before, and at my age," with a shake of her head she clucked her tongue, "I might be kooky to even consider it, but, I have always been interested in law."

Arching a surprised brow, Arista blurted, "You want to be a lawyer?"

"Heavens! No!" Doris laughed. "I'm thinking of becoming a legal secretary." Her brows furrowed, "Do you think anybody would hire an old lady like me?"

"Of course they would hire you."

"They seem to like the younger women."

"Young women create too high a turn over. The bank, where I work, has a distinct preference for hiring women whose families are already established. They stay longer, and it reduces the expenses incurred by continuously training new staff."

Doris lapsed into thoughtful silence. "I don't need money." Partially talking to Arista, and partially thinking out loud, "I just want to use my good health to keep busy being useful to myself and others." Gently twisting her bottom lip between her teeth, she added, "I would also like more social interaction. Sometimes my days are just too lonely."

Arista echoed, "I hate being alone." Blindly staring ahead, seeing uncomfortable possibilities, she admitted, "It scares me to think of myself as someone who never gets married, or has children, and ends up going through life alone."

Remembering how her son had looked at this woman, Doris' eyes widened with surprise. "Why do you think such things?"

"I don't know. A girl I was working with moved back home with her parents and she was thirty five. One of my bosses still lives with his mother and he is fifty."

Looking at Arista's beauty, Doris considered life's twists. Now, heading through middle age at what felt like warp speed, Doris viewed strength and advantage as belonging to younger adults. Meanwhile, the younger members of society typically see authority as belonging to older people. Ironically, it is easy to forget how insecure previous years really were when the older years feel equally unstable.

"One never knows for sure, but, I expect you will find your partner." Knowing Hauk, and acquainting with Arista, she grinned, "He may be much closer than you think." Doris took a sip of her tea, grimaced, and complained, "This tea has gotten cold. I will make a fresh pot if you would like more."

"I've had enough. Thank you." Arista's eyes watered when she was unable to contain a yawn.

"It has been a long day." Doris placed their dishes on the tray and carried it to the kitchen. Arista followed, and when Doris deposited the tray on the counter, she suggested, "I think we should call it a night."

Arista welcomed the idea. Doris turned lights off in their wake, and they went to their bedrooms.

Needing the same cloths the next day, Arista carefully placed her clothing over the wingback chair, gingerly got into the foreign bed, sank into luxurious comfort, and fell asleep instantly.

Day Nineteen - Friday

Arista awoke to sunbeams dancing through the garden doors. She took a quick shower, and wanting to show her appreciation, she wiped the bathroom to a spotless shine and made her bed. Satisfied that the room looked as clean and tidy as when it had been lent to her, she went downstairs.

Doris wrapped her bulky arms around her affectionately and wished her a good morning. Arista remembered the first time she had met Doris, and how Doris had clutched Hauk in an enthusiastic hug. Arista's first reaction had been to escape such smothering friendliness, she now found it comforting.

In the short time they had been together, Arista learnt to value Doris' steadfast presence. Doris gave Arista breakfast, and then brought her to the airport to catch her flight.

Chapter 21

Day Twenty - Saturday

Awaking to bright sunbeams floating through the slats of her horizontal blind, it seemed as though she had only slept for moments despite her full night of rest.

Waving under a slight dizzy spell, she swallowed pain killers and hoped to fend off whatever was ailing her. Running a brush through her hair she let the natural waves cascade loosely. Opting to save yet more energy she left her naturally black lashes without the enhancement of mascara, ran clear gloss over pale lips, and brushed blush onto white cheeks.

Using a flyer and a telephone, she ordered furniture for immediate delivery. She was given an arrival time, and she used the two hour interval to go shopping for miscellaneous household necessities.

The furniture arrived and she spent the next two days setting up her apartment, watching television, keeping a glass of water beside her to wash down an uncomfortable tickle assaulting her throat at frequent intervals, and sleeping.

Day Twenty Two - Monday

Using one hand to adjust some of many pins securing a cluster of curls, and holding a freshly brewed cup of coffee with her other hand, Arista sat down on her sofa. Stifled by the loneliness in her too quiet apartment she flicked a button on her remote control and the television crackled to electronic life.

Flinching at the gruesome depictions greeting her, she shuddered as the news broadcasted information, along with pictures, of countries and peoples torn by war. Another country was struggling with the aftermath of a large earthquake affecting millions of people. Local news headlined violence and robberies.

With a sigh, she turned the television off, got up, poured the remainder of her coffee down the drain, and left. She completely submerged in her job. She plunged into the internet and tracked mutual fund gains and losses looking for the best advice to give her clients. Having been detained by one client, she missed the staff lunch break. Alone in the upstairs lounge, she pressed a button and filled the room with chatter. Voices turned frenzied as gunfire blazed on the screen. Arista turned the television off with a sigh.

After a full day at work, she mixed spinach leaves with mushrooms, yellow peppers, red peppers, carrots, celery, and almond slivers. She topped it with grilled chicken, and made one piece of rye toast. Taking her supper, she moved to her den and her books. Studies blurred into five hours. Her eyes burned from the strain and her muscles crimped from inactivity. Getting up, she stretched, did some light weight exercises to get her blood flowing, and forced herself to jog four miles on her new treadmill regardless of how tired she was. After the first mile and a half her muscles finally fell into momentum and she almost could have slept through the rest. Reeling under a wave of exhaustion she placed her fingers against her throat and counted her pulse.

Frowning, she counted again. Two times she counted her heart rate at one hundred and ninety two beats a minute. Her pulse usually remained under one hundred and forty beats even when she did her cardiovascular workout. Deciding she must be mistaken, she slowed to a walk, placed her fingers at her throat and tried again. It was the same. Turning the treadmill off, she almost cried at the unusual duress her body was displaying with every routine activity she engaged in.

For a number of days she had noticed her complexion paling and circles darkening under her eyes. She showered and laid cloths out for the next day. As a precaution, in case her stomach should decide to go amuck, she chose to eat while she could. She had a tuna sandwich, and went to bed.

Day Twenty Three - Tuesday

At the sound of her alarm she dragged herself out of bed.

"I look like death." She grumbled at the mirror and chose a pale pink suite with hopes of the pastel colour helping to soften the black shadows under her eyes. Slipping on fashionable white sandals, she drank a huge glass of water and ate a dry piece of toast in an effort to settle her nauseous stomach.

Driving to work she kept her speed down as waves of dizziness swept over her. An insane itch assaulted her throat, and she swallowed repeatedly in an effort to wash away the discomfort. The irritation abruptly turned into a vicious bout of coughing emptying her lungs of air only to make her gasp for breath and launch into more violent coughing. Straining to look through watery eyes, she hit the brake, checked her mirrors, coughed some more as tears slid down her cheeks, clicked on her turn signal, and steered for the side of the road.

The next time Arista opened her eyes, she was being jostled on an uncomfortable bed in the closed confines of an ambulance.

"What happened?" She whispered through dry lips. Her surroundings spun with a vengeance making it hard to balance even though she was lying flat on her back.

"You were in a car accident." The oriental woman wearing a navy blue uniform answered, and then asked, "Do you have any allergies?"

"No."

"Are you on any medication?"

"No." Confused, and anxious, denial took hold. "I feel fine."

"That is a good sign. Hopefully the doctors will confirm that there are no serious injuries."

"I don't need a doctor. I'm fine." Arista groaned at the hindrance.

Any shadow of incompetence put her in jeopardy of being replaced by the next person in line, which is Bess. She hated the pencil thin, overly hyper, co-worker vying for her position. Bess, being unduly smitten with her own attributes wore scooped collars, short skirts, stiletto heels, excessive cosmetics, and flashy jewellery sparkling her way into promotions and pay increases lavished on her by male lust.

Bess had a far spreading reputation for being frequently caught in her lewd acts. Married men were transferred to distant branches as punishment for having committed adultery with her. Bess was said to regularly get fired for the sordid affairs, and, always reinstated when the storm calmed. It irked Arista to see Bess profit from the trouble she caused.

Soothing the chafing annoyance, Arista acknowledged her freedom in choice, offering her the ability to engage in the same immoral behaviour as Bess, if she wanted. Shuddering at gross speculations, Arista decided she favoured slow and laborious progress in contrast to Bess's shortcut. She didn't particularly like her job anyway, so, what did she really have to lose?

Remembering the paycheque, she argued, "I really have to get to work."

Patting her hand in a show of sympathetic support, the paramedic encouraged, "The doctor might have you on your way again in no time."

She was admitted into the hospital, blood tests were taken, x-rays were taken, and she was diagnosed with a mild concussion. The room spun, she closed her eyes to the nauseating sensation, and swirled into darkness.

Walking down the hall of her apartment, she flipped the switch for the light. When it failed to turn on, she became aware of the variations from her apartment to this one. Then, she knew. In a frantic effort to drag herself from choking unconsciousness, she dreamed she was biting her arm as hard as she possibly could. It didn't hurt.

Trying with all her might to wake herself, she couldn't pull herself from the dark abyss where bizarre dreams were floating.

Then she saw a car she was in collide with another car. Whisked away in an ambulance she remained incredibly pain free. When she arrived at the hospital, three strangers, who seemed to have been expecting her, greeted her. They invited her to a cottage the three of them owned jointly. Feeling remarkably well, especially for someone having suffered a serious accident, she accepted their offer and left with them for a holiday at their cottage. As they got to know each other, she discovered each of them had been in critical health at one time. One had been in a plane crash, another was born with a serious heart defect, and the third was a war veteran who had narrowly escaped enemy capture. She was talked into purchasing a share of the cottage. When another young woman joined them, the woman attempted to make contact with her family. That's when they all discovered they were dead.

Undistinguishable words from voices clipped with urgency floated into the fog of her mind. Arista heard her name repeatedly and she struggled to surface from the nightmare laden unconsciousness.

"You have finally decided to come back to us." A middle age nurse patted her hand. "Would you like some ice chips?" The nurse plucked a glass from the bedside table.

Her voice failed her when she tried to say 'yes', so she nodded agreement and the nurse slid a few cool, soothingly wet, shavings from the glass to a spoon and into Arista's mouth. Arista remembered the dizziness, the coughing, explosive pain, and darkness. "What happened?"

"Why don't you ask Doctor VanLiev? He's right here."

His name froze in her mind. Her vision fell on the man standing by the door wearing a white lab jacket. His eyes met hers and the world around her faded into the background, and colours brightened. It was an odd sensation.

"Mrs. Shainne down the hall has just buzzed for help." He informed the nurse.

"I'll see right to it." She flashed him a bewitching smile. Turning back to Arista, the spark in her eyes dimmed to professional competence and she informed her patient, "My name is Elaine. If you need anything, press the button and a nurse will come help you."

Hauk looked at Arista with a mysterious glint in his eyes, and a hesitant smile on his lips.

Elaine clipped the device to a convenient spot beside Arista's pillow. Seeing Hauk and Arista absorbed with each other, irritation frosted Elaine's voice when she told Arista, "There's an intercom behind you."

To pacify Elaine, Hauk indicated the intercom to Arista.

Though she couldn't have cared less, Arista twisted her neck and looked at the white box mounted on the wall.

Their compliance soothed Elaine's agitation, and she explained to Arista, "One of the nurses at the desk will be able to answer questions over the intercom, or come to assist you if you need help with something."

"Thank you." Dr. VanLiev politely dismissed Elaine with a subtle nod of his head and turned his attention to Arista. "How are you feeling?"

"Awful."

"Would you like some ice?" He pressed buttons making her bed take the contours of an extremely comfortable recliner, and then handed her the glass.

Sceptically accepting it from him, she feared dumping the chilly contents on herself as it teetered in her shaky hands. Steadying her hands with his, he helped her lift a spoonful of ice to her mouth. Ice melted dry parchment from her throat, and gentle comfort surged from his hand to hers.

Curious, she asked, "What brought you here?"

"I work here." Familiar teasing lights danced merriment in his eyes and warmth into her heart. Then, his expression sobered, "You had us worried. Do you remember what happened?"

Struggling, she closed her eyes and forced her thoughts to move back. "I remember feeling really lousy when I woke up this morning. While I was driving to work, I started coughing, and it was so bad that I could not catch my breath or focus on the road. I was trying to pull over to the side." Closing her eyes she used all her might, but, "I don't know what happened. I woke up in the ambulance."

"A car hit your car from the back. The driver of the car says you suddenly slammed on the brakes and he couldn't stop in time to avoid hitting you."

Crossing her brows with vexation, she asked, "Why was he driving too close to be able to stop? That was stupid of him."

"I agree. People tend to assume things will move in predictable patterns. Assumptions generally prove to be wrong." Cradling her hand between both of his, he explained further, "That car spun your car into an angle that hit the car beside you. The driver of the second car said he had just passed you, you appeared to be making a lane change, and if the first car hadn't hit yours, you should have been able to safely move into the spot that was vacant beside you. Unfortunately, when your car was hit, your foot must have been forced off the brake, and that pushed you forward into the car in the adjacent lane."

"Wow." With a sigh she made an attempt at humour, "I was in a three car pile up, and I missed it."

Hauk lifted a brow, and corrected, "You didn't miss it, and you have a concussion to show for it."

The intercom beckoned for him to attend a complication in the maternity ward. He quickly explained, "I specialize in obstetrics and gynaecology here. Your doctor happened to join me while I was on a break this morning. I noticed your name jotted on his memo pad, and I came to see how you are doing. It's good to see you." He quickly added, "It's not good to see you here. I wish the circumstances were better, but it is good for me to see you again. Do you mind if I come back later?"

Wondering how he could think she would 'mind', she said, "I would like you to come see me when you have time." Sombrely looking into his eyes, she said, "Don't ever think I don't want to see you."

He gave her hand a squeeze, and smiled saying, "I'll be back soon."

Seconds later the door swung open. Hoping it was Hauk, she stared with loathing. "Guy!?"

Hiding the fury in her heart, she lowered her lids over her eyes, her brows creased, and she looked back up with the intention of calmly telling Guy to leave, instead she barked, "Why are you here?"

"Sherry told me where you were working. I stopped in to see you this morning and they said you were here."

Ugly judgments of his personality churned in her mind. Why was he still following her around? How was she going to make him go away?

Seating himself on the side of her bed as though he had every reason to be there, he grinned and his conversation turned to his true interest, "Aren't you going to ask me how I've been?"

She didn't care, but, "How have you been?"

Unaware and unmindful of her indifference, he plunged into dramatics, "When you left, I was devastated." His eyes glittered with deceit.

Taking a slow breath she pressed deeply against the mattress and forced herself to patiently tolerate his presence.

"You know what I did?" Though she didn't answer he carried right along, "I got myself a new apartment, and a job selling cars. I'm making good money," he chortled, "honey."

Every nerve in her body shuddered with repulsion at hearing him use a term of endearment.

Forcing a grin, he produced a tight lipped line. "The best part is that I now live only two blocks away from you." Folding her hand in his he proclaimed, "I've missed you, and now I know I love you."

Choking violently on air, she clutched her stomach. Gasping for air and pressing the button for help, the intercom crackled and a nurse responded, "Is there something you need Arista?"

Emptying her lungs with more coughing and then gasping small breaths into her burning throat, Arista was unable to respond. In seconds her door flew open and Elaine dashed into the room. Tears pooling in her eyes were making it impossible for Arista to focus. The coughing finally subsided to a raw ache in her throat and searing pain in her head.

"Please excuse us." Elaine gave Guy a brief glance expecting him to respond to her polite and direct request.

Elaine was mistaken.

Guy folded his arms over his chest, stretched his legs in front of him and declared, "I'll stay here, thanks."

Elaine froze, turned, stared at him, narrowed her eyes for one slight beat, and stated, "Only if Arista requests your presence." Her mouth pulled into a stern line as she looked to Arista for a response.

"Guy." Arista blinked slowly with mushrooming frustration for his continuous impositions. "I want you to leave."

"Oh. Sorry." For Elaine's benefit he feigned an inclination to please Arista, and he scurried toward the door. The dark glare he fired at Arista said there was plenty of time for him to get even with her later for the humiliation she was subjecting him to. "I'll wait in the hallway."

"No." Arista wanted Guy to leave and Elaine's presence ensured his cooperation. "I feel exhausted and I really don't want your company."

Standing in the doorway, he cajoled, "Sure you do."

"No. I do not"

He smiled as though she were a child incapable of knowing her own mind. "There are some important things I want to tell you."

Arista scowled at his redundant tactics. He never discussed anything, or listened to anyone. He came up with daft ideas and expected the entire world to do his bidding. Silently scorning him, Arista lowered her lids to hide her feelings.

"You will have to wait." Elaine intervened. "She has been in a bad accident and needs to rest."

"Oh. Ok." Putting an effort into portraying a fresh-out-of-Sunday-School look, he failed badly, and anger eclipsed his expression.

Elaine's eyes hardened against him.

Arista saw the hateful glance he shot Elaine. For the first time, she realized he belittled all women. It was strange enlightenment to see that he held disdain and contempt for women in general.

Guy marched out of the room.

"Is he a relative?"

"He's an old boyfriend." Embarrassed warmth climbed into her cheeks.

Elaine grinned, "At least the relationship is over."

Arista smiled and female bonding began.

"Do you want me to place restrictions on your visitors? We are able to ban him from seeing you."

It sounded easy, and good, but, "No." Arista denied the offer. "He would cause a scene and create difficulty."

"Then we call security." Green eyes danced. "We have a woman security officer who could snap him like a twig."

Giggling as she imagined Guy's reaction to being brought to his knees by someone of the sex he deemed weak and inferior, Arista finally shook her head. "Thanks, but, I can manage Guy."

"Don't hesitate to ask for help if you need it." Elaine abruptly transformed to the professional nurse. "What happened to make you cough so hard?"

"I choked on air."

"It may have been too stuffy in here, but I think the air has cleared." Elaine smiled and winked and then concentrated on taking Arista's pulse and blood pressure. "You seem to be fine." When she was satisfied that Arista's condition was stable, Elaine left.

Enormously grateful for privacy, Arista closed her eyes and sank into an exhausted sleep.

It seemed like seconds, but was actually hours, when she awoke to the awareness of somebody's presence. Slowly blinking away the haze of sleep, she recognized Hauk and spontaneously smiled.

"How are you feeling?"

"My head is pounding, my stomach is rolling, and it is making me exhausted."

"You should be back to normal in a few days." His encouraging smile fluttered into her heart. "I hear you had company tonight."

"Oh." She moaned at the unpleasant memory. "Guy."

"Elaine said you were unsettled when he was here."

She grinned impishly. "He's Guy."

"Are you two back together?"

"No." She grimaced, "Sherry told him where I work. People at the bank told him he could find me here."

"Elaine says you are still willing to let him visit."

"He is impossible. I have told him we are finished so many times I have lost count. I don't know how I will make him understand. If he's told not to visit me here, he will wait until I get home. It's safer to deal with him here."

"Your choice of words implies that Guy might be dangerous. Is he?"

Surprised by his observation, she thought aloud, "I don't think so. I didn't mean to suggest that he is. It's just a little strange that he has followed me here."

"Will he be going back home soon?"

Staring at Hauk, and uncertain what to think, she said, "He has moved. He is living two blocks away from my new apartment."

Wordlessly, Hauk's expression communicated surprise, and then contained anger. "Don't worry about Guy. If he becomes problematic we will take the proper channels and force him to stop pestering you."

"Thank you." Closing her eyes against the pain throbbing in her head, unconsciousness pulled her into a grey fog. Without realizing it, she murmured, "I missed you."

Chapter 22

Day Twenty Four - Wednesday

With his sick charge in tow, Ben watched the ground fall further and further below as the jet they were riding soared through clouds and levelled into a relatively smooth flight. Seat belts were unbuckled and passengers made themselves comfortable.

Walking to the washroom, Ben's eyes widened as he spotted Jack three seats down the isle. Jack's eyes instinctively drew to the man watching him. A quick shadow clouded, and he looked back down to the magazine he was reading. Surprised at Jack's presence on the plane, Ben briefly wondered where he was going.

Ben walked to where Jack was seated and greeted, "Hi Jack!"

Jack made no response.

Stiffening his stance for a confrontation, Ben glowered down at the man blatantly ignoring him, raised his voice, and ground out, "Hi Jack!" Aware of having drawn attention, Ben glared belligerently at the passengers staring at him, looked back at Jack, and bellowed, "I said, HI JACK!"

A short, squat man, with black hair hurled himself onto Ben's back in a frantic struggle to tackle him to the ground. To the side of them, a huge brute of a woman clapped her hand over her mouth in terror. In the front of the airplane, a tiny, frail, elderly woman, got up from her seat, turned to see what was going on behind her, and asked in a gentle voice, "Hijack? Are we being hijacked?"

Interceding, a bulky, middle aged man of average height, with greying hair, used one hand to pull the small man off Ben's back and the other hand to grab the collar of Ben's shirt.

Wide eyed, Ben pleaded, "Jack! Tell 'em."

Instead of complying Jack got out of his seat and left Ben with the problem.

"Hey! Jack!" Ben hollered frantically at Jack's departing back.

Another man blocked Jack's path. "Is your name Jack?"

"Yes." He rumbled with restrained laughter. The humour quickly vanished under the scrutiny of the stern set in the man's expression.

Ben was spun around, and his hands were cuffed behind his back. "You are under arrest!" A badge flashed and Ben was read his rights.

Jack was informed of his rights by the second man, and his hands were cuffed behind his back. They were both frisked for weapons. Each seated beside a rigid officer, they silently accused each other with angry glares, which rapidly became a staring contest.

"Ha!" Ben bellowed. "Your eyes flickered."

"They did not!"

"Ha!" Ben chortled. "Ya talked to me." He angled his nose haughtily. "Ya said ya never would." He highly emphasized 'never'. "Now yer a liar, and a braggart."

Jack clamped his fists into iron white squares restrained behind his back and he lunged at Jack aiming to deal a blow against him with the breadth of his shoulder.

His move was quickly intercepted by the officer at his side. Both officers looked at each other with exasperation, and changing seats they put distance between their squabbling charges.

Still fuming, Ben suffered a sting of regret for his outburst when Vinny came into sight with scared eyes glaring against his pale complexion.

"Ben? Why didn't you come back?" The child looked from Ben to the man seated beside him and back to Ben.

Ben swallowed at the enormous consequence of what he had done. "There's an empty seat beside me. Why don't you sit here for the rest of the flight?" He glanced at the man beside him, who nodded agreement.

Once Vinny was seated, the stranger asked, "Is this your dad?"

"I don't have a dad." Vinny's lip quivered and he bit back tears. He remembered being told men don't cry.

Floodgates of remorse opened as Ben observed the child. It was a stupid thing to say, and he had said it on a whim. It felt smart at the time. Now he saw his mistake. Wishing his bad choices would stop haunting him, Ben leant close and whispered, "Sometimes men cry. It's ok."

Still blinking back tears, Vinny turned oversized blue eyes up to Ben, "Have you ever cried?"

"Oh ya. And I expect to cry again."

Large tears rolled down Vinny's cheeks.

Ben blinked dampness away from his eyes. Turning to the officer beside him, Ben informed, "His dad left last year and hasn't made contact since."

"Where's his mother?"

"She had to stay home." Ben shrugged acceptance for the way of life. "She owns the only grocery store for miles. She can't afford to lose her income, and the people need the store to be opened." He tightened his lips with determination to accomplish the mission he was on. "I'm taking Vinny to the doctor for her."

Vinny quickly piped up, "Ben's taking me to see Dr. Hauk."

"Dr. Hauk?" The officer looked suspiciously at Ben.

"Dr. VanLiev." Ben corrected. "Maybe you've heard of him. Dr. Sebastian VanLiev."

"Was there an article about him in the national paper?"

Remembering having seen the announcement welcoming Hauk to the medical team at the research hospital, Ben had thought it made Hauk sound extremely important, and he angled his chin haughtily. "'At'll be 'im. 'E's one of those hot shot doctors in a fancy city hospital."

"Everybody calls him Dr. Hauk." Vinny declared adamantly. "At least all his friends do." His eyes challenged Ben.

"Ok. Dr. Hauk."

"Is the boy sick?"

Concern flicked across Ben's eyes. Effectively hiding it, he looked at Vinny with an encouraging grin, and then back at the officer, "Nothin' Hauk can't fix."

"I have a bad cough." Vinny enthusiastically described, "I cough until I throw up all the time. The other day we were eating supper and I didn't even feel it coming. I threw up all over the table."

Glancing at the man beside him, Ben refrained from smirking when he saw the pallor draining from the stranger's face.

Vinny looked down sheepishly, "My mom cried so I helped her clean it up. Sometimes I can't breathe. Then it sounds like this." Vinny engaged in vigorous gasps. The imitation of it caused a real attack. Suddenly gasping loudly, he clutched the puffer from his pocket and aimed the medication into his mouth. The sparse amount of air he managed to breathe was insufficient for inhaling the needed dose of medication. He sat forward concentrating on regaining his breath for long minutes. The episode made the other passengers fidget nervously.

When his breathing returned to normal, Vinny blinked once, and then, as though nothing had happened, he stated, "My mom cries all the time because she doesn't know what's wrong with me." He squirmed in his seat and then jumped up. "I have to go to the bathroom."

When he was gone, Ben asked, "How am I going to get unarrested so I can look after Vinny?"

The officer looked at him and remained silent.

At the airport their luggage was thoroughly inspected. They were then taken to the police station where statements were made and they were released.

Chapter 23

"Hauk!" Vinny shrieked in glee and burst into a full run ending in a leaping hug as Hauk scooped him up a second before Vinny would have careened into him.

Standing beside Hauk, Elaine seized the opportunity to highlight her feminine qualities and emphasize her maternal instincts by giving Vinny's cheek a playful pinch and asking in a lilting voice, "Who are you?" It was glaringly obvious to her entire audience, including Hauk, that her staged display was intended to impress him.

Hauk ignored the overture.

Vinny hid his face against Hauk's shoulder to avoid more friendly displays from Elaine.

Staring, transfixed, Ben's pulse slowed and then slammed rhythmically at the sight of the most beautiful woman he had ever seen. Right then and there, he knew city life was going to be right for him.

Setting Vinny on his feet, Hauk glanced at Ben and puzzled over the oddity of encountering the pair. Seeing Ben mesmerized by Elaine, and Elaine oblivious to Ben's blatant fascination, Hauk decided Vinny was the best person to ask, "What brings you here?"

Thrusting his bottom lip out with a sorrowful pout, Vinny answered, "I've been sick." Then his expression lit with admiration. "Now we found you, and you are going to make me better. You are the best doctor in the whole world."

Elaine grinned at the absolute sincerity radiating from Vinny.

Regret weighed heavily on Hauk's heart for having left the place and people he loved. After leading Vinny and Ben to an examination room, he instructed Vinny to sit on the vinyl cushioned table covered with a clean layer of crisp white paper. "Now, tell me how you've been feeling." Hauk sat in a leather armchair at his desk.

"I do this." Vinny pretended to gasp. Again, it triggered a real bout of coughing and wheezing. He reached for his puffer, aimed it at his mouth, and the attack escalated. He coughed until he shook, sucked air in with loud noises, leapt from the table trying to get air, looked around wild eyed, and vomited. When it passed, he looked at Hauk, "Sorry."

"It's ok." Hauk called maintenance. Then he asked, "Your puffer is not working very well, is it?"

"It helps a little."

"I'm not too sure." Hauk took the puffer from him and inspected the list of ingredients. "I think the attack is passing on its own by the time you use this."

"I have these too." Vinny pulled a bottle of pills from his pocket.

After reading the prescription label adhered to the bottle Hauk looked at Vinny. "Are these steroids helping?"

"I dunno." Vinny shrugged his shoulders.

Hauk put both medications on his desk. "Did the doctor give you a prescription the first time your mom took you to the clinic?"

"Ya." Vinny looked at the floor sheepishly. "Mom was really mad."

Hauk arched a brow. "Why?"

"Dr. Monroe said you didn't know what you were talking about, when he read the note you sent."

Hauk arched both brows.

Vinny twisted his lips. "He took x-rays and a blood sample, like you said he should." Vinny grinned as he thought it might make Hauk happier to hear that some of his instructions had been followed.

"Did he put a little stick in your nose?"

"No." Vinny's eyes widened with horror. "Was he supposed to?"

"Maybe."

"I'm glad he didn't." Vinny exaggerated a loud sigh of relief. "He gave me this." Vinny dug another medication bottle out of his pocket.

Hauk glanced at the baggy pants the child was wearing and remarked, "Those pockets hold lots of stuff."

"Look how many things I can take with me." Smiling with pride, Vinny took out handfuls of plastic building blocks and mini cars.

Rolling the bottle between his fingers Hauk read the strength of the antibiotic prescribed. "Why did Dr. Monroe give you these?"

"He said the x-rays showed Bronchitis."

Hauk positioned his stethoscope in his ears and walked over beside Vinny. He placed it at the left side of his chest first. "Breathe deep."

Vinny took a scant breath in.

"Deep." Hauk repeated.

Vinny drew in another shallow breath.

"Take a really deep breath." Hauk took a loud, deep, breath as an example.

When Vinny's breaths deepened, Hauk moved the stethoscope over various places on his chest and upper back. Hauk then placed his fingers on Vinny's chest and tapped them with his other hand, which produced hollow sounds. Hauk finished the examination by shining a light down Vinny's throat, and then into his ears.

Stepping back from him, Hauk declared, "Your lungs are clear."

"Why do I keep coughing?"

Ben volunteered, "Dr. Monroe says Vinny has asthma."

"None of these medications are helping, but they do work on asthma. That makes it look as though your cough is viral."

Vinny perked. "Mom will be happy if I don't have asthma. She was really upset."

"I bet she was." Hauk grinned at Vinny. "Your mom loves you a lot."

"I know she does." Vinny radiated.

"Do you cough until you throw up often?"

"Oh ya." Vinny lit with enthusiasm. "The other day I threw up all over the supper table." He grimaced, "Mom was upset."

"I believe you."

"I kinda ruined supper."

"Do you ever cough like this?" Hauk mimicked a limp cough sounding deceptively harmless.

"I don't cough much. I gasp mostly." Vinny perked, "Mom coughs hard."

"What do you mean?"

"She goes onto her knees in the bathroom and coughs until she throws up."

"Does she make gasping noises like you when she's coughing?"

"Sometimes, but not as much as I do." Vinny giggled, "It almost sounds like she's hiccupping really loud."

"I want you to take this." He wrote a prescription and handed it to him. "Your mom should go to a doctor and get a prescription for the same medication." After a few thoughtful seconds, he suggested, "Tell your mom to make an appointment with Dr. Staid. I'm going to be talking with him in the next couple of days, and I will discuss your symptoms with him. For now, I also want you to get blood tests just to make sure there are no infections."

"Sofie is beside herself with worry." Ben stated the obvious. The money she spent flying Vinny to Hauk already testified to the magnitude of her concern. "She doesn't think it makes sense for something like asthma to surface without any previous hints of being present, and there is nothing new in Vinny's environment to trigger it."

Hauk looked at Ben and then at Vinny. With a sigh he sat back in his chair and toyed with the pen in his hand. He wrote notes in Vinny's file. "I want a swab done." Looking at Ben, Hauk informed, "I'm treating Vinny for Whooping Cough."

"You think it's Whooping Cough?" Ben looked at Hauk doubtfully. "I'm sure his vaccinations are up to date."

"It has been resurfacing, mostly in teenagers and adults." Seeing the obvious question in Ben's eyes, he volunteered, "The vaccination wears down over time. Adults react badly to the vaccination, so, until we have something better we will have to tolerate the situation. There are also other forms of Whooping Cough. Some are viral, and they all resist antibiotics. The antibiotics work to make an infected person non-contagious and help stop spreading the disease."

At the mention of 'contagious', Ben instantly worried for his own health, glanced at Vinny, and then shrugged off the concern.

Seeing the reactions flicker through Ben's eyes, Hauk grinned, got up from his chair, helped Vinny off the table, and warned, "The cough might last for a few months."

"I'm going to be coughing like this for that long?"

"The cough should wear down and get less noticeable." Hauk placed a hand on Vinny's shoulder. "Keep taking your medicine, and go see Doctor Staid." Hauk looked at Ben "Tell Sofie he is going to be fine."

"That's the message I was hoping to bring back." Ben smiled at Vinny.

"How have you been?" Hauk asked Ben.

"Me?" Ben grinned. "I'm never sick."

Hauk hoped Ben wasn't jinxing himself with his statement, and asked, "What are you two doing for lunch?"

The three of them went to a fast food restaurant, ate greasy burgers, greasy french fries, and drank fizzy soft drinks. None of it was healthy. All of it was delicious. When they were finished, Ben and Vinny went to find their hotel and Hauk returned to the hospital.

Having enjoyed learning, he had been granted enough scholarships to almost pay his student loans as he progressed, and that made it easier to remain in university long enough to acquire a specialist degree.

Here, in the research hospital, where every doctor specialized in precise fields, so did he. Doing his rounds on the maternity ward, the sound of an agonized scream curdled into the hallway and a nurse came running out from one of the rooms. Seeing Hauk, she instantly bolted in his direction, "Doctor! The baby is coming! We need you!"

Following the nurse into the room he saw the head crowning as a second nurse moved the patient's hands onto the rails at the side of the bed. "Hold onto this it will help you push."

The sweat bathed patient nodded her head, put her head back, gasped a huge breath, held it and pushed with a hard groan.

Quickly scrubbing and yanking sterile gloves on, Hauk looked over his shoulder and saw the head pressing through. "Don't push."

Trying to distract the mother, the nurse told her, "Your baby has black hair just like you."

The blond father instantly looked at the hair on his babies head and smiled, "Maybe our baby will look like my wife. She is beautiful." He gently brushed beads of sweat from her forehead and his eyes filled with pained helplessness.

Ignoring all of them, she again gasped for air and pushed with all her might.

Hauk hurried to the end of the bed.

She screamed.

Hauk told her to stop pushing and, since the pain had relented when the pressure of the head was through, she obeyed. The cord was gently unwrapped from a loose loop around the baby's neck, and then he instructed, "One more push."

As she put out a half hearted effort, he pulled the baby into the world. After cutting the cord, the nurse suctioned the tiny nose, and the precious bundle was placed in his mother's arms.

Seeing pride and jubilation beyond description shine from the young father, Hauk's breath caught. Delivering a baby was always a high point in Hauk's world. He was convinced it was impossible to become indifferent to witnessing the miracle of new life no matter how often it happened.

Chapter 24

Guy waltzed through the door as if he had every right to impose on her. "Hello." He flashed a broad and phoney smile. "I heard you are going home today."

"Yes." Struggling to hide her loathing of him, she sought a diplomatic way to handle the situation.

"I assume you need a ride." His pretentious smile widened over bleach whitened teeth. "I'm here for you." Having overstated his importance in her life, he sat down on the side of her bed.

The nearness of him was repulsive, and his flippancy burnt resentment to the core of her being. Ditching her previous intentions to employ tact, she frowned and barked, "Guy, I do not want to ride home with you."

He jerked slightly, lifted a brow, and then curved the corner of his lip in a mock smile, "You don't mean what you're saying."

"Yes, Guy, I do."

"Why don't you want me to give you a ride?"

"I don't want anything from you. I just want you to leave me alone."

"I didn't do anything wrong!" His pretentious smile tightened into a straight line and his eyes darkened dangerously. "What did I do wrong?"

Watching his every move with a heightened sense of alertness, she rejected caution and flatly stated, "Guy, I do not like you."

With clenched fists he stared at her. "You know you are just talking out of anger. You don't really mean what you are saying."

She rolled her eyes with impatience. "Believe anything you want. Just go away."

Then smug arrogance entered his eyes and a cocky grin slanted his lips. "Are you still mad about the hot chic I mentioned?"

Staring at him in disbelief for his insane approaches, she eventually sighed, "Yes, along with many other things."

Confident of her coming around, he flashed a lopsided smile and cajoled, "What other things?"

"Guy!" Her brows knit tightly and agitation built into an explosion of fury making her want to tell him everything she hated about him. "Do you really want to know?"

"Yes." He chuckled confidently and believed he had the ability to talk his way out of any faults she could point out.

As her mouth leapt ahead of her brain she mumbled, "Only the devil himself can be worse than you."

"What?" Hate flashed from him.

"Guy, why are you here?"

"I don't think I remember."

"Then why don't you leave?"

Neither of them had noticed Hauk walk into the room, stop at the doorway, and watch their confrontation.

"I will," Guy's nose angled with haughty arrogance, "when you are ready to come with me."

Tired, and wanting to be left alone, Arista closed her eyes against mounting impatience. "I do not want to go anywhere with you."

"We've been seeing each other for months now." Glaring at her, his plans flashed through his mind.

He was not going to be deterred from marrying her. She would provide a good living, and he would be free to spend his time having fun. He didn't care that he didn't like her. He could have oodles of girlfriends on the side. Guy believed women saw him as perfect. He would always have hordes of women wanting the honour of his company, and flocking to grant his wishes. Arista was perfect for his image and she was his gravy train. He wasn't about to let her go.

His insanity bounced out of control, and he spat, "You belong to me." Instantly realizing his error, he spluttered, "I didn't say that."

His icy possessiveness chilled her veins, and she accused, "You did say that."

"Nobody owns people. Arista most certainly does not belong to you." Time stopped and motion froze as Hauk stepped into the battle.

The stern set of Hauk's expression warmed Arista with confidence for his sane strength.

Epidemic

Guy's face twisted with determination and he levelled an ugly glare on Hauk.

"I expect you to leave now, and if you don't, I will call security." Hauk commanded with authority.

"I came to give Arista a ride home." Guy stubbornly stiffened his posture in readiness to stand against Hauk. "When she's ready, we will leave."

Expecting Hauk to squash Guy like a bug, Arista watched with keen interest.

Seeing it, Hauk eased his stance and threw more responsibility back at her by pointedly looking at her and waiting for her to give Guy a response.

Flinching, Arista's eyes begged Hauk to throw Guy out.

Reading her mind, Hauk let out a breath of frustration and turned to Guy.

Before Hauk had a chance to say anything, Guy growled at Arista, "You might think I'm stupid, but I know what is going on here."

Lifting one eyebrow, she doubted it, but asked, "What is going on?"

"You are staging this show in front of your doctor to make him take your side."

Scorning the childishness of Guy's though patterns, she rolled her eyes and enforced, "There is no side to take Guy. I want you to leave."

"As her doctor, I'm obligated to report abusive behaviour to the proper authorities."

"Abusive!" Reddening with rising rage, Guy forced a tight lipped smile. "I love this woman." Tautness worked a muscle in his neck, and he stooped to using lucky coincidence and dug into his pocket.

Prepared for combat, suspecting Guy might drag out a weapon, Hauk reeled with shock at seeing Guy's fist come out clutching the sparkle of diamonds.

"You ruined the surprise. I was going to propose to her over a steak supper and romantic candlelight this evening." Seeing the fire of fight splutter out of Hauk's eyes, Guy felt a surge of intoxicating power.

Staring at the scene before her, Arista's stomach dove with nausea.

Enraged with the entire skewed situation, Hauk folded his arms over his chest and glared at Arista, "What is your answer?"

Shocked at being bluntly called on his bluff, Guy stared at Hauk with baffled silence. An immediate answer was not what he had hoped for. Rather, he was only intent on winning the current battle. The war, of making her realize her female inferiority, was one he had planned on waging later.

Looking at Hauk, Arista was confused as to why he would ask her such an unwarranted question.

Hauk repeated, "Are you going to marry him?"

"No!" Anger flashed under her brows and rage surged. A short time ago she would have leapt with excitement at the prospect, now she spat, "I will not marry Guy!"

Hauk winced at the callousness of her refusal.

Belatedly realizing what she had done, she looked at Guy and wondered if she had injured his feelings. He appeared to have one feeling, it was pride, and it was noticeably bruised. There was no hurt in his eyes. The windows to his soul, his eyes, were full of empty, cold, heartless, anger.

Piercing the dismal blackness of Guy's presence, Hauk's voice penetrated the room. "I suggest you leave now."

Wordlessly working his mouth, Guy snorted at Hauk. Then, he pinned Arista under a murderous glare.

Swallowing the discomfort it caused, she watched him spin on his heel and leave the room.

After a few silent seconds, Hauk pulled a chair over to her bedside, positioned it to face her, and sat down. "Are you all right?"

"Why wouldn't I be?"

"You've been sick, and your boyfriend has been a nuisance."

"Guy is not my boyfriend."

The cocky grin she loved curved Hauk's lips, "He seems to think he is."

"He's mistaken."

"He did ask you to marry him." Hauk's eyes teased, "Though I have to admit, it was a nasty proposal."

"Guy is Guy." She shrugged, "You know, at one point in our relationship I actually thought I was in love with him. I don't even like him."

"What happened to make you change your mind?"

Mischief sparked in her eyes, "I started seeing the world in a new light."

Fastened under his all male glare, sizzling sensations raced through her.

Seeing it, he surged with a powerful urge to respond with primitive instinct.

Positive he would remain absolutely professional as long as they were in the hospital, she laughed deliciously as she watched him refrain from launching into sexual innuendoes. Then, seeing male response darken his eyes, she thought he just might throw caution aside despite being in the hospital. Waiting and watching, she relaxed when the intensity in his eyes subsided.

Calmly assessing her, he said, "Your doctor has discharged you. I would offer to drive you home, but I will be on duty for another six hours. You are welcome to wait here."

She said it would be too boring, and he agreed. They set a meeting time for after his shift. She made a telephone call and went home by taxi. When the clock ticked to quitting time, he gave a briefing to the doctor replacing him, threw his lab coat in a laundry bin, glanced at the television screen filled with the latest news of an impending war, and left for Arista's apartment.

Chapter 25

"Hi." Giving Hauk what she thought was a normal smile, Arista stood aside as invitation for him to come in.

Honest welcome radiating in her eyes combined with her smile and magically erased the rest of the world for him. Inside her apartment, Hauk hesitated with uncertainty. Manners and respect demanded that he wait for her to invite him further into her home.

Seeing it, Arista warmed to being treated with consideration, and invited, "Come in." After closing the door behind them, she led the way inside. "I love this place." She brought him through a small kitchen to the dining area where a spiral staircase, set off to the side, circled up to a comfy loft. Instead of going upstairs she walked into her living room.

It was furnished with a sofa, a loveseat, a reclining chair, a large square coffee table, and a big screen television on a glass stand. The entire ensemble had been advertised in the flyer, and Arista had ordered it exactly as shown right down to the arrangement of dry flowers in an elaborate vase on the coffee table. The chair was currently surrounded by a scattering of books and papers.

Squatting on the floor, Hauk flipped the pages of one book open. "This looks complicated."

She pointed out, "Those books are much easier than any medical texts."

"Finances were never my strong point. I would have trouble studying this." He gently closed the book.

"It's boring, but it does provide a living."

A quirk of his brow silently stated, 'there is more to life than money'.

Knowing he was right, she turned her back on the books, went to the kitchen, and set a pot of coffee brewing.

His voice came to her from the other room, "Have you ever thought about going into medicine?"

Hearing his question, she squirmed, a sweat actually broke out on her skin and she asked, "What kind of medicine?"

"I don't know. Maybe you would enjoy nursing. You loved helping in paediatrics."

"I just carried little David until he felt better."

"You have the care giving instinct. You would make a great nurse."

"You think so." Hoping to avoid any further discussion on the topic, she poured two cups of coffee. When she returned to the living room, she found Hauk sound asleep on the plush carpeting and she draped a blanket over him.

She unplugged the coffee maker, and emptied the cups down the drain without either of them having had a sip. He was out to the world. She decided to go to bed.

Still staring at the ceiling at three o'clock in the morning, she tossed angrily, and wondered why her body stubbornly sabotaged itself with constant wakefulness. Knowing she was going to be dragging her feet with exhaustion the next day, she wrestled her blankets with frustration. Clutching her pillow, she roughly pummelled it to fluffy softness, punched it into position underneath her head, and resumed her nightly ritual of staring at the ceiling.

Day Twenty Five - Thursday

Waking to golden sunshine, she remembered last looking at the time at three thirty.

Heading for her coffeemaker, she noticed the blanket folded neatly on the floor. She wondered when Hauk had left. Her doctor had ordered that she take the rest of the week off, so she spent the day studying and sleeping.

Hauk was holding clinic hours and working the maternity ward during the evening and into the night.

Day Twenty Six - Friday

Arista met Hauk for an early breakfast. He was conscious of maintaining a healthy lifestyle. She was concerned with keeping her weight down. He ordered cooked oats, fruit, and toast. She drank black coffee. He winced despairingly at her lack of food and at the other patrons for their indulgences in bacon, eggs, and every other artery clogging fat in existence.

His natural food preferences made healthy eating patterns relatively easy for him to maintain. He jogged at least four miles five times a week. Her lifestyle, which she had thought was healthy, seemed to be sorely lacking in light of his. She ordered one slice of dry, brown, toast.

Finally, they had time to catch up properly on what was going on in their lives.

Arista told him about her job promotion and relocation. The apartment had been in use by bank employees for years, it was vacant, she was given the option of renting it, and she had jumped on the opportunity. She told him she had furnished the entire apartment over the telephone by ordering from the flyer exactly as the layouts were advertised.

Hauk explained the advantages of his relocation, the furnished apartment he had rented, and the sacrifice he had sorely made in leaving his home.

Hauk went to work, and despite her nagging headache, Arista used her day to study.

Chapter 26

Day Twenty Seven - Saturday

Hauk dialled Arista's number with plans churning in his mind. It had been a couple of days since he had gone for a decent jog. Being an exercise addict he missed and needed the boost.

One shrill ring dragged Arista from a dreamless sleep. Looking at the clock, she groaned, "It's only seven thirty. Who is phoning?" The blurriness of sleep was sliced away by a second ring. Plucking the receiver from its cradle, she mumbled, "Hello."

Hearing the sleep in her voice, Hauk looked at the clock for the first time. Wincing, he asked the obvious, "Were you sleeping?"

"Yes." Sleepy or not, hearing Hauk's voice hum across the line was a great way to wake up. A smile curved her lips and she pushed her tousled mop of hair away from her face. "I'm awake now."

"Good. What do you have planned for the day?"

"I was just going to study. I would rather do something else. What do you have in mind?"

Folding her arm under her head she listened to him launch into a detailed description of spending the day bicycling and having a picnic at the zoo. A velvety chuckle danced through the telephone and waltzed anticipation over her.

"We could start with breakfast somewhere along the way. Are you free to join me?"

About to say she would love to, she was abruptly stopped by, "This is an emergency interruption by the operator. Please clear your line for an incoming call."

"I'll call you back as soon as possible."

Immediately after hanging up Hauk's telephone rang and his blood chilled as he answered, "Hello."

"Hi." Doris' voice shook over the line.

"Mom? What's wrong?"

"Everything." She took a long shaky breath. "Those scientists are still here. They say the ground is going to keep moving."

"Has something happened?" It was a stupid question. She was making an emergency call, and he knew it, but it was the softest approach he could think of for getting her to the point.

"Yes." Muffled sobs made her words difficult to understand. "My house is gone."

"It's gone? What has happened?"

"A mudslide pushed it into the lake." Her sobs accelerated.

When she stopped crying, he calmly suggested, "The first thing you need is to find a place to live. You are welcome to use my apartment. I never did get around to subletting."

"Oh." She sniffled and giggled at the same time. "I'm calling from your place." Looking at his belongings brought a smile to her lips. "All your stuff is here. It feels as though you should be walking in the door any minute." Missing him intensely, fresh tears ran down her cheeks. "I wish you were here."

He wished he was there.

"It has been so strange around here lately. First it was your cottage. Now it's my house." Her mouth curved downward in deep sadness.

"Where were you when the mudslide hit?"

"I was in town." About to tell him of her having submitted an application at the local college, she stopped.

Hearing the hesitation, he knew she was keeping a secret, and in respect of her privacy he ignored the curiosity tempting him to ask questions. "Are you going to be all right?"

Ready to fall apart any second, she lied, "Of course. I'm a grown woman and perfectly capable of looking after myself."

He knew it was true. His mother was one of the strongest women he knew.

Arista accompanied him, and they caught the first flight to his home.

Waiting for their departure to be announced, the two scientists immersed in studying their notes.

"This is amazing." The tall well conditioned man shook his head. "Everything went exactly as expected. It was a classic textbook shift." Clint's lips briefly pressed together and he removed and carefully folded thickly framed reading glasses. "It's too perfect."

He knew science to be a kaleidoscope of unproven theories with unexpected twists presenting a constant mockery of the human quest for knowledge. Studying his notes, graphs, and printed readings, all from highly technical equipment, Clint instinctively searched for an unnoticed detail. "What are we missing? There must be something."

"Flight number fourteen is now boarding at gate four." The announcement beckoned.

Gathering stacks of papers, he was haunted by the nagging certainty of having overlooked some important element.

"Don't worry." His lanky, balding, colleague slapped him on the back and smiled reassurance. "We can be back here in a matter of hours if we find something new."

Across the shiny heavily waxed tile floor, at the other end of the airport, Doris barrelled toward Hauk. Wincing at an impending collision, Arista was surprised to see Doris bring her bulk to a graceful stop just before impact, and, rather than bowling Hauk over as Arista had expected, she grabbed him in a hearty embrace and blue eyes, exactly like his, shone with moisture. "I'm so glad you are here."

Watching the sincerity, Arista felt her heart tugging with admiration and a deeper twist of emotion whispering a longing to be part of their tight knit bond.

Moving to give Arista a hug of welcome, Doris abruptly stopped. A rumble filled the air and a hard, sharp, jolt hit them. Having inherited keen alertness and an instinct for fight from her mother, Arista leapt into action. Grabbing Doris with one hand and Hauk with the other she rushed for shelter. The floor moved against her as she sought protection for them under the nearby doorframe.

Debris splintered away from the ceiling two stories high. Lights rocked dizzily. Looking at the exterior wall made of multiple windows, Arista's stomach churned nauseously as she watched the building swing drunkenly. It rocked in one direction while the ground outside seemed to lurch in the opposite direction. They came back into brief alignment and passed into opposite directions from each other.

The air exploded with the sounds of pained moans, terrified screams, overwhelmed sobs, and groans from the building, but mostly, a thunderous roar as the ground quaked beneath them. The whole of it happened in a flash. It felt like years. Powerless to do anything else, they clasped hold of each other and hoped to be spared in the vengeful upheaval. Then, there was an eerie silence.

Throughout the city, emergency response crews leapt into action and faced disaster of a magnitude they had been trained for but never experienced. Off duty doctors and nurses rushing to the hospitals stopped to help injured people along the way. Off duty police officers and paramedics made their way through the city. Sirens wailed. Lights flashed. Motorists sped through intersections. Chaos reigned. Traffic lights stood colourless and telephone communication failed.

In the airport, people slowly began moving. They cautiously stopped to look at each other with confusion shadowing their eyes.

"Please! Help me!" A plea came from a few feet away.

Hauk responded instantly. Moving to the frail elderly gentleman he announced, "I'm a doctor." Crouching and inspecting him, he found the problem in seconds. "You have a broken foot." He checked and found a pulse in the surrounding tissue. "This is best left until we can get you to a hospital." He smiled reassurance.

A shrill scream pierced the air. Looking in the direction, Hauk saw a young woman holding a small child.

"Stay here and try not to move too much until we can get you to a hospital." Hauk quickly instructed and straitened to his feet.

"I'm a nurse." A slight woman with shimmering brunette curls ran to the woman. "What is wrong?"

"He's bleeding!"

Professionally inspecting the child the nurse smiled, "It looks worse than it is. He will probably only need a few stitches." Looking at the walls in search of a first aid kit, she saw none, and asked the woman, "Do you have any bandages in your purse?"

"Bandages?" The distraught mother began screaming. "Are there any bandages?! Please! Somebody!" Hysteria pitched as each word became more frenzied.

"He's going to be fine." The nurse calmed the frantic mother.

"Can I help?" Hauk stepped in and introduced himself, "I'm Dr. VanLiev."

"A doctor!" The woman shrieked with relief. "My son is bleeding."

Hauk arched one dark brow as he inspected the cut on the boy's forehead. "It's a very minor superficial injury and will heal with either a few strips of tape or a couple of stitches."

"Are you sure?" She dubiously looked at blood trickling from the wound.

"He'll be fine."

A thin young man dressed in the uniform of a ticket salesman for one of the airlines approached at a run, "Who needs bandages? I have a first aid kit here, and there are more over there." He pointed to a counter where employees were stacking boxes marked with the universal sign of a red cross.

Before he could answer, a blood curdling scream sliced the air.

Looking, and seeing blood pooling quickly around a young girl, both Hauk and the nurse raced to her. On their knees in one fluid movement, they instantly found the gash on her forearm. Holding pressure on it, Hauk studied the wound, took the girl's pulse, and checked her eyes and her breathing.

"Do you want me to stay here and keep pressure on it while you go help others?"

It was exactly what the girl needed since a tourniquet could result in the loss of her limb. "You know what to do if the bleeding proves to be uncontrollable?"

"Yes." She had been trained to maintain a calm appearance in the midst of crises. Despite reeling under the same anxiety as everyone else, she produced a gentle smile and assured him, "I'm a qualified nurse."

Recognizing her experience, training, and natural ability, Hauk squeezed her hand as his own controlled emotions rioted under a composed exterior.

The floor shuddered. The building creaked and with abated breaths people waited for falling objects. None came. Relieved sighs accompanied refreshed movement and most decided it was a good time to leave the building. Within a few minutes only people with injuries and those helping them remained inside.

Arista stood looking at the scene surrounding her. Hauk was busy splinting a broken ankle with a dislodged bone blocking circulation and needing immediate attention. The nurse was still with her young patient. A young man, Arista guessed to be in his mid twenties, with dark hair, and a tall athletic build, looked at her with uncertainty shadowing his eyes. When her eyes met his, he shrugged with a half smile silently saying, 'I don't know how to make myself helpful.'

Hauk hollered, "Arista!"

Instantly locking eyes with him, she heard him ask, "Please come and help?"

She had already begun moving toward him at the sound of his voice.

"Put on some gloves." He slid a first aid kit over to her that had rumpled latex gloves tousled in a heap. As soon as she had them on, he instructed, "Hold this." Pressing her hand down hard on a bloody rag he watched her and his patient. "You will need to apply pressure."

Relaxing her body in preparation for a lengthy duration of maintaining her hold on the rag, she was surprised when he said, "Be prepared." His eyes locked with hers and he flashed the briefest grin before squaring his jaw. "There is going to be a hard tug and you have to keep applying pressure."

She braced her hold. He positioned his hands and gave a sharp hard yank. Her hand slipped, blood gushed, she got the rag back to where it belonged and applied hard pressure. Sweat poured over her skin and she shivered with icy coldness.

Hauk gave her a quizzical look. He relaxed the mood with a grin, "At least we know full circulation has returned."

Hearing sirens, they both looked through the glass wall to the outside where help was shrieking into the vicinity from all directions. Tightening her hold, Arista blew air upwards from her mouth to move loose strands of hair away from her face and she closed her eyes with gratitude for the arrival of screaming sirens and flashing red lights.

"How are you holding up?"

It took a few seconds for her to comprehend his question. "I'm fine." Thinking about it, she thought she was perhaps better than she had ever been, even if she felt like death and her legs were like rubber. She was in her element.

"You look pale."

"We've just had an earthquake." She grinned at him with mischief in her eyes.

"What do you have here?"

Glancing up at the sound of a stranger's voice, Arista lit with relief at the sight of a woman dressed in dark pants and a white shirt with patches identifying her as a paramedic. A tall man wearing a matching uniform stood a slight distance to the side of her.

Hauk answered, "He has a broken ankle with a ruptured artery. The bleeding is being controlled, and he needs surgery as soon as possible."

Both paramedics hesitated, glanced at each other, looked at Hauk, and then they crouched beside the patient.

"I'm Dr. VanLiev." Hauk stretched out a hand of welcome.

"It's a pleasure to meet you." Shaking Hauk's hand, the six foot tall paramedic introduced himself, "I'm Paul Grayston."

"It's great having you here." Hauk grinned with sincerity.

"My name is Shelly Lang" She stretched out a hand and Hauk shook it in friendly and respectful greeting.

"This is my friend Arista." Hauk honoured her with a warm smile, "She's been very helpful."

Firmly shaking her hand, Paul stated, "We need all the help we can get." Checking the gloves on his hands, he momentarily looked frazzled, and then plastered an emotionless expression on his face.

Hauk and Arista glanced at each other as they realized the problem encompassed more than just the airport. Hauk asked, "How bad is it out there?"

Shelly glanced at Paul and nodded agreement to the soberness of his expression. "It's worse than any mock disaster could ever have prepared us for."

"We're lucky the hospitals are fully functional. Generators are replacing downed power lines to keep electricity running."

Visually surveying injured people scattered throughout the building, Hauk drew attention to another problem. "We haven't even checked upstairs."

Paul turned and looked at the stairway leading to the second floor. "Let's hope most of the people have come down here."

Paul left. Shelly busily got equipment ready for transporting their patient. Paul returned almost immediately and spoke with a group of fire fighters. The fire fighters disappeared upstairs and soon reported there were a number of injuries on the second level, no fatalities, and the injured people were being tended to by a group of nurses returning from a vacation.

People in need of immediate medical aid were transported by ambulance. Leery the building may collapse people with less critical injuries were taken outside to await transportation to a hospital.

Chapter 27

"How are you feeling?" Taking her hand in his Hauk searched Arista's face for signs of excessive strain.

Loving the nearness of him, she basked in his warm comfort and said, "Fine. How are you doing?"

The energy radiating from her almost irked him and he confessed, "I feel exhausted." With a withering look he grumbled, "You don't even look tired."

"I love this." Being at peace with what she was doing was providing a fountain of strength. "This makes me feel alive."

"You like disasters?"

"No." She cuffed his arm playfully. "I like to know that what I am doing is helpful to somebody. I usually feel that I am wasting my time, and I wonder why I bother doing the things I do."

His vision wandered around people grouped comfortably on the grass waiting for shuttles. He spotted the scientists distanced from the crowd. They were surrounded by large papers and open laptop computers. He vaguely wondered if all their training had equipped them to predict the earthquake before it struck.

It rankled to think they might have had the ability to warn people. Giving it a second thought, he acknowledged how all the residents of the area were fully aware of the fault. With or without warning, they chose to take their chances and there was no blame due to anybody.

Returning his attention to Arista, he pointed to one group of people telling jokes and laughing. "You could have been over there enjoying a few good laughs instead of holding bloody rags in place with me."

Arching both brows, she scolded, "I would rather be, holding bloody rags, as you put it, with you."

"I don't know why." The truth was, he did know.

She challenged, "Why did you choose to be a doctor?"

He gave her a sideways look beginning to spark with humour, "I want the money."

She laughed softly. "You must have made a fortune all those years you were working seventeen hour shifts in a rural hospital."

Deep laughter rumbled from him. "No. I didn't."

"I didn't think so." She let her head rest against his shoulder. "I suppose you are making a small fortune now."

"I make more money than I need." He let out a long sigh. "I sure miss working in this city."

"You mean you aren't warming to the smog and blaring horns of the big city?"

Cupping his hands together and leaning his chin into them, he propped bent elbows on his thighs, and he weighed the error of taking oneself too seriously. Nobody was irreplaceable, including himself.

Leaning on her arm she angled herself to watch him without straining. "I was teasing you. You are exceptionally talented, and I expect your skills are being fully utilized where you are working."

"The challenge is great, and I love having the opportunity for personal growth." He gave her a wan smile.

Made nervous by his soberness, she began babbling, "I guess we should just follow our hearts."

It instantly sounded hypocritical considering her life. Her heart would have led her on very different paths than the ones she had taken.

Frustrated, she grumbled, "Our heads just make a mess of us."

"It is possible to over think things."

With a soft laugh she hugged his arm.

Looking down at her, merriment danced in the depth of blue eyes and he teased, "You might be right. You listen to your heart, and you make me feel good."

Uncaring of the crowd scattered around them, she cupped his face in her hands, lifted onto her knees to bring her face level with his, and she pressed her lips greedily against his.

Without hesitation, his lips drank from hers with unquenchable thirst.

Obnoxiously loud throat clearing grated into their warm embrace.

They parted with only enough space for a breath between them, and looking up Hauk asked, "Doris is everything all right?"

"It is for the moment." She answered with obvious discomfort for being an intrusion, and stubborn determination to remain one.

They waited for her to leave.

She stayed.

The mood chilled. Arista moved back and sat beside Hauk.

"I came to tell you there are school busses here to provide shuttle service. The ambulances are also returning."

Seeing the end of this ordeal approaching, his energy revived along with a surge of anticipation for his apartment, his coffee maker, and the refrigerator Doris was sure have stocked lavishly in the short time it took for him to get home.

A slight tremor shuddered through the ground, everyone tensed, the earth stilled, and ease returned. Assessing the situation, Hauk knew it would be impossible for him to relax at his apartment as long as the city was in chaos. Nobody from the hospital would ask for his help, most people didn't even know he was here. Still, his mind would be on what was going on there, so he would ultimately be more relaxed putting his energy into helping get this situation under control.

Arching a brow, Hauk watched a shiny new black Cadillac pull alongside the curb. He snuck a sidelong glance at Doris. Her face lit like sunshine with pink hues of delight climbing into her cheeks. A tinted window slid down with electronic ease.

"Would you like a ride?"

"Yes. Please."

A tall, well built, man with greying hair, got out of the car and walked around to the passenger side where he opened the door for her.

Doris' politely restrained smile glowed. "Thank you so much."

Arista observed the attraction flashing between them. Doris was beautiful from her outer appearance right down to the core of her being. She would be a treasure in anyone's life.

The man closed the door after Doris was settled on the seat. Turning to them, he smiled, and asked, "Would you like a ride?"

Arista and Hauk both emerged from the same distracted musings. "Thanks." Hauk grabbed Arista's hand and they got up at the same time. They walked over, Hauk opened the back door for Arista, and he introduced, "Tye, this is Arista. Arista this is Tye."

"It's a pleasure to meet you." Richly thick, but not pouting, lips formed a smile oozing with magnetism, and his voice waltzed charm into every word he spoke.

"It's nice to meet you." Arista mumbled as she glimpsed some of the attributes she suspected Doris found appealing about Tye. She also noticed the absence of a ring on his left hand.

"He's the best lawyer in the area." Doris beamed with admiration.

Surprise widened Tye's hazel eyes for only the briefest second. Instigating even the tiniest visible reaction in a lawyer was commendable, so, Arista assumed Tye had a high regard for Doris' opinions. It also explained Doris' interest in law.

Then a confident grin spread as he advertised, "I like to think you are right."

Refraining from chuckling at the arrogant statement, Arista commented, "If I ever need a lawyer-"

"Give me a call." Tye interrupted. His ready grin flashed with ease.

Sliding onto the leather car seat, Arista watched Tye walk around the front of the car. Hauk got in beside her and closed the door. Tye had all the polish and sophistication a person could possibly acquire. Still, there was something more. He was gifted with irresistible charisma.

No sooner had they pulled away from the airport then they were staring in shocked disbelief. Roads were cracked. Traffic was congested. Police were directing motorists at intersections where traffic lights were without power.

Fortunately, it was a small city only three miles long and three miles wide. The population thinned rapidly at the outskirts and dwindled to nothing within a short distance. Sirens wailed from all directions.

At the airport, Clint pointed to the map of underground plates. "We didn't look far enough."

Following the movement of Clint's finger, Mark's complexion paled.

"You see it."

"I see it." Doom hung in the air.

"What do you suppose we should do?"

"We must warn the people here."

"What if these computer projections are incorrect? What if the plates don't move?"

Staring at each other, they both knew nature was unpredictable. No matter how high tech the equipment, or how smart the computer, or how many scenarios were run, nature never did the exact same thing twice.

With a shrug, Clint stated the indisputable argument, "What if it does move?"

"You're right."

With a tight lipped nod, Clint initiated action, "First we will talk to federal emergency departments."

Telephone calls were made and government departments said they would be able to verify the information, ". . . in a couple of days."

After hanging up and relaying the inadequate response, Clint asked, "Do you think we have a couple of days?"

Solemnly considering it, Mark half laughed and half growled with frustration. "For all we know it may be a couple of centuries."

Squinting with deep thought, Clint compressed his lips, relied on his instinct, which he had learned to trust above logic, and he said, "It could happen in a couple of hours."

Paling at the recognition of one of Clint's intuitive analysis, Mark let a slow breath out pursed lips. "Let's warn them at the hospital and then at the police station. Even if they don't believe there's any importance in what we have to say and they think we're fanatics, they will know what's happening when those plates move."

"They will move." Clint squared his jaw.

Chapter 28

"Are those the scientists studying underground activity in the area?" Doris drew Hauk's attention to the two men walking into the hospital.

Looking at their dusty and unshaven appearances, it was hard to envision them having inspired Ben's desire to attain a fashionably slick city style. Suddenly noticing the obvious, he looked at the dust clinging to Doris and Arista as well.

Looking at Clint walking purposefully toward him, Hauk's mood drooped in expectation of trouble.

"Are you a doctor?"

"Yes."

"May we have a word with you?" Clint looked around searching for a remote corner. Spotting none, he added, "In private."

"Come with me." Hauk led them to an office.

Clint and Mark informed Hauk of their findings on the impending disaster.

After the two men left, Hauk called Arista to the office, retold their concerns, and asked, "What do you think?"

"They said nothing might happen, right?"

"Yes."

"Is it justifiable to move out an entire hospital on a hunch?"

Running a quick internet search, Hauk found published articles by the men, complete with pictures of them, and scads of information about their accomplishments and backgrounds.

"Can we ignore the warning in light of our circumstances and their experience?"

"I don't know." Arista considered the weight of this decision. "Why don't you call an emergency meeting with the administrators and let them decide?"

Knowing the administrators, the warning was sure to be ignored. The budget was of top importance to those people, and evacuating was expensive. Hauk opened the word processor on his computer and keyed alerts stating the danger, naming the scientists predicting it, and listing their outstanding credentials.

"What are you doing?"

"I will print these and distribute them anonymously. The majority will rule."

After dropping them onto various desks around the hospital, he looked at Arista, "Shall we go to the cafeteria and get ourselves some coffee?"

A relaxed break sounded like the perfect suggestion. Nodding agreement, she hummed, "I will get coffee and yogurt." Just mentioning it teased a delicious craving for the creamy treat.

In remarkably short time the hospital was buzzing. Some recipients were throwing the notices away with the belief that the worst was over. Other people silently observed events and waited for more information. The next group sprung into pessimistic motion and frantically believed the end was at hand.

"Did you hear?" The receptionist blurted, "Scientists say a 'big one' is going to hit any minute."

"Isn't it scary?" A nurse scurried over.

"We are at the bottom of a mountain. What if the whole thing just falls over?"

The nurse paled, gasped, and squeaked, "Oh! This is terrible."

In another half hour, the environment was almost normal. Nothing immediate was happening. Not even a twitch beneath their feet. Most people were placidly returning to a tired, but comfortable, state of mind.

All missing persons were reported as accounted for. There were no fatalities. There were no critical injuries. The aftermath included an abnormally high number of pregnant women experiencing the onset of labour.

In the background, invisible to the public and most of the staff, the administrators were holding an emergency meeting. Dr. Jenk, the board chairman, looked around the room with solemn concern. "The reason I have called this meeting is to discuss this day's events." Pausing he glanced at the paper in his hand, and then displayed it to the other six board members. "How many of you have seen these?" All six members nodded they had. "We are unable to take any action without authorization from the proper emergency and health officials. This includes choosing to ignore the warning. If we decide to evacuate and it causes any negative set backs for our patients there will be difficult consequences. If we take no action and disaster strikes, there will be equally difficult consequences. Do you all understand the position we are in?"

Dr. Dale squirmed nervously and asked, "Are we going to request an evacuation?"

"No!" Dr. Monroe spat staunch opposition.

The others silently looked down, or raised eyebrows to the quick and rash response from the stout, elderly, pale man reputed to drink to excess, before, after, and while, on duty.

"We should seek permission to have some patients moved to nearby hospitals. We are filled past capacity and unable to handle any further complications." Spoken quietly, Dr. Mansh's logical suggestion commanded attention from the others.

"Are you ready to make a motion?" The board chairman, Dr. Jenk, looked expectantly at Dr. Mansh.

"I motion. We request permission from the proper authorities to transfer patients to nearby hospitals thereby removing the overload currently taxing our staff, equipment, and facility."

Dr. Hadj lifted a hand, "I second the motion."

"Are we all in favour?"

In show of agreement all hands raised, except Dr. Monroe's.

"Dr. Monroe?" Dr. Jenk approached the problem with a gentle smile.

"I'm not in favour of moving any of our patients."

"Do you want your vote on the record?"

"Sure." He shrugged obstinately.

Dr. Jenk looked pointedly at the recording secretary. "There are five in favour, and Dr. Monroe is contrary. Carried."

"Off the record," pausing to glance meaningfully at the recording secretary, who then put down the pen, Dr Dale expounded, "the patients remaining here will primarily be intensive care, maternity, and palliative care patients. Thus, we will be equipped to handle incoming emergencies, if there is another crises situation."

"Good point." Envisioning the necessary rescue response needed for a stronger earthquake, Dr. Jenk looked at Dr. Dale, and then at each doctor seated around the table.

"I move that we keep our paramedics and ambulances available to us here. We will release all patients able to get transportation from family and friends."

Glancing at her colleagues, Dr. Lind suggested keeping the full emergency response unit available to the city.

The members launched into disorderly discussions with each other around the table.

"Then nobody on oxygen or intravenous will be transferable."

"We need to maintain our full staff in the hospital."

"We are too short staffed to send attendants with patients."

"It is important to keep our rescue vehicles here in case we need them."

"I second the motion." Dr. Dale lifted his hand.

"Are we all in favour?"

Dr. Monroe kept both hands on the table as the others each lifted one.

"We have five in favour, Dr. Monroe contrary, carried." Standing up, Dr. Jenk seemed to fill the room with his six and a half foot height of muscular girth. "I move that this meeting is adjourned. We all have important work to get done."

"I second the motion." Dr. Lind volunteered.

All hands lifted in agreement.

Within two hours the city was declared to be in a state of emergency. Busses rolled onto the premises for transporting patients to surrounding hospitals.

Helping patients prepare for transfer, Arista walked into Mr. Storm's room with a cheery, "How are you?"

Standing beside his bed, dressed in sweat pants, an oversized tee shirt, and runners on his feet with no socks, the elderly gentleman was finishing packing the scant belongings he had with him into a duffle bag. Barely flicking a glance at her, he complained, "I feel terrible."

Smiling with perky cheerfulness, she encouraged, "You'll be feeling better soon."

"I don't know. They can't seem to find what's wrong with me." He shook his head forlornly. "This morning was terrible. It felt like the whole world was rocking."

Looking at him quizzically, she considered the oddity of his remark, decided to take it lightly and chuckled, "Earthquakes tend to make us feel odd."

"There was an earthquake?" His faded blue eyes stared at her with confusion and fascination.

She stared at him with amazement. "Didn't you know?"

"How would I?" He closed the zipper on his duffle bag. "I get very dizzy sometimes. I thought I was just having a really bad spell. It scared me. I stayed in my room, closed my door, and haven't talked to anybody since. Nobody has spoken to me either, except a nurse who opened my door just long enough to tell me to get dressed and pack my belongings. I thought they were sending me home."

"You are being moved to a different hospital. This hospital is full over capacity."

"I was wondering why there were so many sirens earlier today." His eyes widened with incredulity. "I thought it was probably one of those mock disasters these places have."

"No." Arista lifted both brows, remembered their plight at the airport, and assured him, "This one is real."

"No wonder I felt so odd." Seeing him staring out the window, she stood quietly allowing him to sort his thoughts. He looked at her sheepishly, "You must think me a very senile old man."

"No." She looked at him in earnest. "I think you must be very ill if you mistook a large earthquake for one of your spells."

"Well." He grinned. "I suppose this morning was worse than usual. There was no reason to tell anyone how I felt. They haven't been able to figure out how to help me." He shook his head sadly. "They have tried everything. Some tests have come back with abnormal results, but they don't know why." His eyes suddenly lit and he chuckled, "We had an earthquake?"

"Yes. It has the entire city in confusion and we have been declared to be in a state of emergency."

His expression changed to sobriety, "Is there a lot of damage?"

"Oh yes." She told him, "You will see."

"Where are they going to take me?"

She realized, "I don't know." With a shrug she stepped forward to help him get ready. "There are busses waiting outside to take mobile patients to hospitals in surrounding areas."

"Isn't an evacuation an overreaction if the earthquake is already past?" Searching her face as though he might be able to derive information if he looked hard enough, he asked, "Do you know why we are being evacuated?"

"The ground is still unstable. They need to free hospital beds in case there is another quake."

"That's why they're bothering with an old guy like me." He pushed his slippers into the duffle bag. "If I wasn't in the way, they might just leave me here to die."

Arista stared at him. She was one of the many people remaining here to keep order. She did not expect to die for it. "Let's hope they are mistaken and things don't get any worse. There have not been any fatalities."

"Oh." He looked over sheepishly as he realized her circumstances were different from his. "When are you leaving?"

"I will only leave if they evacuate the entire city."

"Earthquakes are impossible to predict." He belatedly tried to encourage her. "Look at how long they have been calling for 'the big one' and it hasn't happened. Everything will probably settle back down."

"I hope you are right." Feeling exhaustion tugging at every part of her, the only thing she wanted was the return of normality.

"You look tired."

"I am very tired."

"Will you be staying here to help for a long time?"

Slightly shrugging she admitted, "I plan to be here as long as my help is needed."

"Why don't you go home and rest?"

"Everybody has been working very hard today. We are all tired."

He lifted his duffle bag. "If you tell me where the bus is, I will go there. Then you will have one less person to look after. I hope you are able to go get some rest soon."

In a couple of hours most of the patients were moved and the next shift was arriving. Spirits began climbing as exhausted workers headed for the cozy comfort of their homes. The next shift was anticipating an easy night. The hospital was emptier than it had ever been.

"Are you ready to go?"

"Yes." Looking into blue eyes, relief flooded through every part of Arista's body.

"It's been quite the day." Hauk held the door open for her.

"It feels like about ten years." Trying to make light of the situation and smile, she found her lips producing a strange feeling of tightness she was sure must be unattractive. She stopped trying to force pretence.

He wrapped his arm around her shoulders. She leant against the reassurance of his warmth, and sighed with a feeling of bliss.

Looking down, he saw contentment on her face. "You look awfully relaxed and happy for the kind of day it has been."

"Of course I'm happy." A smile came easily as she looked up at him and snuggled against him. "We are still alive."

Momentarily stunned, he contemplated it, gave her shoulders a slight squeeze with the arm draped over them, and conceded, "True."

"Never take things for granted." She mumbled through a yawn without giving any thought to what she was yapping about.

He took it to heart and pondered just how many things he had taken for granted. Even the life he had built for himself here. He had tossed it aside in hardly more than a blink. Arista would be long gone from his life if God hadn't brought their paths back together.

Engrossed with being together, neither of them noticed all the curious eyes watching them leave the hospital. Nor were they aware of the intense speculation building in their wake. Hospital staff was zealously buzzing over the blooming romance catching their interest. Some said the relationship was doomed for failure. Others dreamily predicted a lifetime of perfection in a bubble of unfailing love. The bitter sector, the people who no longer believed in love, scorned the couple and the onlookers.

Chapter 29

Watching frenzied activity clogging the small city, Arista remained silent. Hauk carefully wove his way through a congestion of tangled traffic. People madly preparing for, 'the big one', were successfully wreaking havoc.

Hauk waited patiently as, along with numerous others, he drove only a few inches every couple of minutes in a backlog of traffic blocked by streams of vehicles forming a line up for gas pumps two blocks away.

Arista wondered what difference a full tank of gas could possibly make if the mountain should decide to hurl them all down to the centre of the earth. Glancing at the needle on their fuel gage, she was relieved to see it at three quarters full, and decided there was logic in wanting to be able to make it to the next town.

Stores were forced to close as shelves emptied of produce, and the owners wished they had more on hand to sell. Greedily hoarding their supplies, the majority of people chose to dine out. Restaurant supplies became sparse.

People unwilling to wrestle with another earthquake were choking the highway in their panicked exodus.

Grating into her mental meanderings, the air crunched with the sound of metal slamming into metal. Arista's shoulders slumped in weary defeat as the insanity surrounding them drained the last of her energy. Hauk's hands pressed into a white knuckle grip on the steering wheel and frustration boiled in his eyes as he glared at the jumble of traffic blocking the road. Seeing him assess their surroundings with one fluid sweeping motion of his vision, Arista knew he was looking for an alternative route. Glancing at the jam of traffic, she doubted he would find one.

Equally impatient, four huge men converged and grabbed the small sports car responsible for the accident, hoisted it off the ground, and carried it to the sidewalk. The other car made horrible clunking sounds, but the owner managed to get enough life out of it to drive it off the road. Traffic began moving immediately.

As they passed a sporting goods store, Arista was shocked to see how many shoppers were coming out laden with tents, camping stoves, and all other paraphernalia. "What are they doing?"

"Only they know." Hauk arched a brow at seeing a gap in the traffic and slid his car into it before the opening could close. Eventually Hauk parked and turned off the ignition. Watching him rest his head against the back of the seat and let out a long sigh, Arista remained still and silent.

"You know," he looked over at her, "I'm so tired, I will hardly be able to get up to my apartment. I hope the 'big one' stays away for a few hours yet."

Giggling at his understatement, she replied, "I hope it stays away for a few centuries."

"I'm glad you're still smiling." He took her hand into his. "I'm not sure what I would do if you would ever stop."

She grinned impishly, "I'll never stop smiling." Intuition whispered against being too assertive in making predictions. She might stop smiling. If she believed in premonitions, she would have been alarmed, however, she considered the lot of it to be nonsense, and so, she ignored the fleeting hint of something being amiss.

Her hand remained in his as they walked through the underground parking area, rode the elevator to the twelfth floor, and walked down the hallway to his suite. When Hauk opened the door, they were greeted by a warm and heavy aroma of food cooking.

Hesitating, he remembered his mother was living with him. It was a major detail he had forgotten. Frustrated with circumstances continuously creating a lack of privacy in his life, he momentarily indulged in a longing to heat frozen pizza, put on his slippers, watch television, snuggle with Arista, and get a very long sleep.

He faked chipper energy, walked around the corner into the kitchen, let go of Arista's hand, and greeted, "Hi Mom."

Grabbing him in a shaky hug, Doris didn't know how delicately frail she suddenly felt to him. Hauk changed his mind and decided he was glad Doris was with them. It would save him from worrying about her.

Patting him on the back, Doris forced a smile and tears pooled in her eyes. Trying to blink them away and put on a brave front, she moved out of the hug and said, "I made us a pot of chicken noodle soup, some baking powder biscuits, a garden salad, and fresh apple pie." Ignoring the tears spilling down her cheeks, she smiled bravely.

"Thanks Mom."

Finding pleasure in being useful, a shaky little laugh escaped Doris, and she immediately began ladling soup into bowls. It was rich with orange carrots, green celery, an abundance of chicken chunks, and thick noodles. The biscuits were flavourfully enhanced with a sprinkling of parmesan cheese, parsley flakes, and garlic salt. Lettuce salad was tossed with cheese chunks, mushrooms, celery, shaved almonds, grated carrots, and topped with croutons. Everything Doris had made was embellished with a dash of something special. The food combination was warm and delicious. It worked its magic and before long they were all struggling to keep heavy eyes from closing with sleep.

"I'll get the table cleared." Doris lifted the salad bowl and the plate of biscuits from the centre of the table. "Then I'll cut the pie for desert."

Muffling a yawn and a groan, Arista placed a palm on her stomach. "I ate too much! It was a fantastic meal. Thank you Doris."

"You're welcome." Doris beamed. "I love cooking when there are people to share the food with."

"It was good. Thank you Mom." Hauk looked at his mother with obvious love and respect, and Doris glowed.

Observing them, Arista easily read the expressions. Looking down and absently playing with her cutlery, Arista pondered the generosity and kindness deeply embedded in Hauk and in his mother.

"You are very deep in thought."

The deep velvet of Hauk's voice thrummed into her reflective meditation. Looking up, her thoughts suddenly felt readable, and she babbled, "I'm just tired." With a quirk of her brow she grinned, "I was sleeping with my eyes opened."

"I think we are all ready to wind down from the day." He got up and gathered plates and cutlery.

"Is there anything I can do to help?"

"No. Thank you." Glancing at the kitchen, he once again wished they could find a margin of space for themselves.

Exhaustion pulsed through his veins and fatigue shadowed her face. Taking her hand, he silently led Arista from the table and out to the patio without bringing Doris' attention to them. There he soberly looked down at a profusion of tents dotting the city.

"Why are they setting up tents?"

"In a tent, the ceiling can't fall on you, or, if it does it won't hurt."

"Oh." She laughed softly. "I never would have thought of using a tent."

Drowning in her eyes, he impulsively murmured, "You are the most wonderful, and," about to say, unpredictable, he paused to use the more cautious, "exhilarating woman I have ever met."

Compliments were a rarity in her life. Hearing them from someone as fine as Hauk had an extreme effect. She knew she was not wonderful, or strong, or any of the other things that make people stand out and shine. She wished she was. For just a few minutes, Hauk made her feel like she was out of the ordinary in a good way.

The screen door scratched along the track and Doris shrilled, "There you are."

Hauk's spirit groaned. Covering it with a crooked smile, he assured Doris, "We will be in shortly."

"I've never seen anything like this." Brushing past them, Doris leant against the rail and looked out at the vast number of tents pitched within the city.

Disgruntled at the persistence of Doris' intrusion, Hauk grumbled, "I'm going to get a piece of pie."

Knowing she had interrupted a private moment, Doris felt a glimmer of victory for stalling the inevitable, and silently rebuked herself for being selfish.

"I'm going to get a cup of coffee." Arista followed Hauk's lead.

Doris remained a constant presence throughout the dessert of apple pie and coffee. Later, when Hauk prepared his bedroom for Arista, Doris clucked during the entire process. Despite Doris' objection to Arista being given the bedroom, Hauk insisted on sleeping on the futon in his den. He said he had some paperwork to finish.

As soon as she could do so politely, Arista plopped into Hauk's bed and fell into a deep sleep. Guy's face invaded her night with abstract dreams of thin grey shapes circling. One leaned forward from the group and almost pressed its face against hers while taunting, "I loved you."

Trying to back away from the shape, she mumbled, "No."

It followed, with its face in hers, laughing and insulting, "What if nobody ever loves you again?"

"Get away from me!" She screamed at the phantom.

Rubbing his eyes, Hauk walked into the dark room. "Arista?"

"Leave me alone! Go away!"

Moving to the bed and trying to nudge her into wakefulness he asked, "Arista?"

Epidemic

"No! Leave me alone!" Her voice boomed in fury.

"What's going on in here?" Doris flicked on lights and eyed Hauk with suspicion.

Arista squinted against the sudden flood of brightness.

"She was having a nightmare." Hauk defended as he stared at Doris with disbelief for her having hinted at the worst.

Seeing his eyes cloud, Doris felt instant guilt for even briefly having suspected him to be anything less than chivalrous. She was certain he would only be in Arista's room with good reason, or an invitation, which may be in the process of being retracted.

Finally surfacing to wakeful awareness, Arista ran her hands over the quilt covering her and subtly checked to make sure her body was decently concealed.

Sitting on the side of her bed, Hauk took her hand in his, studied her complexion, and looked into her eyes.

Watching, Doris' heart tugged warmly. She saw them as the cutest couple in the world. She probably knew Hauk better than anyone else, and the adoration he felt for Arista was clearly visible. As his mother, it seemed only natural to accept and cherish the woman holding her son's heart captive.

Drowning in attention when all she wanted was sleep, Arista looked at Doris, puzzled over why she was watching her endearingly, and then looked at Hauk and saw tension in the deepened lines around his mouth. Wanting to erase it, she squeezed his hand, opened her mouth to reassure him, glanced at Doris, and kept silent.

Seeing it, Doris began a graceful exit, "Are you going to be all right?"

"I'm fine." Arista smiled at her sleepily and her grip on Hauk's hand tightened.

Doris noticed and excused herself with, "Then, I'm going back to bed."

Hauk's eyes perked.

Doris noticed.

"Good night." Even though he was glad she was leaving them alone, he loved his mother dearly and it warmed his smile.

Doris read his expression for what it was. "Good night." She smiled at Hauk. "Good night Arista." Smiling with feigned relaxation, Doris felt her throat constrict as she accepted the new stage of life they were entering. Being the kind of man he is, Hauk would freely give his full devotion, support, and loyalty, to the woman in his life. It was the natural and proper order of things.

"Good night." Arista smiled back and she silently hoped these wonderful people would continue to grace her with their kindness.

Doris closed the door when she left. Hauk studied Arista and drank in every detail while absently and gently moving a strand of hair off her face and to where it belonged.

"I'm feeling much better. I needed some sleep." Smiling at him, she basked in the relaxed atmosphere softly beating with tranquil intimacy. "You still look exhausted. Haven't you slept yet?"

"I did get some sleep." With a grin, he teased, "More than I ever got when I was on my internship."

It was hard to imagine any day being more gruelling than this one. Grinning she said what she thought to be truth, "At least things can only get better from here. I mean it really can't get any worse than what it has been."

He looked at her sceptically.

"If 'the big one' comes," she chuckled, "it will create an overload on this city, and we will all have to leave."

"You think so?"

"What other options are there?"

"I'm a doctor."

"Yes, but, you are not able to hold up mountains." Though, she almost believed he might be able to find a way if it was important enough. Dreamy admiration hazed her thoughts.

"Let's hope the earth is finished moving for a long time." Without conscious intent, over the course of the conversation he had slowly reclined, and was lying propped on an elbow beside her.

Knowing he should go to his den and get some sleep, the energy to get up and walk those few feet seemed like more than he had. Sinking under a wave of tiredness almost beyond endurance, he vaguely wondered why he was so deathly exhausted. He couldn't remember ever experiencing such an overall sense of lethargy. He forced his eyes open, and was going to say he was leaving. Seeing her sleeping beside him, he relaxed to watch her for a few minutes.

Chapter 30

Day Twenty Eight - Sunday

Waking to sunshine flooding the room, he looked down at the dark mass of crumpled hair under his chin. Feeling the warmth of Arista snuggled against him, he lay still in the quiet comfort.

Sensing the wakefulness in him, she rolled away, rubbed her eyes, and opened them. Closing her eyes against the sunlight, just as he had done, it took a few seconds for her to look over. When she did, a warm smile curved her lips and her eyes sparked with pleasure at seeing him.

His arm automatically circled her and drew her close. She cuddled against him, and her libido jumped. Seeing the heavy droop in her eyelids, knowing the cause, his lips found hers.

Loud crashing assailed from the kitchen. He hugged her, she snuggled into him, breathed the aroma of his skin, they got out of bed, and they left the room.

Seeing them come out of Arista's bedroom, Doris made assumptions and gave them an odd look. Her cheeks flamed with discomfort. Being from the 'old days', she believed a man and woman should be married before engaging in physical relationships. She busily flipped pancakes on the grill.

Arista would have taken delight at the sight of pancakes if she had come out of her bedroom alone. She remained silent in the awkward atmosphere.

Hauk wished his mother didn't need his help at this time in his life. He walked over and draped an arm across Doris' shoulders, "Pancakes." He beamed with appreciation.

"After yesterday," she shrugged and smiled sadly, "I thought we could all use an energy boosting breakfast."

Striving for friendship, Arista offered, "Can I help?"

"You can set the table." Doris accepted Arista's assistance with a warm smile.

Drowning in uncertainty, Arista looked around the kitchen, and wished she knew where to find things.

Seeing it, Hauk opened one large cupboard door and displayed, "All the dishes are in here." Sliding a drawer open he told her, "The cutlery is here." He moved to another cupboard, "Glasses and cups are here. There is cereal in here." He opened a large drawer. "Bread is in," he shrugged, "that wooden thing on the counter."

Arista and Doris grinned at each other. Turning in time to catch it, Hauk silently dared them to say anything to him about his description of the contraption. They continued sharing their amusement. Seeing bonds form, Hauk let them enjoy themselves at his expense.

They ate ravenously and drank oodles of coffee. Dishes were cleaned up, and then, they all left together. Hauk was heading to the hospital. Doris was getting a ride from him to the shopping mall. Sitting in the passenger side of the front seat, Arista glanced at Hauk. She was looking forward to tagging along with him for the day. She planned on volunteering her services at the hospital if they could use her help, otherwise she intended to go investigate the tiny malls in the surrounding area and meet Hauk for lunch. Hauk offered Arista the use of his car. Doris suggested she meet up with her at the main mall. Arista was hoping they would put her to work at the hospital.

Still feeling severely tired, Hauk kept his concern to himself. He thought he might talk to his doctor and get some tests run.

Lost in her own mental meanderings, Doris considered an upcoming appointment with her hairdresser. She was hoping to find a new look neither ridiculously young, nor drearily old. Mulling over different ideas, uncertain what kind of cut to go with, she wished she had more of a flair for style.

In a heartbeat they lurched against straining seat belts and the ground jumped. A deafening roar filled the air and the earth opened into a giant mouth. Sounds mingled into a drone of horror as the air thundered, people screamed, metal folded like match sticks, and cement crumbled like autumn leaves. The earth took one big bite of civilization and spit dust at the bystanders.

Surrounded by deathly silence, terror clutched Arista's throat in a boa constricting vice. "Hauk?"

Deafening silence answered.

Stretching over as far as she could, she was unable to reach the warmth of Hauk's body. She fidgeted with her seatbelt. When it refused to budge, she angrily jerked at it, twisted it, and finally pounded it, all to no avail. The tears streaming down her face were unnoticeable in the shroud of black darkness worse than anything she had ever imagined. Panic leapt to life in her veins, over her skin, and into her thoughts. It was a monster overpowering logic and threatening to smother her. Closing her eyes, she forced regularity into her breathing. As rhythm returned the quiver left her veins. Envisioning her favourite place, in Hauk's arms, she struggled to move to his side.

Gingerly letting her hand explore as far as she could reach, she grasped a thin strap. "Please be my purse. Please be my purse." Pulling it to herself, she half held her breath with fear of it being something else. Dragging her purse into her hands she almost shouted with joy, but the dank cloak of darkness enforced depressed silence.

Rummaging through her purse, she finally found her manicure scissors and chopped at the seatbelt until it let go. Afraid to dislodge something by shifting her weight, she moved with cautious slowness. Nothing budged. In seconds she was at Hauk's side.

She felt the warmth of his skin, found a pulse, and whispered, "Hauk?"

No answer came to her. Afraid, and unable to see through the darkness, she folded her feet underneath her, propped up on them, and very gently moved her hands around his head, over his face, carefully around his throat, and over his chest. She paused at the shallow quick breaths he was taking. Swallowing a lump of trepidation, she vaguely acknowledged the unusual warmth of his skin and she continued her exploration down his abdomen, over his arms, down his thighs, and his calves.

"Arista?"

Jerking to the sound, she listened carefully in case it had been imagined.

"Arista?"

"Yes." Wanting to launch herself against him and grab him in a hug, she refrained. She feared the possibility of an injury in his neck or back.

"I think I'm in serious trouble here."

"No." She whispered and her blood chilled to ice. "You are going to be fine."

"Can you find anything wrong?"

"No."

He took a deep breath and tears burnt in her eyes.

"I can't feel my legs."

Terrified, she didn't know what to say or do. She sat still and silently prayed for miracles.

He let out a slow breath and asked, "How is Doris?"

Doris? She had forgotten about her. "I don't know. I haven't been in the backseat yet."

"Go check on her."

Crawling over the seat, she froze when the roof of the car made a grinding creak testifying to the crushing weight above them. It subsided and she continued making her way over the back of the seat. "Doris?"

"Owww."

"Where does it hurt?"

"I hurt everywhere." Doris moaned quietly as she slowly moved each part of her body.

"Are you bleeding anywhere?"

"I don't think so."

Cringing, Arista realized she wouldn't know if she was either. It was impossible to see anything. "Are you able to run your hands over your body and check?"

"Yes."

Hearing clothing rustling, Arista assumed Doris was feeling for blood and Arista quickly ran her hands over her own body.

"Hauk?"

No reply came to Doris.

Arista told her, "I was just talking to him." Then, she lied, "I think he is all right." She hated saying, "We shouldn't waste air talking." Crawling back over to the front seat, she shuddered at the eerie silence.

"Hauk?" Arista whispered beside him as she took his icy cold hand.

"Huh?"

"How are you doing?"

"I feel horrible."

"Do I hear him talking?" Doris had to know.

"How are you doing, Mom?"

Though she couldn't see it, and didn't know if he had the strength for it, Arista vividly imagined the special smile he always had for Doris. Tears rolled down her cheeks. When one splashed on Hauk's hand, his hand reached for, and found, her cheek.

Chapter 31

Above ground, sirens shrieked. Rumbling black clouds filled the sky. People fearfully whispered to each other.

"Why are you talking so quietly?" One child asked her mother.

"I'm not sure." The mother pondered the question and was unable to find a reason.

The crowd stood staring in confused silence as each individual struggled to absorb what had happened. Dust burnt their throats, lungs, and eyes. Emergency routes exiting the area became congested as people fled with the intentions of driving, and driving, and driving, in any direction going as far away as possible. Others milled about in confusion. Authority figures remained loyal to their community and worked diligently at maintaining order, providing medical help, or implementing emergency procedures, whichever department was their responsibility.

Paramedics stood nervously waiting. Hospital staff bustled in preparation for a swarm of wounded people in need of assistance. Silence and inactivity prevailed. It was the worst possible aftermath.

A few men purchased shovels at a corner hardware store and came back to wage war against the earth. A stunned crowd watched them dig. First the onlookers responded with pity. It seemed impossible to make any headway in the task those men were undertaking. Within minutes more men left, and then returned with shovels. Soon women joined the effort. Droves of youth came to help. The area filled with people of all ages and lifestyles working, crying, praying, and hoping together.

The rescue effort organized itself without a word of instruction. The will to help was abundant. All the people had needed was the leadership provided by example. The mob of helpers didn't know the first men had begun with few expectations of accomplishing anything other than venting anger for what had happened and staging rebellion against it. The initial attitude quickly changed as growing numbers of helpers gave hope.

Then, a man shouted, "I see a bumper."

Spurred by encouragement, people pushed their shovels deeper and faster. Dirt was hauled out of the area in wheelbarrows and piling high around the perimeter of the site.

Grocery store delis and restaurants offered aid by bringing food, water, and coffee. Churches brought folding tables to hold the incoming stream of food. Children too weak to help with the physical work were put to the task of taking water and sandwiches to those too engrossed in their efforts to leave.

Flashing yellow lights joined the flickering blue and red lights of emergency vehicles. Large chunks of cement were targeted for removal. Immediate attention remained focused on the trunk of the vehicle they were working to free.

Arista was too excruciatingly tired to keep her eyes opened. As heavy lids drooped, she carefully leaned away from Hauk to avoid moving into him and jostling him in any way. Doris had fallen unconscious a few minutes ago. Hauk was constantly drifting in and out of consciousness. Glancing toward the back of the car, utter darkness appeared to have a glimmer of something else. Rubbing her brow, Arista told herself it was a hallucination.

Wanting to save herself the effort of moving all the way to the back seat to check on Doris, she whispered, "Doris?"

"Huh?"

Relieved at hearing her, Arista struggled to breathe and longed for sleep. Blurry confused thoughts focused on a sudden shaft of light. Thinking it was the bright light signifying death, she whispered, "Hauk, I love you."

She thought she heard him say, "I love you." She thought she heard the familiar chuckle lacing his deep velvet voice. If it was a dream, she wished to stay in it for a long, long, time.

A burly bear of a man dressed in denim coveralls and a flannel work shirt with the sleeves rolled high onto thick biceps held his shovel up commanding attention and shouting, "We have the car! There are people inside!" Flashlights jerked frantic beams of light in all directions as they darted from the car to the crowd and back to the car. "There are three people!"

"They aren't moving."

Through squinting eyes, the bear of a man glowered at the young boy for voicing unacceptable pessimism. The boy looked fearfully back at the man. The man lowered himself onto his knees for a closer look.

Shovels frantically clawed the ground. Racing time, cranes prepared to remove chunks of broken cement.

"Everybody must leave the area!" Through a loud speaker the order repeated three times. The bear of a man refused to obey. He dug his shovel into the ground faster.

Four police officers approached. Three stood back. One stepped forward, "You are going to have to leave this area!"

"Why? These people need our help."

"We know." The officer's lips pinched and he forced himself to do his job. He wanted to pick up a shovel and assist the man. "We will get back to this car in a few minutes." He looked at the crane waiting to do its job. "There are many more cars under this rubble and we need to move the heaviest obstacles. The people buried here are all running out of time and we're wasting precious minutes right now."

Tears mixed with dirt crusted on weather worn skin and the bear of a man picked up his shovel, bowed his head, and obeyed instruction.

All four police officers swallowed hard and wiped escaping tears from the corners of their eyes. The officers escorted him safely away from the area.

Cranes positioned, men wearing hard hats stood directing the operators, and cement boulders were removed.

The car jerked violently and the muffled sound of metal against metal creaked. For the briefest second, Arista thought she heard a baby cry. Opening her eyes, she sucked in several large gasps of air. Thinking she was alive, stunned with the possibility, she pinched her arm hard and welcomed the pain it caused her.

Glancing at Doris, Arista saw her chest moving. Then she looked at Hauk. Seeing him, after thinking she never would again, her breath caught. Impulsively moving to grasp him in a hug, she remembered, stayed still and looked. His position was different from the feel of it had been. Checking where her purse was, she realized it had also moved. Guessing the car must have jostled while she was unconscious, she swallowed a lump of fear. Unable to bear thinking of the possible consequences, she concentrated on telling herself they were all going to survive and return to perfect health.

Black lashes quivered, and Hauk's eyes slowly opened. Arista smiled at him and waited to see him flash his usual smile. She wanted to see his eyes dance with familiar mischief and confidence. Her heart broke when his eyes remained shadowed.

"Hauk?" An ocean of tears slid down her cheeks. "What is wrong?"

"Do you want an educated guess?"

There was a familiar glimmer of his usual perkiness. Smiling through her tears, she prodded, "Yes. Tell me what I can do to help you."

"You can't help." He smiled a weak and wan smile. "I feel ill. If I go into a coma, tell them to look for botulism."

"You think you have botulism?" She doubted the accuracy of his diagnosis. He was an extraordinary medical doctor, and he knew how he was feeling. Perhaps he was right.

"I have the symptoms. Nothing I've eaten seemed spoiled or questionable."

Interrupting, Doris gasped, "Oh! No!"

"What's wrong?" Arista turned with alarm.

"What if my canning is making him sick?"

Arista factually and undiplomatically stated, "Then we better tell the doctors. They need to treat you too, before you get sick."

"I'm not worried about getting sick." She sobbed. "I love him. What if I made him sick?"

Wanting to ignore the emotional upheaval, but, taking pity on the beseeching look in Doris' eyes, she asked, "What do you can?"

"I always have home canned pickles and tomatoes."

Struggling for patience, Arista asked, "Do you can any high risk foods like meats or vegetables?"

"No."

Cranes efficiently lifted cement boulders and dropped them a safe distance beside the site. The bear of a man descended on the people he was determined to save. Paramedics followed with stretchers. With assistance, Doris and Arista clambered out of the vehicle. Hauk was unconscious. Afraid of jarring a possible broken back or neck, the process of removing him from the car was agonizingly slow in a void where minutes felt like years. Arista and Doris watched helplessly.

Standing beside a man with a shovel, Arista remembered, and whispered, "I thought I heard a baby cry."

"A baby was crying?" A teenager looked over sharply.

"I don't know. I may have imagined it."

Shovels sank into the ground swiftly. Bobcats came to help speed the removal of dirt. Within minutes light reflected from a door handle on a car submerged sideways. The first scream of sirens sliced the air as Hauk was taken away by ambulance.

Chapter 32

Glaring at Doctor Munroe, Arista insisted, "He said he suspected botulism."

"You need to be calm." Dr. Munroe scolded.

Arista stood her ground and stared right back at him.

Wanting her to stop pestering him, Dr. Munroe rudely snapped, "We have to run tests to identify his illness. We cannot simply begin treating him according to your diagnosis. What medical degrees do you have?"

Turning her back to him, she marched away with tears streaming down her cheeks. Panic tightened her breathing and guilt clenched her chest.

"Slow down!" A hand grabbed her arm.

Looking over her shoulder, she saw a huge man, wearing a long white medical coat.

"I'm Doctor Staid." He held out a hand of greeting. "I heard you talking to Dr. Munroe. I have worked with Dr. VanLiev and I've never known him to be wrong."

Her hand took his in hearty welcome of the introduction.

"Do you know why he suspected botulism?"

"He said those were the symptoms he was experiencing."

Knitting heavy black brows together, he asked, "Was he lethargic or having difficulty breathing?"

"He said he couldn't feel his legs."

"He had paralysis?"

"I was worried it might indicate a broken back or neck."

"We've taken x-rays. There don't seem to be any broken bones." Dr. Staid walked with a confident stride and calm expression while silently contemplating Hauk's diagnosis. Stopping at the next corridor, he turned to tell her,

"I'm going to test Sebastian for botulism right now. Will you be staying in the hospital?"

"Yes." Quickly mapping plans she could stick to, she informed, "I want to go see Doris, and then I will go to the cafeteria."

"Good." He grinned. "I'll know where to find you."

Anxious to hear the results, time seemed to drag endlessly as she sipped at a steamy, creamy, cup of coffee, and wished Doris had been awake. She held her chin firmly square and looked around the cafeteria at the many people. Most of them were dressed in medical uniforms and sitting by themselves.

Sirens wailing progressively louder drew her attention to the row of windows lining the cafeteria. Watching the white and red vehicle approach with flashing red lights, she wondered what the injury count was going to climb to before the day was done. So far it was at 37 wounded, 50 missing, and, as of yet, no fatalities. Stirring her coffee, she reflected on the cry she heard underground and how coincidental it was to have heard it just long enough to have given the rescue workers information alerting them to the vehicle's location and leading them to bringing the mom, dad, and baby to safety.

Looking out the window at the haze of dust lingering in the air, flashing sirens of an ambulance, and seeing the tired daze in the eyes of those around her, she almost could have believed she had been transported to some tortured planet closely resembling and vastly different from Earth. Unnerved by the weirdness of her thinking, she gulped down the last of her coffee.

She wandered over to the food bar. A chubby brunet, wearing the cafeteria uniform of a navy and white striped shirt, navy pants, a navy apron, and a striped cap, asked, "Can I help you?"

Arista glanced at an assortment of pizza, pasta, and other hot foods visible behind glass panels. "I'll have one slice of pizza please." It was the first thing she saw, and she wasn't hungry, so she didn't care what she got.

Workers were taking breaks whenever time allowed. It created a trickle of doctors coming and going, nurses doing likewise, same with kitchen staff, and cleaning staff. Picking at her pizza and slowly putting minute pieces into her mouth, Arista waited.

Three nurses walking in together were deeply immersed in lively conversation with each other. More flashing lights swung up the drive.

Brown eyes faltered uncertainly, "I'm sorry, I never asked your name."

"Arista." She informed while standing up and anxiously waiting to hear his diagnosis.

"We are treating Dr. VanLiev for botulism." Pulling out a chair, Dr. Staid asked, "Do you mind if I join you?"

"I would like very much for you to join me." Sitting down, she watched him do the same.

"We will have to confirm our suspicions, but, the most likely source of contamination seems to be potatoes, if it is botulism." He continued to explain, "Improperly handled potatoes wrapped in foil provide an air tight environment for the bacteria to grow in."

"I've heard of it, but," leaving her sentence trail off, she strongly doubted the accuracy of his diagnoses. The whole of it was too unlikely.

"Sebastian is conscious, and he told us where he has eaten in the last few days. One of the restaurants has been in question before for contamination of their potatoes. We are looking into the matter." He grinned and told her, "Sebastian was asking if you were in the hospital."

Wanting to jump from her chair and race to his room, she forced herself to remain seated long enough to request permission, "May I see him?"

Dr. Staid warned, "He might be asleep again."

Unable to wait another second, she was on her feet. "I'll go see."

"I'll come with you."

On their way, she asked, "How is he doing?"

Dr. Staid's broad face took on a sombre expression. "Botulism is a dangerous poisoning. Mild cases usually disappear in a few days without leaving permanent damage. Severe contamination may necessitate months of hospitalization. We are hoping botulism is not involved." His eyes held a silent pity. "We are administering antibiotics to him for mild pneumonia. We are also expecting to hear an announcement declaring a full mandatory evacuation of this entire area within the next few days."

Swallowing hard to curb her emotions, she struggled to optimistically belief that Hauk will bounce back to perfect health. Fear insisted that she and the people in her life were all as susceptible to tragedy as the next person. She silently prayed.

When a quiet voice in her heart asked why Hauk should be spared, her heart pleaded, "I love him."

Guilt racked to her core, her heart took control, and she blurted, "If I ask you to treat him with a specific medication, will you?"

Looking at her as though she had lost her mind, he remained silent.

She told him the symptoms and complications she was expecting Hauk to encounter as well as the medications she thought would be most effective.

"How do you know to suggest those treatments?" Suspicion veiled his expression.

"I've read articles on the internet." Her lie triggered a powerful stress overload throwing desensitization into her mind and body. Thankful for the fog of disorientation, she blissfully sank into its murky depths.

"You need to sit down."

Feeling him direct her step by placing his hand on her elbow and guiding her, she blindly followed. Sitting in the chair he led her to, she stared blindly at the floor. She hadn't noticed him leave, but he was suddenly offering her a glass of water.

"This might help you feel better." He placed it in her hand.

Holding it, she kept her eyes on the floor and her mind swirled with confusion. She looked up at him. He plastered a professionally reassuring smile over serious concern. She lifted the water to her lips.

Seeing pink creep into the stark whiteness of her complexion his mood eased and he assured her, "He's a strong healthy man. Hauk has a good chance of being out of danger in a couple of days."

Hauk? It was the first time he had used the nickname. Looking at Dr. Staid with fresh curiosity she asked, "Are you and Hauk friends?"

With a quirk of his dark brow, he grinned, "Very good friends." A spark lit in his eyes. "We used to play hockey together." Laughter rumbled with memories. "He never believed in inflicting injury. He avoided physical contact, but, he had an uncanny knack for manipulating the opposing team members. One time," merriment caused his words to tumble over each other rapidly as he got caught up in remembering, "there were two seconds of game time left, we had our players in position, and wanted to break a tied score. Hauk skated against the man with the puck, acted as though he had it, took an imaginary shot at the net, and when the confused opponent went to intercept a nonexistent puck it created the opening our man needed." Hearty laughter robbed his breath and made his eyes water. "You should have seen the reaction. The opposing team members were so angry with their player for falling for Hauk's bluff. The guy walked away with such a dumbfounded expression."

Loving the story, but loving Hauk more, she got up, "I really want to see him."

He walked with her to Hauk's room.

Slightly deflated at finding him sleeping, she opted to stay in the room with him. Sitting beside his bed, able to do nothing other than watch and wait, her heart ached over the grey paleness of his skin, the severity keeping him unconscious most of the time, and his unresponsive state when he was awake.

She almost buckled with relief when Dr. Staid prescribed one of the medications she had requested, and it began flowing intravenously into Hauk's veins.

Doris joined her at Hauk's bedside as soon as her doctor was satisfied with her state of health. Although they spoke very little to each other, they provided silent support for one another. Doris read anything and everything she could find from books, to magazines, to newspapers. They both loved Hauk, and their shared concern grooved a special notch in each one's heart for the other.

The sun went down, came up, set again, and rose. Hauk drifted in and out of wakefulness. He didn't talk, and he fell back asleep almost as soon as he awoke. Her shins were achy from having walked miles on the hospital floors. Her back burnt from sleeping in the chair. Doctors and nurses came and went. Some of them watched her with concern. Numbness grew in her body, her mind, and her emotions.

Their heads were bent together and they were discussing a magazine article Doris was reading. Arista glanced over at Hauk and tightly gripped Doris' arm with speechless excitement. Doris immediately looked at Hauk, and they both leapt to his bed.

Hauk was finally looking at them, and with a weak smile, he gave Arista a look she would never forget. Love shone in his eyes, and he whispered, "Hi Hon."

Seeing his eyes fixed on Arista, Doris felt a painful little sting at being placed a healthy second. When Hauk reached for Doris' hand, love swelled in her heart for the man she still saw as her little boy.

"What happened?" The weakness in Hauk's body forced his eyes closed and he struggled to remain conscious.

"You have been dangerously ill." Doris clutched his hand tightly.

"You have finally come back to us." They all turned at the sound of Dr. Staid's voice coming from the doorway.

"What happened to me?"

"You don't remember?" Dr. Staid had previously explained the condition to Hauk, twice.

"No."

"You have been very sick. You probably don't have the energy to remember." Charting Hauk's lack of memory, he explained, "You have pneumonia."

Glancing at the monitors he quickly assessed Hauk's vital signs. "It looks as though you are making a turn and beginning to recover."

"I feel like death."

"You were nearly there."

Hauk shot Dr. Staid a withered look. "This is not funny Marty."

"I hate my name."

"I know, Art."

"I won't bug you if you don't bug me." With a smile, he patted Hauk's shoulder.

"Don't be condescending."

Dr. Staid chuckled with good humour. "It is good to see you getting back to normal."

Hauk smiled despite the exhaustion shadowing his eyes.

"Now I have to get going. I have patients to look after who are actually sick." Flashing a grin at Hauk, he winked at Arista.

"I saw you trying to flirt." Hauk teased with feigned indignation. "You're not her type."

"It would be wise to get back on your feet soon." Art winked at Arista again, and Arista bubbled with soft laughter at the innocent provocations he was aiming at Hauk.

Feigning absolute earnestness Hauk told Arista, "He wouldn't be as brave if I was able to get out of this bed."

Art countered, "I most certainly would. Just wait and see."

"Go do something useful with yourself."

"I do have an overload of work waiting for me." He walked to the door and turned, "I'll be back later. Tell the nurses to call me if you have any problems." Honest concern glimmered.

"Thanks." Appreciation and trust sparked in worn dullness. Then, Hauk's eyes closed and he drifted back to sleep.

With one hand on the door handle, Dr. Staid turned to Arista and Doris, "It looks as though he is out of the woods. He will need plenty of rest."

He left and Arista looked at Doris with a mixture of relief and uncertainty. They had been at the hospital for days. As all consuming fear began ebbing to relief, smaller concerns were remembered.

"I talked to Hauk's landlord."

Arista looked over at Doris in dread of what might be coming next.

"He says the building has been inspected and there is no major damage." Feeling the desire for creature comfort, she silently studied her son's face. "You should go there and have a break." Seeing Arista preparing to argue, she reasoned, "I will stay here while you go take a shower, change into clean cloths, get some sleep, and when you come back, I will go do the same."

Feeling weariness ache in her bones, and wondering if Doris was hinting that she smells bad, Arista dearly wanted to take Doris up on her suggestion. Looking at Hauk, seeing the improvement of his health in the colour of his skin, and glancing at the monitors showing stabilized readings, she wanted to leave, but her heart whispered a desire to stay and she was powerless to act against it.

"Hauk will be fine."

"I know." Realizing she meant exactly what she said, her heart warmed and her eyes shimmered as she smiled at Doris. "He really is going to be all right."

"I know."

Doris' eyes clouded with emotion. Arista went to her, and hugged her. It was the only way to share the vast relief they were both feeling.

Wiping a tear from her cheek, Doris asked, "Are you sure you won't go take a break?"

"Positive."

"Then I will leave for a little while."

After Doris was gone, Arista floundered in unexpected loneliness.

"What's the matter?"

Looking toward the voice, she grinned at seeing Hauk awake. "Your mother left. I was just missing her."

"You like her?"

"Yes. She's so nice. Everybody must love your mother."

Hauk chuckled. "She can be difficult if she wants to be."

"I can't see Doris ever being anything other than friendly and accommodating."

"Oh." He arched an eyebrow, and Arista's heart skipped at seeing the familiar gesture. "She has her enemies." He grinned with admiration, and said, "She is a staunch ally to have on your side." After only a brief silence, he declared, "Life is too precious to waste time on insecurities. I want you to know I love you."

After a lengthy silence, Hauk's skin crawled with the chill of pending rejection. Hiding it, he gave the prompt, "This is where you say," he lifted his voice to a squeaky soprano, "Oh Hauk, I love you."

Love and fear instantly overwhelmed her being.

Seeing tears pool in her eyes, and her smile falter, he misread her reaction. He flatly stated, "I guess you don't."

"I don't what?"

"You don't love me."

Stunned that he could miss the powerful emotion she thought was glaringly obvious, she spluttered, "Of course I love you. Why else would I be here?"

For the first time, he noticed the worn look on her face and the crumpled state of her clothing. Their feelings for each other were clarified to his satisfaction, and he asked, "How is Mom holding up?"

Reeling from the abrupt changes in his conversation, she looked at him, studied his expression, and saw nothing out of the ordinary. Going with his swings, she answered, "Your mother is fine. She is a tower of strength."

His eyes saddened. "She is a strong person, but don't be fooled, she hides her weaknesses. Where did she go?"

"She went to your apartment to take a shower and get some sleep."

"Good." Reassured of Doris' well being, he drifted back to sleep.

Chapter 33

Stepping out of a steamy shower, Arista reached for a bleached white hospital towel, dried, and basked in the fresh crispness of clean blue jeans, and a white sleeveless cotton jacket zipped over a pale peach tank top.

She was thankful that Doris had brought her fresh clothing, and that the staff had breached the rules by letting her shower in Hauk's private bathroom. She lingered for a moment before stepping back out to the odour of disinfectant overriding the sourness of illness. She took one final whiff of the steamy air filled with the scents of soap and shampoo. Then, she waltzed into the other room on a cloud of pleasure for her fresh cleanliness and an air of joy for the return of Hauk's health.

Seeing Doris glancing over at the sound of her entry, she smiled, "Thank you so much for bringing me my stuff."

"You are welcome."

"It smells nice in here." Hauk's eyes locked with hers, and simultaneously each of them radiated their welcome for each other's company.

Sitting on the edge of Hauk's bed and holding his hand, she heard a man walking past the room striking notes with his voice as though tuning his vocal chords for a specific reason.

The three of them looked at each other with amusement dancing between them.

Arista thought it would be aggravating to hear those strange sounds on regular intervals.

At the opposite end of the spectrum, Doris knew who had walked past. She was also aware of the country band he sang for, and the concert they were planning to perform later that evening. To Doris, the salt and pepper hair, tall lankiness, swarthy walk, and deep rich tones of the man's voice, mixed into a pleasant package. Doris dreamily relished the thought of hearing him humming 'good morning' over the first rays of sunshine in the beginning of a new day seeped with the aroma of freshly brewing coffee. Her eyes instinctively turned to the watchfulness of Hauk, and then to the unabashed curiosity sparking from Arista.

"Was that Tye?" Hauk broke the awkward silence and playful lights glimmered over his seemingly innocent question.

"Yes." Keeping her chin squared and level, Doris answered without ado.

Unspoken and warm teasing danced in Hauk's eyes.

Arista swallowed back a giggle.

"I wonder what the commotion is in the hallway." Doris brought their attention to the sudden sound of voices and activity buzzing around them.

They all turned when Dr. Staid stopped at their doorway.

"What's happening?" Hauk asked as he absently lifted himself into a sitting position.

Noticing the motion Hauk seemed oblivious to having made, Arista silently celebrated the speedy recovery he was making.

"How are you feeling?" With his attention focussed on the chart rather than Hauk, Dr. Staid's question seemed detached and unimportant until he looked at Hauk and waited for him to answer.

"I feel lousy."

"Your vitals are holding." Dr. Staid checked the monitors. He moved to Hauk's side and studied him closely. "Are you up to moving?"

"I haven't tried."

"Let's see if you can walk."

"Shouldn't one of the nurses be doing this?"

Dr. Staid shrugged his broad shoulders, "They are too busy."

Slowly swinging his legs over the side of the bed and belatedly realizing what he was wearing, he mumbled under his breath, and asked, "Will you please give me a second hospital gown to wrap around this gaping contraption?"

"They're in the cupboard behind you." Dr. Staid motioned to the cupboards lining the wall behind Arista.

She searched the cupboard doors and saw the label, 'gowns.' Piles of blue, green, and yellow gowns were stacked on the shelves. She plucked one out and brought it over to Hauk. He swung it around his shoulders, and got up with caution and embarrassment. The comical display of clumsy modesty made Doris and Arista grin at each other in good spirits. The small act of characteristic modesty, nurtured her love for him yet further.

Looking down at the floor, she gained a moment of privacy behind the hiding shield of her lids and pondered the strength of small and unplanned moments in their relationship. Those little details speeding by in a second, that can be missed just as quickly, were fast becoming the roots of her admiration and adoration for him.

"How does it feel to be on your feet?"

"Great." Hauk began trusting his strength and cautiously stepped further from the bed.

"Are you dizzy?"

"No."

"Do you feel nauseous?"

"No."

"Do you have any discomfort or difficulty breathing?"

"No." Hauk grinned as, tongue-in-cheek, he asked, "Does this mean I will be going home now?"

"No."

Detecting something amiss, Hauk locked eyes with his friend. "Where are you planning on sending me?"

"A mandatory evacuation has been ordered. Emergency procedures are underway and I trust you know the proper earthquake route to exit the city from this location?"

Shock vibrated through all of them as they listened.

"There hasn't been any more movement." Arista whispered.

"Scientists are picking up bizarre activity on their fancy machines and they say we must get out of here." Looking over his shoulder at Arista and Doris, Dr. Staid asked, "Will you be able to manage him?"

"Of course we will!" Squaring her shoulders, Doris' rigid stance resembled an army Sergeant. The sad tiredness of her eyes was a different picture.

"We will be fine." Arista wrapped a supportive arm across Doris' shoulders.

"Here's the wheelchair you asked for." A nurse scurried toward Dr. Staid.

"I feel well enough to walk." Hauk stood in protest. Looking down at the hospital gowns, he said, "I need my cloths."

"Will you please get Dr. VanLiev's personal items out of the closet?"

The nurse looked into an empty closet. "His cloths are not here."

Doris blushed. "I'm sorry. I took his cloths home and threw them away." Her embarrassment deepened to crimson. "They were filthy from the earthquake." Then, she beamed, "I brought a clean change of cloths." Picking up a bulging overnight bag from the floor beside her, she glowed with pride as she informed Hauk of her thoughtfulness. "Your wallet is in the zippered pocket of the pants."

Hauk grinned with obvious pleasure. He loved the pampering Doris bestowed on him.

Arista impulsively asked, "You couldn't possibly have been expecting him to leave today?"

"No dear." Doris' smile reflected her comfortable amiability with her own personality. "Procrastination is an option I try to avoid." She placed the bag on Hauk's bed. "The way I see it, delays only offer three possible outcomes. Stress caused by having to finish something in a rush. Avoiding a task until it disappears, which may save some effort but it usually costs comfort. The third possibility is to be saved from a chore by dying before the work gets done. None of those appeal to me."

"My mother has her opinions." Hauk arched a teasing brow.

"They have mostly all proven true over the years." Doris tilted her chin belligerently.

"It works for you." Hauk grinned at her indulgently.

Watching, Arista saw love glowing behind Hauk's light hearted words, and she thought about what she was seeing. Regardless of circumstance, Hauk has the ability to generously bestow kindness and respect on the people around him, and the esteem brings honour. Generating a rippling effect, Hauk's attitude demands that the people in his life treat each other with respect. His personality creates a noble and healthy environment.

"When will you be ready?"

"We should be out of here in about ten minutes." Hauk looked at the doctor, and asked, "Are you leaving soon?"

"I will be attending in one of the ambulances. We will go as soon as possible."

"I will hurry and get out of your way."

"You are not in my way. We are still discharging a number of patients able to travel with friends and family." Inspecting Hauk's complexion, he reached over and took his pulse. "Get as much bed rest as possible for the next few days. If your symptoms persist or intensify you should seek further treatment." Dr. Staid handed him a prescription. "Get this filled when you are safely out of the area. Take one pill four times a day for the next ten days."

Being the healthiest one in the group, Arista took the wheel. Hauk was given the back seat where he could easily lie down when he needed rest. Doris sat in the front passenger seat.

As they were skirting the edge of the city, Doris asked, "What's happening to the lake?"

Waiting for a break in the traffic, it finally came, and Arista looked down at the lake nestled in the valley beside them. Visually skimming the area, it looked normal to Arista.

"Look." Doris' voice hushed to a whisper of foreboding. "The water is boiling."

Hauk looked out the window with sudden alertness.

Concentrating on the traffic congesting the road, sweat bathed the wheel under her chilly hands and Arista waited for Hauk to verify what Doris was seeing. Noticing other drivers looking at the lake instead of the road, she pressed her foot on the brake.

"Everyone is looking and I want to see what is going on." She drove the car onto the narrow gravel shoulder where she brought it to a stop.

"Look." Doris whispered.

"The middle of the lake is boiling." Arista stared at clouds of steam rising from the water. Arista again fell under the odd feeling that this planet only vaguely resembled Earth. Dreary clouds filled the sky, and water boiled on the lake's surface, and steam from the bubbles licked up at the air. It used to be tranquil water and blue skies in this place that had been near perfect.

Hauk suggested, "We should keep moving."

Arista struggled to regain sanity. She took deep breaths, focussed on the traffic, and manoeuvred their car into the congestion of automobiles. She was thankful for the slow speed. The distraction of the lake was bound to cause accidents, and at least damage should remain minimal.

Hauk made an attempt at being rational. "This is most likely to be resulting from underground sulphur pools changing with the recent ground shifts."

Arista numbed with trepidation.

Doris spoke with a welcome breath of sanity. "We have no control over what is, or is not, going to happen. We will just have to keep driving away from here."

Arista loved the calming effect of Doris' honest approach.

They reached the highway. Automobiles automatically distanced from each other and increased their speed. Miles sped by with each of them engrossed in their own thoughts.

A sudden and strange movement grabbed Arista's attention. In her rear view mirror she immediately saw acute physical distress in Hauk's spasmodic jerking. She jammed her foot onto the brake, tightly gripped the steering wheel and held it as the nose of the car angled sharply down to the pavement. She yanked the car over to the side of the road, put the gear in park, pressed the button turning on her emergency flashers, exited the car and entered the back seat in an instant.

Recognizing the paralysis in his lungs as a complication of the virus invading his system, she immediately began rescue breathing. Checking, at the appropriately timed intervals, she always found his pulse. His breathing remained in arrest. She continued forcing air into his lungs.

Sirens screamed and stopped in front of the car. Paramedics assessed the situation, and took his pulse, and she kept counting the breaths she was administering. They asked if he was able to breathe on his own. She nodded he was not and she took another breath and then pushed her air into his lungs. They moved him onto a stretcher and she moved in unison. Then she was replaced with an apparatus rhythmically swishing air into his lungs.

"How did you know we were in trouble?"

He looked at her with a puzzled expression and answered, "We had a call."

"I used my cell phone."

She had forgotten about Doris. Arista climbed into the ambulance behind the stretcher.

"What will we do with the car?" Doris glanced back as she prepared to follow Arista.

Pausing for the first time, Arista looked at Doris and requested. "Please bring it to the hospital and meet us there."

The ambulance was loaded, doors were closed, and Doris stood watching in a fog of shock as the air filled with the screech of sirens and the ambulance sped away.

Inside, Arista issued a string of instructions. The attendant attempted to give her a stern look. Her complex knowledge of medicines and dosages dulled his ability to be authoritative.

He hesitantly informed her, "We are unable to take orders from anyone other than a qualified doctor."

Staring at them for the briefest second, she glanced at the duress assaulting Hauk, and snapping under pressure she unzipped her purse, pulled out a wad of identification, and handed it to them. Never having seen so many letters representing medical degrees behind a name, the paramedics stared at her.

"Is this for real?" A chunky, middle aged, balding, paramedic looked at her doubtfully.

Pulling out more identification to add extra weight to her credentials, she staunchly stated, "Until very recently I was employed with one of the most advanced international health organizations in the world."

"Why are you not employed there now?"

"I know what the virus is, and I know the best way to treat it." She glared at him, "Would you please stop wasting time." She looked around the ambulance. "I'm sure I can do this myself."

The paramedics looked at each other with uncertainty.

Hauk's body jerked in violent spasms.

"If I leave this to you, we are going to lose him." Arista assessed the monitors blinking his vital signs, saw his blood pressure drop dramatically, and his oxygen level slipped as alarms beeped urgency. Arista removed the breathing mechanism from Hauk's face and tried breathing for him. His respiratory passages refused to take in air.

About to tear the ambulance apart in search of what she needed, she met cooperation and the paramedics began administering the drugs she had previously requested. She resumed rescue breathing, and the air went into his lungs. The oxygen machine was put back in place and a rhythmic hissing indicated healthy airflow to and from Hauk's lungs.

Anxious to get their patient to the hospital where they would be relieved of their stressful responsibility, the paramedics turned their attention to Arista.

The second attendant, a chubby woman with stern set features warning of a domineering personality, bravely asked, "What does he have?"

"It's a virus." Looking at the woman, and angry about everything, Arista blurted, "It is extremely contagious."

Silence descended thick as night.

With a sigh, Arista relented, "It is unlikely many people will suffer a violent reaction like Hauk is doing." Looking down at him, tears spilt onto her cheeks. "Most people infected with the virus will not have symptoms any different from a common cold."

Assuming her knowledge was real and had come from her previous employment, the balding man asked, "If the scientists know about this, why is the medical profession not being warned and receiving instructions?"

Dazed by the lab's conflicting viewpoints on the matter, she shrugged her shoulders that she didn't know. Assessing Hauk's vital signs, she saw that the lab's unproven theories were accurate. The medical treatment they had been working with had saved Hauk's life.

Sirens screamed. The ambulance arrived at the first hospital outside the earthquake zone, and the paramedics moved as quickly as was humanly possible to get Hauk into the emergency entrance. There he was immediately assessed and admitted to the intensive care unit.

The paramedics retold the events in the ambulance, and the doctors decided to act on the side of caution. All people known to have come into contact with Hauk, including Arista, Doris, the ambulance attendants, doctors and nurses, were placed in quarantine. In consideration of the high contact she had had with the virus, Arista was granted permission to stay with Hauk.

Over the next five days, Hauk regained strength and his health stabilized. When it was necessary to enter his room, hospital staff donned special suits to protect themselves from becoming infected. As an added precaution, used suits were destroyed instead of being sterilized and used again.

Chapter 34

Hauk and Arista spent days watching constant news updates flashing across the screen suspended from the ceiling in their hospital room. High numbers of people were succumbing to a mysterious illness. Authorities were implementing extreme measures to protect the public. All labs properly equipped to handle contagious and deadly viruses were urgently analyzing the epidemic rapidly spreading throughout the nations.

The cell was soon discovered to have distinct characteristics of Whooping Cough. It was much larger and hardier than the known strains, and it was resistant to the standard vaccination.

Quarantines were enforced worldwide. Planes were ordered to be grounded if any passenger displayed cold symptoms while in flight. In such an event, the plane would be quarantined, and passengers without symptoms would remain together for ten days, until the threat of spreading the disease was passed. Passengers were advised to carry latex gloves, hand sanitizers, air masks, and disinfectant sprays. These were to be used for protection from the disease if they became subject to quarantine. Travel was banned between countries. Cities and economies suffered as scared people remained in their homes.

Highly acclaimed medical experts suggested using antibiotics in an effort to make infected people non-contagious, using steroids for the prevention of chronic lung damage, and prescribing puffers to counter the attacks similar to asthma. For the first time in decades, penicillin was used without restraint.

The onset of the epidemic was traced to Lee Yates. The lab refrained from informing the public and the world governments that the disease had stemmed from research on the Neanderthal man. Their 'top secret' findings were that the Neanderthal man had died from an attack of arrested breathing brought on by the virus. Now, millenniums after his death, the same lethal virus was revived and thriving.

To cover their reputations and their work, the elite scientists staged public reports describing ancient drawings suggesting the symptoms of such a disease having plagued primitive man. In an effort to be prepared in the event of it resurfacing, research had been underway as, and they emphasized, 'a precautionary measure'. They went on to say how fortunate they were to have had the project in place. Their work had streamlined the efficiency of classifying the virus when it did strike. As, of course, they had suspected it might.

Arista watched the news in numb confusion. She explained to Hauk, "It was my job to analyze reports. Funding was provided by numerous governments, but the organizations financing the research were seldom given true details of the experiments."

Looking at her with keen interest, Hauk asked, "You worked in that lab?"

"The secrecy was smothering. Their continuous justifications for withholding information, their misleading implications, and their outright lies, agitated me throughout my employment with them. The man preserved in ice was a grand discovery. The finding of a potentially lethal virus should have been told. Viruses lay dormant, in the ground, waiting for favourable conditions enabling them to resurface and thrive. This virus could, and probably would, rebound without the Neanderthal man having ever been found. Why not research it openly? The people in charge had their reasons. I disagreed with them."

Seeing memories clouding her eyes, and her vision on a faraway place invisible to him, Hauk silently listened.

"During my years in medical school I had dreamed of being an outstanding doctor. I wanted to help people. I had extraordinarily high marks that gained the attention of prestigious universities, and I accepted choice offers as they poured my way. My grades continued to soar. Universities waived tuition fees to get me into their faculties. I came into contact with people in ranks I had never known existed. My aspirations grew. Joining scientific teams equipped with outstanding labs, I set out in search of discovering miracle cures for devastating diseases." Her goals had been honourable. None of them were realized. She had grown to feel like a fly trapped in a web.

"Research for ordinary cures was left to what my superiors had considered to be 'lesser' labs. My affiliates dedicated themselves to making discoveries by means of remote scientific projects no other organizations knew about. They aimed to bask in the glory of their work, and share rewards of distinction with nobody. It had all been futile vanity." Her convictions had differed from the stance held by her superiors.

"Still, I probably would have plugged away at my job for decades, hoping to stumble onto at least one miracle cure. Then, Dr. Yen joined the team. He arrogantly thwarted procedure. I voiced my concerns to other members of the team. The team leader brought the matter to our supervisor, and reported to the team that there was nothing he could do. Dr. Yen's contract of employment was too tight to be breached without incurring great expense. Dr. Yen was there to stay. My lawyer found a loophole in my contract, and I left the lab."

Confused, Hauk asked, "Why are you working in a bank?"

Staring at him with blind eyes, the past hazed to the present, and she eventually focussed on Hauk. "I hit mental burnout. I had worked very hard, and sacrificed everything. It was all for nothing. I wanted to leave it all behind and start fresh."

Chapter 35

Day Thirty Seven - Tuesday

Driving away from the hospital in a rental car, Arista relished fresh air, bright sunshine, and freedom. "Doesn't this feel good?"

Hauk's appreciation went further than hers. "I forgot what it was like to feel good." She glanced over at him, and he continued, "I honestly didn't think I was ever going to be healthy again."

Chills frosted her veins at the memories of terrifying moments. "You were critically ill."

"Perhaps it will make me a better doctor. I will be more empathetic now that I understand how my patients feel."

The evacuated city had suffered a major earthquake during their absence. It had sustained intense damage, it was time to rebuild, the scientists were gone, Hauk's apartment was deemed safe, and they were returning. Warned by a sign indicating a steep grade on the road, Arista moved her foot to the brake in preparation. Pressing her foot slightly on the brake brought no response. She pressed harder. Then, she put her body weight on her foot and pressed as hard as she could.

"What's wrong?"

"I have no brakes."

Swiftly gathering speed on the decline, Arista moved the gear to neutral and clutched the wheel for the battle she could not avoid.

"There's a runaway ahead."

Looking for it, she concentrated on keeping her car on the road while it gained wild momentum.

"It's straight ahead." Hauk pointed to a narrow length of sand.

Seeing a red sign telling her to stop at the intersection they were speedily approaching, she cursed unknown and illogical authorities for putting it right before a runaway. It would make more sense to have stop signs at the road intersecting the bottom of the steep decline. Praying for the path to stay clear of unsuspecting vehicles, she braced her hands on the steering wheel.

In a cloud of dust, all she could do was fight to hold the car straight as the wheels sank into soft sand. It did effectively stop them, and quickly. At one point she thought she felt the organs of her body moving with the momentum and slamming into her bones.

Staring in stunned disorientation, she came back to awareness of her surroundings when Hauk gently asked, "Are you all right?"

"Yes." Looking over at him, remembering how ill he had so recently been, an overflow of emotion flooded her cheeks with tears. In a flash, she was wrapped in the strong warmth of his arms.

Hauk used his cell phone to call for a tow truck, and they waited. The tow truck arrived, pulled the car onto a flatbed, and the driver brought Arista, Hauk, and the car, to a garage. They checked into a nearby hotel, where they could comfortably wait for the car to be repaired or replaced by the rental company.

Relaxing in a bubbly and soothing hot tub, in the bedroom of the suite, Hauk broke the silence by suggesting, "What if you take what you have learnt to a research lab that works strictly on finding cures for existing illnesses? You must know many advantageous techniques."

It was a prospect she had never considered. Running from her work had been too great an obsession. There had been no room or energy left for contemplating alternate possibilities.

"The people you worked with, and went to medical school with, are absolute geniuses." He gave her an odd look.

She didn't know he was thinking she must be one too. She felt incredibly stupid.

"You must have gained a great deal of knowledge from them. You would be able to achieve amazing accomplishments with that expertise."

"I have never had the chance to try achieving anything. Everything we worked on was so utterly futile. They sought nothing more than empty prestige." In an instant, waves of memory washed through her mind. "The mathematical calculations were astronomical. We worked through probabilities and possibilities until our minds felt as though they were spinning on perpetual motion. If I could try using those methods in true medical research, something, somewhere, just might help." The rebirth of old dreams breathed life into a fresh flame of aspiration. "If I could help just one person overcome a devastating illness, then everything I have done would become meaningful." Blankly staring into her vision, she whispered, "At least once, I would like my efforts to produce something worthy."

"The work you did probably saved my life."

Staring at him, she realized it was true. The lab had established an accurate theory for treatment, which she had implemented. Her medical training and experience had been crucial at the most important moment she had ever encountered.

"How did you end up working at a bank?"

"When I left the lab, I took the first flight back to Canada, and stayed where it landed. I checked the newspaper for job openings, sent out resumes, and the bank is where I got a job." Her mind spun at remembering her disorientated thought patterns. "I just wanted to get away from where I had been. I didn't put any thought into where I was going. Aimless chance brought me to the bank, and to Guy. It's probably a good idea to stop and look carefully at a situation instead of moving ahead haphazardly like I did."

Emotionally overwhelmed, sudden exhaustion hit her with the force of a freight train. Bubbling hot water caressed her skin, and her eyelids drooped heavily.

Looking at her was making Hauk equally tired. Without a word he took her hand in his, they got up and walked out of the hot tub, dried, and wrapped themselves in hotel robes.

She climbed into bed in a daze, wrapped herself in blankets, and whispered, "I need sleep."

Hauk walked to the door, turned, and said, "Good night."

Almost asleep, she mumbled, "Good night."

He watched the late night news on television. She slept in the bedroom, and he fell asleep on the sofa.

Day Thirty Eight - Wednesday

The day began with the mechanic informing them that her brakes had been tampered with. The brake hoses were loosened, it had to have been intentional, and whoever did it had known the brakes would only work for a few stops and then fail completely.

Looking at Hauk, Arista asked, "How is that possible? It is a rental car. Nobody could have been targeting us."

Replaying the morning in his mind, Hauk remembered, "When we stopped for gas, we both went inside. The car was unattended, and that would have given somebody time to loosen a few screws."

"Who would do that?"

Hauk figured the lab was a prime suspect. They were powerful enough to be dangerous if they felt threatened by Arista's knowledge of them.

Instead of saying that to her, he suggested, "Let's go to the police and see what they advise us to do."

The police took statements from them, and that was all they could do.

They got a different rental car, and agreed that one of them would stay at the car at all times.

Driving, Hauk asked her, "What is the best way to hide from your enemy?"

"Crawl into a cave and grow old hoping to never be found."

Laughing softly, he pointed out, "If you are being chased by someone with evil intent, you are to run to the busiest street in the area and draw attention to yourself. Never hide in a secluded spot."

"Right now, hiding in a dark and empty corner of the planet seems like the best idea possible."

With a slight and negative shake of his head, he countered, "The best thing you could do is go public, give your credentials, and land the kind of job you always wanted. At the same time you could say how fortunate you have been to have had the fine associates you did. Give them the praise they crave. Leave their secrets intact and reaffirm your alliance with them by way of public statements. Then, they might trust you enough to leave you alone. If you give them enough prestige, you will probably reap the rewards of highly sought and envied references from them." Seeing the sceptical look in her eyes, he added, "You would be telling the truth. The skills they taught you are what you will use to pursue your avenue of interest in the medical field."

"Do you think it is the lab that is after me?"

"I think it is a strong possibility."

"I'm not so sure they would do that. I really don't know who would. I do know that I do not want to face a bunch of reporters. Do you have any other great ideas?"

Mischief danced in his eyes. "I have one more."

Thinking he was taking this whole thing too lightly she stared at him, then tilted her head at a haughty angle, and asked, "What?"

He drove the car onto the shoulder, stopped, put the gear in park, turned to her, and asked, "Will you marry me?"

Stunned at his words, at a time like this, she didn't know what to think or say. She asked, "Why?"

"I love you, and you love me, and when a man and woman love each other they get married."

The simplicity of his reasoning sent her thoughts jumbling into a swirl of dysfunctional confusion. Looking into his eyes, she saw his love for her, and her love for him swelled.

"Besides," he took her in his arms, "I want to-"

Her lips assaulted his with abrupt and intense desire. Without thought, she took what she wanted, and her tongue wrestled with his. Moving her hand to position herself closer to him, the horn blasted insistently. She jumped at the noise, he chuckled at seeing what was happening, she removed her hand from the horn, and the piercing noise stopped.

"Does that mean you will marry me?"

Her heart answered, "Yes, I will marry you."

Chapter 36

Day Forty Five - Wednesday

Obeying the travel advisories, Arista packed a carryon bag with latex gloves, disposable masks, disinfecting spray, and hand sterilizer. Their flight was marvellous. It gave her an intoxicating rush when the aircraft slowly crawled along the runway, rapidly gained momentum, and, her favourite moment, lifted off the ground angling toward the heavens. Levelled at 35,000 feet, they hit slight turbulence, and the rocking plane lulled Arista to sleep.

Hauk looked at the field designs far below them. He dreaded their mission. Arista had taken his advice and telephoned the media. They were more than accommodating in their reception of her. A press release was scheduled to take place two hours after their landing, which would be in another three hours.

Taking the ring box out of his pocket, he considered the magnitude of events they had suffered. Snapping it open he thought about his having searched for the perfect ring, and putting a rush on having it sized. He was planning on giving it to her later today, when they celebrated the end of this press release. Right now, all he wanted was to get their problems behind them and move into their future.

Time sped them to their mission. Wearing her hair pinned in a sophisticated twist, and an immaculate ivory skirt and jacket with a pale pink blouse and enclosed ivory heels, Arista looked beautiful. Hauk felt pure terror as he watched her in front of the news cameras airing the live broadcast.

Questions rushed at her, "How did you know about the virus?" "The public has been informed that research was underway before the virus broke out." "Was the lab researching this virus when you were working with them?"

"Yes."

"Is the statement they made, of suspecting it had plagued early man, accurate?"

"Yes."

Questions erupted from numerous reporters at the same time, "How did they know this?" "Exactly what made them aware of the virus?" "Is this a cover up?" "Was the virus produced in a lab to be used for chemical warfare?"

Arista halted the questions by lifting an elegant hand requesting silence. "I can assure you the virus is completely natural in structure. It is definitely not a mutated cell created in a lab."

"What led to researching this virus?"

"As you know there is continuous exploration revolving around new discoveries of how life has evolved over time. There are many theories on different changes and how they may have come about. Information is obtained by uncovering remains in various forms. By studying certain conditions they found signs of an epidemic having plagued early man and they began researching possibilities."

"When will there be a cure?"

"Discoveries are always unpredictable. Some cures take a long time to find, and others come unexpectedly quickly."

The questions seemed endless. Finally, they were wrapping up, and the last question was, "Was the research beneficial in battling this virus?"

"Yes." Arista grinned with confidence. "I applied the theories that were developed for treating the disease and the hypothesis proved to be life saving."

"Then there is truth to the rumours of you pulling rank on medical personal and demanding specific treatment for an infected patient?" Without waiting for an answer they asked, "Was it Dr. Sebastian VanLiev whose life you saved?"

Arista sternly reprimanded, "The identity of my patient is strictly confidential."

"Why did you leave your former employment?"

Here was her chance, and she was taking it. "I am hoping to restructure my career and dedicate my training and experience to medical science rather than exploratory research."

"Did you leave your employment on negative terms?"

"No." Her plastic smile came to the rescue. "I expect them to give me a positive reference when I embark on a job search."

Hauk's advice proved true. Her colleagues flooded the next three days with well wishes and letters of recommendation. They followed their calls by mailing gifts in acknowledgment of her upcoming wedding.

Job offers poured her way.

Day Fifty - Monday

She accepted a part time job in a lab. They gave her free reign in choosing her projects, and her first choice was to join in the battle of seeking a cure for cancer. She also accepted a part time position allowing her to practice as a general practitioner in the emergency unit at the same outstanding hospital where Hauk was working. She was finally on an avenue allowing her to do what she had always wanted to do.

In the morning, Arista was busy negotiating the terms of her employments. Hauk made arrangements for Doris to sublet his apartment from him, and he gave Doris his furnishings. Mady had found Bud wandering forlornly after the mudslide, taken him to her place, and grown attached to him. Mady was granted permission to keep Bud. When Hauk was finished tying loose ends, he made reservations for supper at his favourite restaurant.

When she was finished with business, they went shopping. He bought a new black suite, blue shirt, and striking tie for the evening. She bought a playful red dress, shiny red and white polka dot platform shoes, and flashy rhinestone jewellery.

From there, they went to Hauk's apartment, showered and changed, and left for supper.

The restaurant was impressive with dim lighting, a lit candle on every solid wood table, soft red velvet chair cushions, and a fireplace filled with crackling flames in the middle of the setting. People were slowly starting to come out of their houses and move about, but there were few others in the restaurant. Even so, Arista was aware of numerous people coughing.

Their host displayed perfect manners. The service was memorable. He was never intrusive, barely visible, and they were never lacking. Water glasses were filled, food was brought with perfect timing, and used dishes were soundlessly whisked away.

Positively content, Hauk and Arista walked toward his car with his arm around her shoulders, and her arm around the indent of his back. A sudden commotion, the air piercing shrill of his car alarm, and a man on the run, grabbed their attention.

Vaguely recognizing the shape and posture of him, Arista leapt into reactive action. "Uh-uh. This is not going to happen." She sprinted after him in a dead run.

Momentarily stunned, Hauk watched the scene unfold, launched into pursuit, and heard someone shout, "He slit the tires on this car."

Arista was fast. She quickly closed the distance and was gaining on the man. Hauk was struggling to catch up to them.

The man abruptly stopped and turned on her.

With full recognition, Arista growled, "Guy!"

He lunged at her, made a fist, swung, and she moved out of its path. One fluid motion connected her shoe with his groin, and he was flat on the ground.

Siren's screamed their approach. Guy was arrested. The police contacted her later, and informed her that Guy was guilty of previously tampering with her brakes. Guy also confessed to having broken into her apartment and ransacked it. She hadn't been back to notice yet.

Chapter 37

Day Sixty Two - Saturday

Looking through the blur of white netting, floating in a cloud of shimmering satin, her eyes met the most beautiful blue eyes in the world.

The same people were in attendance of all events in the community. Today there was one newcomer. Elaine was seated beside Ben. Mady was watching Ben from two pews back. Personalities were predictable, and when Klarissa stepped from the pew, Arista was ready for her. Her sister had explained how Klarissa admired bridal couples and considered them the equal of queens and kings. Recognizing the honour of being held in such high regard, Arista paused and turned, Klarissa's sister swallowed a lump of dread, and Arista whispered instructions to Klarissa.

Proceeding forward, Arista locked eyes with Hauk. Visions swam of a splendid marriage. Even if they could live a thousand years, they would never become bored with each other. Never look elsewhere. And never stop loving each other. When she reached his side, she moved her bouquet to Klarissa, who handled the bundled long stem roses as though they were a fragile treasure.

Klarissa quietly stepped to the side and adored the couple she was engrossed in watching. Seeing the high esteem bestowed on Klarissa, her sister smiled with heartfelt gratitude. Hauk took hold of Arista's hand, his eyes seared into hers, and her soul melted. Come what may, life was grand.

". . . to love and to cherish . . ." Hauk's vows bathed her in love.

Then it was her turn.

After a brief and intense ceremony they walked out of the church, with her arm wound into his, as husband and wife.

Endless cameras flashed, guests' appetites were satisfied, the three tier cake provided by Doris was cut, and they were away.

Adorned in the glamour of her satin gown and his grand black tux, they walked into the bridal suite of the best hotel in town. Lit candles were abundantly placed throughout the room in preparation for their arrival. Tiny flames licked warm shadows against petals of pink and white roses filling numerous vases. Arista was being treated like a queen, and her king was perfect. She watched Hauk pop the cork from a bottle of champagne and fill two crystal goblets with the pale effervescent liquid.

His lips found hers and tugged playfully. He drew back slightly, looked at her, she opened her eyes, and silent messages flew between them. Melding to each other their embrace tightened with the demands of raw hunger. Champagne sparkled untouched on the table. His lips delved into her sweetness with an unquenchable thirst. In another second he swept her up into his arms. Their tongues wrestled playfully.

He eased them onto the bed in a pool of white satin. He took a moment to admire the beauty of his wife. Desiring more than admiration, she arched her body to his and her lips ravaged his. Slipping satin away, he marvelled at her milky smooth flesh. His hands followed the trail of his eyes over the gentle indent of her waist, along the flaring path to seductively curvy hips, and to the sleek tapering of shapely legs. Her toenails glistened with the same silver sheen of painted colour as her fingernails. The simple detail infused his blood with heat.

His thorough exploration of her body was producing sexy little moans from her. Unable to wait another second, she tightened her hold on him, saw him look at her, took his lips with hers and positioned herself over him where she could easily slip onto him. Shocked at the sudden move, amazed and infatuated with it, he let his wife do as she wanted and he positioned his hands under her buttocks.

Feeling the magnificent strength of hard muscles sent hot sparks coiling in her stomach and her body launched into driving need. Just when she didn't think she could ever get enough, she flashed to ultimate ecstasy and he thundered with her.

When they were spent and relaxed, she looked at him. His eyes met hers and her smile was alive. He loved the way she was always receptive to him, and the way she looked, and the way she tumbled with him under the covers, and everything about her.

For a lingering second he imagined what it would be like when they had little children running about, and then grandchildren. Perhaps someday they would be blessed with great grandchildren and celebrate their sixtieth wedding anniversary. Looking at her, her eyes met his, and he saw his hopes and dreams reflected in their depths.

The End

Dear Reader:

The events and characters in Epidemic are fiction. The story imitates life as difficulties strike in rapid fire of each other. Unexpected problems surface without neatly waiting for previous troubles to be resolved. Every circumstance connects to the next. Even situations that seem meaningless play a vast role in taking the characters to necessary physical and emotional destinations.

When life is moving along paths I would rather not take, it is encouraging to remember God's promises. Romans 8:28: "And we know that in all things God works for the good of those who love him, who have been called according to his purpose." NIV

CPSIA information can be obtained at www.ICGtesting.com
Printed in the USA
LVOW10s0810111214

418210LV00009B/112/P